THE CATASTROPHIST

THE CATASTROPHIST

— a novel —

LAWRENCE DOUGLAS

Other Press · New York

Copyright © 2006 Lawrence Douglas

Production Editor: Robert D. Hack
Text design: Natalya Balvova
This book was set in Janson Text by Alpha Graphics of Pittsfield, NH.
ISBN-13: 978-159051-219-7

10 9 8 7 6 5 4 3 2

Library of Congress Cataloging-in-Publication Data

Douglas, Lawrence.
   The catastrophist / by Lawrence Douglas.
      p. cm.
   ISBN 1-59051-219-7 (hardcover : alk. paper)   1. Young men–Fiction.
2. College teachers–Fiction.   3. Marital conflict–Fiction.   I. Title.
   PS3604.O928C38 2006
   813'.6–dc22

2005024339

For R-F

PART 1

One

The Amtrak from Montreal to New York thunders by at three thirty every morning, the only train that still runs on these once-busy tracks. The couple across the hall has grown accustomed to the noise, though their child has not. When the train rumbles off, the girl's muffled sobs and the mother's calming voice filter through my thin walls. In my case, it's not the train that wakes me, but the anticipation. Come 3:27, I'm up, charged. Unfortunately, my biological clock is more accurate than Amtrak's timetable: often I must wait fifteen or twenty minutes, sometimes as long as an hour, for the first distant whistle. Then I kick off my sheet and hurry to the kitchen window. The rumble builds before the train bursts from the pinewoods into a clearing, roaring past in purplish silhouette. A great old diesel, its headlight carves a cone of light, stirring memories of an imaginary childhood. It turns a bend and disappears into a dark grove. I go back to bed.

In the morning I get up whenever. For breakfast I munch dry Froot Loops while padding about the small living room in my underwear. The shabby apartment is Rosalind Roth's old place. After she moved out, it sat vacant. The college disposed of the overt mess, leaving behind only traces of the deeper chaos: a crumpled box of Lucky Strikes in the bedroom closet, a layer of grit in the tub, and a lingering, ineradicable odor, like cat urine mixed with a hint of vanilla. The housing office offered to replace the kitchen's Spam-colored vinyl floor and the gold-flecked Formica countertops, but I declined. As my mother would say, they're authentic period pieces. And they hide the dirt.

After breakfast I dress – generally speaking. Since moving in, I've been steering clear of my office; in fact, I've hardly been out at all. News travels fast around the college, at least news of collapse. The campus ripples with stories about the young star who harassed his student, fabricated his past, and cheated on and then bloodied his pregnant wife. Even the *Times* ran a tiny news item:

ART HISTORIAN RESIGNS BERLIN COMMISSION

(Berlin) The Holocaust Memorial Commission of Brandenburg announced yesterday the resignation of Daniel Ben Wellington from the six-person Memorial Planning and Selection Committee. Wellington, an expert on war memorials at Franklin College in Massachusetts, was the sole American appointed to the committee charged with choosing the design for Berlin's planned Holocaust memorial, to be the largest in Europe. The Commission cited "personal reasons" for the sudden resignation. An international competition sponsored by the Commission has attracted over 700 designs from leading artists and architects from around the world. The winning design for the five-acre memorial is to be announced this fall.

I clip the piece from the paper with a pair of nail scissors and file it away in a folder neatly marked, *Me: Decline and Fall of*. The college hasn't initiated disciplinary action yet, but it will. It's just a matter of time. For now I can be grateful that hardly anyone is in town. The tennis camp and summer school have disbanded, the lawns have yellowed, and the faculty has retreated to the Cape or the Maine coast for the final respite before the onslaught of SUVs that will deposit the students and their sound systems on the North Quad. Even so, everyone knows and has an opinion. E-mail traffic brings equal measures of censure and pity, often both. I'm a pariah and an outpatient. The gossip mill couldn't ask for more.

*

And yet they all have the facts wrong. Let's start with the first of my so-called personal problems: my alleged infidelity. My wife did not throw me out for lying about an affair. The affair *was* the lie – it never happened. It was all . . . how should I put it – a *joke*.

So those who peg me as the Restless Husband self-destructively lashing out against the confines of domesticity couldn't be more off the mark. Monogamy suited me fine. In all my life I've never had a one-night stand – at least, not by choice. Years ago, in my first semester of graduate school, I met a woman at a party who asked me to walk her back to her apartment. The woman was from the South, Kentucky I think, and was working toward a degree in Italian literature. She spoke with a nasal twang, often swallowing her words, and her features were plain: small blue eyes, puffy cheeks, and blond hair cut in a lank pageboy. By the door to her apartment, I grazed her cheek with a dry peck, but she answered with a firm kiss, then whispered in my ear, "I want to blow you to Kingdom Cum." Astonished, I let myself be led to her room decorated with posters of Siena and horses in waterfalls. There she wasted no time seducing me. I can still picture the girl's eyes: closed, blissfully absorbed in private pleasure as I lay beneath her, watching. The next morning, she seduced me a second time. Again I felt as if I had moved to a place far off, detached not just from the act but from myself as well. Only later did I realize a simple truth: while most men might have been thrilled, it seemed I needed the love, too.

Not my wife. R. was drawn to adventure, conquest. On our honeymoon in Poland, it was R. who insisted that we travel first to Bialowieza, the last patch of primeval forest on the continent. There we saw black storks, peregrine falcons, and a single European bison grazing by a stand of towering alders as dark and mysterious as a Cranach landscape. Later, with Warsaw as our hub, we took day trips to the sites of the former death camps – Auschwitz, Treblinka, Sobibor, Chelmno, and Majdanek – so I could research and photograph the memorials for my planned book, *Art and Atrocity*. Most spouses would have complained, but not R. She accepted the quiet power of the memorials, in particular, the seventeen thousand slabs and shards of granite that jutted defiantly from Treblinka's lush green fields; and she liked the idea of a honeymoon that baffled and possibly appalled her extended family. Come evening, we'd bus back to Warsaw. After a dinner of borscht and sauerkraut pierogi, we'd retire to our drab room in the formerly state-run hotel and its narrow Stalinist bed. Only we did little in the way of sleeping. Once, R. pitched against me so forcefully that I suffered a slight case of whiplash. Later she sucked my tongue into her mouth with such violence that I tasted blood: her kiss had torn a thread of skin that anchors the tongue to the sublingual fold. I had to gargle with hydrogen peroxide.

After a couple years of marriage, though, R.'s desire had exhausted itself. Twice a month, every other Saturday night, she would issue the blunt command: "Stick it in." If we missed a Saturday night as the result of, say, a cold, there were no make-ups. Although nothing chills the spirit of Eros more than the weight of routine, this is the way R. came to want things. On all other nights, she would permit me to lie close and place my hand on the thrilling rise of her naked hip. If my hand strayed, the rebuke was gentle but firm: "Wrong."

How we arrived at this arrangement is hard to say. If it's natural for married couples to be less passionate than newlyweds, this still doesn't explain the dismaying erosion of R.'s interest in physical intimacy. Experts observe that women, particularly when settled into domestic rhythms, prefer the quiet of cuddling to the slap and sweat of "genital activity." But not R. Lavender-scented candles, Tibetan incense, and comfrey massage oil all left her equally indifferent. The default explanation was that R. had fallen out of love, a charge I sometimes leveled in the hope of prodding her to some tender rebuttal. R. would pat my arm and say, "Poor baby, of course, I love you. But I'm more a cat person. Too much touching makes me claustrophobic. You're more doglike. Now go to sleep, little hound." Then she'd place my hand on the crest of her hip, and close her eyes.

Not that I ever really doubted her. In other matters our marriage was strong. If anything, her apathy was a sign not of love's defeat but of its triumph. Unfortunately, it was not until R. began to lose interest in me that I was free to discover my erotic appetite; her lassitude aroused me as her desire never had.

Two

Two years before my "affair" in Berlin, R. began acquiring creatures – first dead, then living. We were coming off a fierce winter, and though the calendar promised spring, the fields surrounding our house remained heavy with snow, the nights windless and clear. One afternoon, while cross-country skiing, we chanced upon the remains of a porcupine. Astonished I watched R. kneel by the snow-dusted carcass and tug loose a handful of quills.

"Aren't they beautiful?" she said. "Like tiny javelins. Did you know that porcupines are born with all their quills? It's strange to think of this incredibly sharp thing growing inside something warm and soft."

I envied R.'s uncomplicated relationship with the natural world. Earlier that winter, we had gone to a play, a one-man comedy about relations between the sexes. The comedian had traced all marital discord back to the anthropological fact that men were designed to hunt and women, to gather. From an evolutionary perspective, the pleasure men get from whacking balls and racing cars is a vestigial display of hunting behavior; the fun women have shopping reflects the genetic legacy of the gatherer. The theater rocked with laughter as couples recognized themselves in the comedian's simple anthropology. After the show, though, R. and I both re-marked how imperfectly it described our marriage. True, I'm an avid sports fan, and R. generally shunned competitive games. But when it came to our careers, we broke stereotypes: as a freelance science writer for magazines like *Geo* and *Smithsonian*, R. worked in a man's field, while my discipline, art history, is now dominated by women. When it came to clothes, R. was basically indifferent, throwing on whatever she grabbed first, while I could waste an hour finding a tie to match my socks. As for household repairs, R. always wore the tool belt. We lived in a two-hundred-year-old New England farm-house that we bought shortly after I began teaching at Franklin. The house was a classic colonial – five bays, central chimney, slate roof, butter yellow clapboards with black shutters. The previous owners had had ambitious plans to renovate that were derailed by a combi-nation of bad investments and alcoholism. When we bought the house, it looked less neglected than abandoned – walls had been left half-sheetrocked; you could draw a line on the eighteen-inch-wide pine floorboards where the power-sander had abruptly quit. Even before we moved in, R. set to work, wiring a fan in the bathroom, cutting holes for switch plate covers, replanning warped doors, and finishing the floors. I handled the painting.

Once the house was in reasonable order, her attention shifted to animals. The quills were only a prelude. One day I discovered a long, stiff, black plastic bag in the freezer. Around its irregular shape, packing cord had been carefully wound.

"What is *that*?" I asked.

"A fox," she said.

"Come again."

"A red fox – a real beauty. I found him by the side of the road. The poor thing was still warm. A car must have clipped him and bro-ken his neck. He looked like he could have been sleeping."

"You put road-kill in our freezer. Next to the Ben & Jerry's."
She smiled.

"Why?" I asked.

In the coming days I got my answer. After lugging the package down to her workbench, she sawed the animal open, eviscerated it, and tried her hand at amateur stuffing, following the steps outlined in *The Home Guide to Taxidermy and Tanning*. ("Black lacquer followed by a coat of clear shellac brightens the appearance of nostrils and lips.") The experiment came to an end when the mothproofing agent putrefied the carcass. The odor in the basement, a baleful, gullet-constricting stench of meat rot, exiled us briefly to a motel; the odor, meanwhile, lingered for weeks in the basement.

R. was not easily deterred. As the milky spring sun dispatched the last of the snow, she set about building a coop next to our garage.

"We're going to have fresh eggs," she announced. "There's nothing more delicious in the whole world than an egg still warm from the hen."

She brought home three adorable chicks that grew swiftly into three hideous chickens. Never before had I observed a chicken up close: the flaming malignant wattle, the orbiting eyes, the Jurassic feet. The claim that chickens are simply superannuated dinosaurs no longer seemed all that ludicrous. I suggested "Psycho," "Little," and "Fricassee," but R. gave each chicken a sensible, utilitarian name, and carefully monitored their respective laying habits. "Red" laid with great regularity; "Brown" laid not at all; and "Reddish-Brown" would, after several barren days, deliver frightfully over-sized and misshapen offerings – eggs like bars of soap.

True, the fresh eggs tasted better than the overpriced ones from the organic food co-op, and they made convenient gifts for friends, neighbors, and colleagues. But it was also clear that the chickens sym-bolized a longing on R.'s part for something more than a Sunday omelet. For no sooner had they reached adulthood than I found a manual on her nightstand, *Vietnamese Micro-Pigs: A Primer for Owners.*

"They're very companionable and have unusually flexible snouts," R. explained.

"Flexible snouts?"

"And you know pigs don't have fur – they have hair, so they wouldn't aggravate your allergies." Quoting from the book, she pointed out that pigs are uncommonly intelligent, far smarter than dogs. The Vietnamese breed also was said to be clean and self-sufficient – in short the perfect household pet.

R.'s excitement was infectious. During the drive to the breeder, we imagined the sound of cloven hoofs nimbly clicking across our kitchen tiles. But we were in for a disappointment. The breeder's farm turned out to be no more than a small fenced enclosure at the back of a tract house. On a modest patch of trampled grass, a dozen Vietnamese pigs rooted and snorted. The adults looked very much like your typical pig – bloated, filthy, vaguely obscene. Eager to demonstrate her pets' intelligence, the breeder barked a series of commands, none of which had any observable influence on the pigs' behavior. One piglet affectionately circled my ankles, then ate my shoelaces. The others soon had to be shooed inside her house to avoid sunburn. The house, a revolting mess, smelled of rancid Chinese food. A pig was sleeping soundly on a worn, stained recliner in the living room. Another was nosing around an outlet covered in a frayed Union Jack of duct tape. Grudgingly the breeder admitted that her pets had the regrettable habit of chewing through electrical cords.

We drove back in silence. The pigs were never again mentioned. And one morning when R. went to retrieve the day's supply of eggs, she discovered that a raccoon had slaughtered Red, Brown, and Reddish-Brown. She buried their remains in a corner of the overgrown pasture.

Three

"What's next on you list?" I asked. We were lying in bed. It was a morning of soft, cloud-filtered spring light. "A human being?"

"You mean, instead of a llama?"

"Is that the other choice?"

"Yeah – that or a peacock."

I thought about this. "Aren't llamas supposed to be pretty nasty creatures?"

"Well, they *are* known to spit and bite. And they're not well suited to New England weather. They're good in the snow and high elevations, but freezing rain can give them hypothermia. It's strange – they can survive the fiercest blizzards in the Andes, but not a little New England sleet." R. shifted closer to me, dropping a leg across mine. Our house was large, far more space than two people needed. We each had our own study, and that still left a room empty. It was impossible to ignore how R. had begun fixing up that room. Her foot curled around my calf. Her eyes were radiantly dark. "Of course, peacocks make an incredible racket."

I reminded her that she once described herself as a woman without a strong maternal instinct.

"It's true," she said, smiling. "Baby in the abstract never moved me. But baby with you – I like that. Want."

"But shouldn't we wait till after tenure?" My promotion review was a year off and I needed to complete my book, *Art and Atrocity*.

R. pulled the sheet taut across her breasts. "I'm nearly thirty-five. I don't see why we should let your department decide whether we can have a family."

In fact, R. had only recently turned thirty-two. A friend of ours had just given birth at forty-four. But this was R.'s way: once her mind was made up, she became short on patience.

"That was Stephanie's *third* child. That makes a huge difference. The longer you wait for the first, the greater the dangers. You know that. Anyway, I don't want to be retired and decrepit when my child starts college."

"I'm not talking about a long time," I said. "Just until things are more settled professionally."

"Tick, tick, tick," she said.

"But you're healthy, in great shape – I wish *I* still got carded." In addition to being an extremely handsome woman, R. looked remarkably young, having inherited her grandmother's fine, creamy, wrinkle-free Hungarian skin.

"I don't see what my complexion has to do with my reproductive organs," she said. "These things shut down, dry up, malfunction."

*

Initially there was no urgency to our efforts: R. simply stopped inserting the "frisbee." After months without results, though, she became more methodical, monitoring her temperature and cycle. On circled days, sex was mandatory. R. did her best to enliven these acts

13

with a repertoire of new lingerie; unfortunately, once her reproductive window shut, so too did her erotic interest. Her approach was all very goal oriented. R. was nothing if not purposive.

This went on for the better part of a year – flurries of reproductive activity followed by weeks of abstinence.

It was all for naught. Once, indulging a spirit of scientific inquiry, R. suggested examining my semen under a microscope deaccessioned from the college. Expertly she prepared the slide, and at 430× we watched the little swimmers lash energetically, then quickly fall inert. I assumed that the sperm had succumbed to the heat from the microscope's light; R. entertained other theories. She clipped an article from *Geo* that linked the destruction of the Brazilian rain forest to a global decrease in human sperm motility, then scheduled me for a battery of exams. A matronly nurse regarded my modest contribution to a specimen jar dismissively, but could discover no problems. Tests on R. likewise uncovered no structural flaws. The doctor, who thought it relevant to mention that he had *four* children, encouraged us to "keep plugging."

The medical exams gave the idea of having a child an urgency that neither of us had felt at the outset. R. assembled a small library of books: *Taking Charge of Your Fertility, The Fastest Way to Get Pregnant Naturally, The Fertility Diet, Fertility for Dummies.* She investigated elaborate clinical interventions and called several of my colleagues who had journeyed to formerly Soviet Georgia and to the interior of China to adopt; she contacted an agency in the plains of Lanzhou.

For the time being, we kept trying. The exotic undergarments fell by the wayside; the candles remained unlit. Our postcoital routine, formerly a time of caresses and dreamless sleep, now turned into a show of preposterous gravity-defying calisthenics, anything to aid the desperate upstream odyssey.

As our third anniversary loomed, R. spoke of the Almighty. We both came from secular Jewish families, though her family's Judaism had a distinctly Lutheran flavor – the only religious holidays her grandparents had recognized were Christmas and Easter, which they celebrated with Germanic austerity. R. herself rarely spoke about God, and yet one evening she said, "Maybe He just didn't intend it to be."

"Or maybe He just wants us to keep trying," I said. "Maybe He's got other things on His mind with the holidays coming up."

"I suppose neither of us was all that gung-ho to begin with. And who knows what the future holds in store. I mean, here we are, living in the midst of the greatest species die-off since the Jurassic Age – every day, dozens of life forms going extinct, vanishing forever, and nobody even blinks an eye. Maybe it's wrong to bring a child onto a dying planet."

I wasn't sure how to reconcile R.'s eschatology with her evolutionary fatalism. But I respected this about her – she wasn't one to waste time with self-pity. She always knew how to pick herself up and move on. True, she discouraged easily; it was part and parcel of her impatient side. In this case, though, her thinking was closer to my own than I acknowledged. Despite the reassuring results of the medical examinations, I was secretly convinced of my sterility, certain of some systemic flaw. In part I suspected this was a consequence of the masturbatory excesses of my adolescence. But at the core was a feeling that I wasn't evolutionarily suited for fatherhood, that mine was a design not worth replicating. It was hard to say where this certainty came from, yet it remained as unshakeable as it was obscure. The knowledge saddened me, though not for myself; I could imagine a life without children easily enough. It was R. I worried about. Though maybe not the cuddliest person, R. was so profoundly competent, so grounded and commonsensical, that there was no doubt she would have a gift for mothering.

As a temporary measure, I found a surrogate. At a local animal shelter I discovered a three-year-old calico cat with extra digits on her front paws. Sweetness, by name. Her fur was splashed with autumnal colors – orange, ginger, and a brown of leaves just past their peak. They say that cats have expressive faces, and when I knelt to stroke her, I was sure she lifted her jowls into a grateful smile. Then she stroked *my* arm, delicately retracting her claws into the pads of her freakish paw.

We celebrated our anniversary in our traditional venue. Housed in a venerable New England inn, the Graylord was a restaurant popular with New Yorkers heading north for leaf season and with parents visiting their children at the nearby Hartfield boarding school. The decor was Colonial Highbrow – chintz swags, fretwork molding, pewter napkin rings, and a waitstaff that hovered just outside the narrow arc of warm candlelight. Dining there provided us with a welcome opportunity to put on something other than Patagonia fleece: R. wore a long, sleeveless, beaded dress, a recent addition to her collection of vintage gowns. Around her neck hung her grandmother's pearls. More than just attractive, R. looked sturdy. Her arms were beautifully rounded and toned, not from trips to a swank gym, but from her heroic struggles to subdue and extirpate the Virginian creeper, Japanese Knotweed, and chokecherry that threatened our garden and pasture. On her forearm was a quarter-sized patch of bubbled salve and glistening rawness from poison ivy. She was in good spirits, although she refused to join me in a glass of expensive wine, a 1993 Nuit Saint Georges.

Admittedly, our conversation faltered.

"How's your salmon?"

"Very good. What about your quail?"

"Delish. You want to try a bite?"

"Just a tiny one."

At the next table, a woman, an executive type with neatly scalloped blond bangs, dined with her teenage son in his studiously rumpled Hartfield blue blazer. "Have you tried that medicated shampoo?" I heard her ask, slapping dandruff from his shoulders. "Why do I send you these things if you refuse to try them?"

Waiting for dessert, I gave R. her present: a leather collar with a brass, heart-shaped tag. On it were engraved the words: *SWEETNESS. I belong to* . . . R. examined the collar with a broad smile.

"You see, I got us a cat," I explained. "Her name's Sweetness. Didn't you always want a cat? She's even a bit deformed."

R. beamed. "A deformed kitty. I *do* love you. But what about your allergies?"

"I think I'll be fine. I kept her on my lap for an hour and didn't get too congested."

Then R. handed me a box of identical size. I tore open the wrapping, half expecting to find a "Gift of the Magi" puppy collar, then removed a sweatshirt from Yale, my alma mater.

Baffled, I held up the sweatshirt. Size: XXS. R. was smiling madly. There was some brilliant joke that I didn't get.

Then I got it.

I struggled to say something. I leaned over and strafed R.'s forehead with a kiss and said "Jesus." Then I rose, pointed wordlessly to my stomach, and hurried to the bathroom, only suddenly to change course and stumble out the restaurant's front door. A waiter was smoking a forbidden cigarette. The night sky was moonless, pocked with stars. I shivered but not because it was cold. It was as if I had stumbled into a dark lake with hidden channels of warm and icy water. From the direction of the Hartfield dormitories I heard a rhythmic percursive sound, a bass drum being pounded, then realized the sound was my own heart. A creature, beetle-like, scuttled down my back, then another: sweat. I loosened my collar, but the feeling of constriction persisted, as if my skin had shrunk after a washing. The tightness spread to my chest. An invisible ratchet was cinching in my ribs. Several steady clearing breaths loosened the grip, but then a bolt of adrenalin struck, making my heart scamper madly. The stars turned enormous and liquid: my eyes filling with tears. I remembered feeling this way only once before when, as a ten-year-old, I discovered the webbing between the second and third toes of my left foot. In school we had started to learn about genetics, and the discovery of the extra flap of skin, waxily translucent in the glare of the flashlight I kept by my bed, paralyzed me with precocious dread. Engrossed in morbid study of my abnormality, I became convinced that the webbing had spread to toes three and four, and so had quit my bed and dashed outside, quieting my sobs by hugging the tallest tree in our yard, a great oak. There my mother had found me, and, guiding me inside, had revealed her secret: the identical mis-design, hers on her right foot.

The memory filled me with a strange sad nostalgia for my own childhood. On the quad was a giant sycamore. I dashed toward it, and throwing my arms around its trunk, held tight. The tree's bark was both scabrous and smooth. It smelled like a closet, a comforting odor of neatly stacked sweaters and folded blankets. I pressed my lips against the bark, and chewed. The flavor was like smoked licorice, an exotic Asian tea. So I stood, embracing the tree, face pressed to the bark, when I heard a voice: "Excuse me, sir, are you okay?"

Startled, I turned and backed into the trunk, as if edging away from an attacker. Bits of bark were still on my tongue.

The figure in silhouette repeated an offer for assistance, only abruptly to interrupt himself. "Professor Wellington . . . ?"

As he pivoted into the light, I recognized the young man as an incoming graduate student in my department. He was tall, extremely thin, and vaguely androgynous; when I had met him a few weeks earlier his face had reminded me of the young Mick Jagger.

"I really didn't mean to alarm you," he said. "It's just, it seemed – "

"You don't have to apologize," I said, still struggling to regroup. "I appreciate your concern – that back spasm just came out of the clear blue."

This hung for a moment in the night air.

"Uh, I've heard those can be very painful," he said.

"Yes, they're pretty awful. I was having dinner at the inn with my wife, when it happened. I get them from time to time, the result of an old cycling injury. It feels like a bayonet jab."

"Ouch," he said.

"So I came out here. A physical therapist taught me that exercise with the tree. I guess it must have looked pretty strange."

"To be honest, it made me think of my mom. She used to, uh, bray at the moon."

I wasn't sure if I had heard him correctly. "Bray at the moon?"

"Yeah, but that's kind of a long story . . ."

He seemed to regret having mentioned it. I did some vague stretching, as if flexing a sore back.

"I once kind of injured my back," he volunteered. "Running track. It was here, actually. I'm an alum."

I nodded or said something like, *Huh!* or *Really?*

"Yeah, it's kind of a family place – father, grandfather, you know, one of those dreary legacy things. The headmaster asked me back to teach an art history overview this term. I figured I could use some extra income. Uh, is your back feeling better?"

"Yes, thanks. The air does it good." Just then a breeze stirred the drying leaves.

"I read in the school's propaganda," he said, "that this is the largest sycamore east of the Mississippi."

"Really? Well, it *is* a magnificent tree. And my physical therapist did strongly recommend that I do the stretches using something deciduous."

He didn't laugh or even smile – he seemed to take me seriously.

"Well, I should be going," I said. "Dessert's waiting."

"Yeah, okay. Feel better, Professor. I'm sure I'll see you back at the Department."

As I hurried back to the inn, I followed his long-limbed stride across the quad.

R. was tracing patterns on an empty plate. At my place sat the chocolate mousse she had ordered for me, untouched. The cat collar still lay on the table. The tiny sweatshirt had been refolded and replaced in its box. Gone were the mother and son.

"You okay?" R. asked. Her brow was fixed in a complex pattern of wrinkles, both horizontal and vertical, that formed a tick-tack-toe-like grid.

"I think so. I'm not entirely sure. It could have been the salmon."

"We should go," she said. "I've already paid."

"No, please. Let's have some tea. Or decaf. The mousse looks delicious, thanks. Don't you want some herbal tea?"

She signaled to the waiter and ordered a chamomile.

"I guess I'm just a bit overwhelmed. Wow. This is great, absolutely unbelievable."

"You're sweating," she observed. "A lot."

"I know. I can't help it. It's very strange. But I'm feeling much better, really. Jesus, this is great. Do we know the due date?"

"I haven't been to the doctor yet, but it should be around April fifteenth."

"The Titanic," I said.

"What?"

"I mean, when did you find out? How?"

"What about the Titanic?"

"Nothing. That's when it went down, April fifteenth. It just flashed through my head, I'm sorry. So how long have you known?"

"Christ, Daniel. Thanks for that tidbit, I can't wait to share that with my parents . . . Anyway, two days ago, I couldn't sleep. It's hard to explain, but my body just felt different. I thought to myself, either I'm coming down with something or I'm pregnant. So in the middle of the night, I took a test and watched the little dot turn blue. Look . . ."

From her purse she removed an envelope. In it was tucked the test strip. R. was awfully organized. I stared at the indigo dot, as bright as an alert eye.

"Just like that, all by yourself. And you didn't wake me?"

"I wanted it to be a surprise. I guess I've succeeded all too brilliantly."

"I'm sorry, love. I don't understand what just happened. I really think it might have been the fish. But this is the greatest present I could possibly imagine. Honest."

"Okay. Just keep your voice down. I'm right here."

Later, as R. undressed, I scrutinized her body. Her stomach was as flat as ever, and her hips looked no wider. But her breasts were different – not simply fuller, as in the days before her period, but transformed, her lovely nipples larger and more protuberant. It occurred to me as I lay watching that I *had* noticed this change a couple of nights earlier, but thought nothing of it. Now I cursed myself for remaining oblivious to the other small signs. At a recent dinner she had complained of nausea, only to devour my watery spinach soufflé. And her refusal even to sip the wine! How could I be so dull?

It was customary for us to have sex on the night of our anniversary. R. considered it something between a marital ritual and an obligation, and she surmised that the *only* day her parents still had sex was on their anniversary. (For me, imagining my parents in any coital configuration triggered a cognitive screen-freeze, a complete brainlock.) My meltdown notwithstanding, R. still intended to respect precedent. In the bottom drawer of her dresser, she kept two distinct sets of night-wear. The first were floral, opaque, and one hundred percent cotton. The second were lacy, diaphanous, and preponderantly black. She climbed into bed wearing a new spider-motif black camisole.

"Are you sure this is okay?" I asked. "Are you sure you're not feeling nauseous?"

R. laughed. "I feel great. How about you?"

"Fine. Much better – really, I swear."

But nothing worked. Nothing.

"I'm sorry," I said.

"You're just nervous. You've never screwed a pregnant chick before."

"Umm. That must be it."

"Don't worry, everything will be fine." R. turned on her side; my hand found its place on her hip. "Now go to sleep, my love."

Four

In the following days, I managed to stave off another full-blown anxiety attack, but felt nothing approximating calm, much less happiness.

I couldn't account for my feelings. I hadn't stumbled when it came to marrying. I liked kids, respected parenthood, had no ideological truck with the concept of family. So why the dread? A colleague in the philosophy department, Jonathan Stein, tried to put things in perspective. "You think this is any way unusual? Your reaction borders on cliché. Nine months is a long time – a lifetime for many creatures. Gerbils have a gestation period of three weeks."

"I guess I should be grateful that I'm not a rodent."

"You joke, but you know why I'm Mister Expert about gerbils? Because I have a pair. And that's all I have. The contrast couldn't be more poignant. You – about to embark on fatherhood, maybe a little nervous, maybe a little impaired by neurosis, but basically traveling on life's gravy train. Then there's me – over the hill without even the benefits of the climb. No, I just burrowed straight to the other side where it's all downhill."

In fact, Jonathan was only in his early forties, not that much older than me, but he often acted as if his life were essentially over. He wasn't bad looking – his eyes were slate-colored, alertly intelligent, and he had a warm smile and a firm, reliable chin. Only he had a skin condition that required an ointment that turned his face vaguely green, and he always wore the same frayed blue-and-yellow Michigan sweatshirt from his graduate student days. He lived alone in a small clapboard college house where he had installed a satellite dish so he could watch sports and weather from around the globe. His mother, who had been born in Vienna and had fled Europe via Shanghai, now lived in a retirement community not far from the college. Jonathan dutifully visited her every day. Besides these visits, Jonathan had little personal life. He dated a fair share of women, though these relationships tended to fizzle for no apparent reason. At times he referred to himself in the third person and the past tense. "And one day Stein sold off all his books and things, bought a Titanium RV with a big dish on top, and just drove straight off into the desert." He didn't like to talk about his own life, but his insights about others were sharp. He was one of my few campus confidants.

"Fears about having a child are normal – it would be weird not to. Look at my sister, Ms. Ambition-and-Career." Jonathan had one sibling, a sister who wrote for the *Frankfurter Allgemeine* in Germany. From our one meeting I remembered her as a surprisingly spry and sexy woman married to a dreary corpulent German bureaucrat. "When she found out that she was carrying twins, she very nearly lost it. She was certain that two at once would ruin her beautiful blossoming career. She looked into culling, all sorts of crazy ideas. Remind her of that now and she shudders . . . Don't worry, you'll come around – you're basically too normal not to."

Prior to the news I would have agreed. Now I wasn't so sure. The pregnancy made for more than just emotional upheaval. In a matter of days a sickle-shaped scaly patch – raw, red, and itchy – appeared on my back. The lower eyelid of my left eye developed a slight quiver, imperceptible to an observer, but distracting to me. My vision seemed oddly impaired: objects appeared at a distance, as if seen through a pair of second, more interior eyes. My voice also sounded different, by turns reedy and insubstantial, then nasal, as if altered by chronic allergies. During class the sound of this murky alien voice filling the lecture hall would cause me to lose my train of thought. "What was I just saying?" I'd ask my puzzled students. Few could answer.

Work on *Art and Atrocity* stalled. The manuscript was nearly completed, but I balked at the conclusion. I'd stare at a single sentence until the luminous signifiers disassembled themselves into phonetic mush. A serviceable clause would present itself in my mind just as the screen saver activated, blotting out text and idea, causing me to punish the mouse. After hours of this, I'd go online, and pretending to be a sociologist, pose the question to myself: How easily can a student gain access to cyber pornography? Office door locked, I'd fritter away the rest of the day surfing porn sites. If someone knocked, I'd click on my text and answer impatiently, as if disturbed from concentrated intellectual labor. Once the student had been shooed away and my door relocked, I'd dash back to *Pamela's Poontang Playground*.

All the while, thoughts of the baby loitered at the edge of my consciousness. The fear that a child would cost me tenure now hardened into a certainty. Of course, the baby wasn't disrupting anything, except R.'s sleep and digestion. But the fear that it would ruinously disrupt my work was ruinously disrupting my work. I was willing into existence the very state of affairs I dreaded most.

Gradually, even Jonathan Stein became baffled by the compulsiveness and tenacity of my worries. The tenure concern, he insisted, had to be epiphenomenal – a screen for a subterranean fear of fatherhood, which, in turn, probably masked a yet deeper anxiety. Stein confessed that he didn't particularly like small children, but pointed out the crucial difference between mild dislike and paralyzing terror.

"I'll admit it, you're not in great shape. It's getting time to turn the corner."

With a referral from my primary care facilitator, I sought out a therapist who specialized in the treatment of academics. For several weeks I worked hard at puzzling through the patterns of my past, trawling for evidence of early harm and hurt. The first sessions went well – I left almost elated, not because of any tangible breakthroughs, but because I was encouraged by the very act of trying. Quickly, though, I lost all hope for success. Part of the problem was the therapist. He was a kind man, with a thin brushstroke of moustache, distinctly un-Freudian, who seemed intelligent and remembered clearly what I told him. But he always wore the same pair of shabby Rockport loafers in desperate need of a re-soling. His office was sparsely furnished with fake teak woodwork. There was a bookcase largely free of books; maybe this was designed to create an environment unthreatening to professors, but in my case, it backfired. The few titles he had – Norman O. Brown's *Love's Body*, B. F. Skinner's *Beyond Freedom and Dignity*, and Eric Berne's *The Games People Play* – seemed like curiosities of an early-1970s Santa Cruz education. Relative to other therapists in the area, he charged less, a fact I learned only after I started and that further eroded my confidence in the treatment. When I needed to rearrange an appointment, his schedule was disturbingly accommodating. And once, when I stole a peek at the notes that he sparingly recorded on a yellow legal pad, I saw that he had written, *Milk ½ gal.*; *Chicken, 8 pc. family pack.*

The real problem was me. I lacked material. At times I longed for a distant catastrophe to blame for my present struggles, some unmastered ur-trauma, which now had resurfaced to make life untenable – the loss, say, of a sibling when I was a little boy. If anything, though, my childhood had been drearily bereft of all those defining disruptions that make impairment and neurosis wholesome responses to life. Although my parents had frequently bickered, their clashes lacked a morbid subtext or compelling organizing logic – no compulsive gambling, sexual derangement, or alcoholic excess. To find the stuff of drama, I had to travel back a generation to my aunt's death and grandmother's suicide when my mother was a teenager. Even then, how could I lay claim to a tragedy that was properly my mother's and about which she had chosen to remain largely silent? Perhaps my current anxieties had a far more obvious reason: I genuinely did not want a child. A shibboleth of self-help is to "listen to your feelings." Even if I didn't like what they were saying, wasn't it my responsibility to pay attention? I felt bad about denying the therapist a needed stream of income, but after two months I broke off the treatment.

There were glimmers of happiness. Standing in the checkout line at our local organic food market, I felt a tiny paw graze the back of my head. Turning, I looked straight into the startled lapis eyes of an infant. The baby had freed an arm from his mother's elaborate Scandinavian swaddling to play with my hair. "Hello, little creature," I said, unable to suppress a smile at the sight of this impossible humanoid. But minutes later, as I loaded the groceries into my car, the dense fogbank of gloom regathered about me.

R. asked, "Still suffering from dread head?"

"I think I'm better now that I've quit therapy. It's strange though – I never would have predicted feeling this way. It's like discovering an unknown part of your self."

R. pressed her lips together. She wasn't a big believer in unknown parts of the self. She was an intelligent woman with what she called "horse sense." Introspection, the dissection of inner feeling, the probing of a soul's dark interior – none of this was her strong suit. She tended to ascribe psychic woe either to faulty wiring or self-indulgence. It was a bit crude, but so sturdily defended that I loved her for it. "You must be looking forward to this to some degree, aren't you? I mean, even you should be able to feel happy about this."

"Don't be ridiculous, of course I am."

"Look me in the eye." R. had a theory that whenever I lied I slightly averted my gaze. I stared at her directly and said, "Scout's honor."

"I mean, try to think about the small things. Didn't you always want to have a son so you could sit on the floor and play with Matchbox cars?"

"Sure, of course. To be honest, though, I think I've always wanted a girl. Then there wouldn't be all this pressure to make sure the kid can fungo and throw a tight spiral and sink a jump shot."

"Yeah, boys can be real villains," R. said. "But at least they got dicks. They have so many more opportunities, even today. You can take a hike alone without worrying about being attacked by a psycho. And girls can be cruel, really truly vicious." In fifth grade, R. had been the teacher's pet and the most popular with the boys. In her desk one day she found a note signed by every girl in the class. *We hate you and hope you die from your next nosebleed.* Even her best friend had signed it. "Of course, it would be cute to dress up a little girl in adorable outfits and tie red ribbons in her hair . . . Anyway, I don't feel all that strongly. As long as he or she is healthy."

"Definitely. That's all that counts." I scratched the scaly patch on my back with a hanger. "And as long as it lets me get my work done."

R. patted my wrist. "You'll finish your book. Professors aren't a celibate class. Believe it or not, people can actually teach and write *and* have children."

I wasn't about to contradict her, though I had noticed that as a demographic matter, remarkably few professors had successfully procreated. The tenure process took most of the women on the faculty out of their childbearing years. One colleague, on hearing of R.'s pregnancy, had commented, *Oh, really? How weird!*

"Yes, I know," I told R. "It's just the timing . . ."

"There's never a perfect time for having a child. Look at Klara – even she's coping. What does she have to say about your worries?"

"I've only spoken to her a couple of times. I haven't really told her all that much."

"Well, maybe you should."

This was an astonishing comment coming from R. Klara and I had met in Berlin during my fellowship year after college. She was studying painting, and we were both enrolled in "The Grotesque in the German Pictorial Tradition," a course taught by a fading emeritus. From the first, her face fascinated me. Certainly it was beautiful – delicate crescent eyebrows, full lips, cheekbones shaped by an ice cream scoop – but it was something else that attracted me. Aesthetics teaches that beauty resides in symmetry, but Klara's face challenged this. Her eyes appeared to belong to different people. One eye was Aryan blue: candid, cool, decidedly uncomplicated. The other was a kaleidoscope of blue, gray, and hazel, all dashed together – sinister, indolent, full of unruly, disruptive emotion. After class one day I offered to squander Fulbright money if she'd dine with me at Berlin's most expensive Vietnamese restaurant. She arrived with a PLO scarf wrapped around her neck and a painful sinus condition. Shortly thereafter I moved into her decrepit Kreuzberg apartment.

From the beginning we got along badly. Perhaps I had never before known a complicated person. I'm extremely simple. Once you grasp my basic operating program, my behavior is entirely predictable. Not so with Klara. Her internal states always seemed unrelated to external stimuli and events. At any given moment it was impossible to say whether she was about to explode into laughter or tears. She would walk city streets barefoot and befriend deranged strangers on the

S-bahn. When we married and moved to New Haven (she needed a Green Card, and we figured that marrying was the easiest way) her closest friend was a fourteen-year-old member of a street gang who convinced her to donate money to a variety of radical, violent, and wholly spurious causes. After his arrest, she took to sleeping twelve hours at a shot. One day she announced that she had fallen in love with a sculptor who had cooked her pork chops. I helped her pack. It was all very amicable – too amicable from R.'s perspective. And now R. wanted me to solicit Klara's advice. This suggested deep, even profound concern.

"So I'm supposed to help you find peace in your fevered brain?" Klara said over the phone.

"I guess."

"What about your therapist?"

"I stopped going."

"That's a positive step." Like R., Klara rejected therapy, but for opposite reasons. R. found analytic models too involved; she couldn't understand why desire would choose the path of indirection and subterfuge. Klara, by contrast, found all such models gross simplifications, impoverished caricatures of unfathomable human depths.

"But I'm not sure things are any better . . . You know what I now think about? That the baby will be born with some kind of defect."

"That sounds like a normal fear."

"Only it's not exactly a fear. I almost find myself secretly wishing for it. I start thinking how much easier it would be to have a sweet little child with Down syndrome who would grow up to bag groceries at Stop & Shop, and would be spared learning what a fraudulent and mentally ill loser his father is. Doesn't that sound completely sick?"

"I suppose . . ." She didn't amplify or explain. We both fell silent. She exhaled slowly – smoking.

"I thought you'd stopped."

"I had briefly. But it's such a pleasant way to upset my neighbors, these narrow little Pawtucket morons. Anyway it relaxes me. When it does not make me too agitated." She and her sculptor-partner lived in Rhode Island. It seemed incredible, but she already had three children, all under five. In the background I could hear their squeals. Without bothering to cover the receiver, Klara shrieked, *"Anna! Hör sofort mal auf! Laß doch das Baby in Ruhe!"* To me she added, "So, you hear what it is like – always kinetic."

"And you like it?"

"You mean the constant noise and chaos? It's completely enjoyable."

"But doesn't it frustrate you, not having time to paint?"

"I did a nice little portrait of Kai, but that was . . . I don't know when. Anyway, Oliver is a finalist for an impressive commission, so we keep our fingers crossed. If he doesn't get that, maybe I'll go back into the studio." She painted tiny still lifes and portraits, executed with terrific technique – so profoundly passé as to be cutting-edge. Yet despite her talent she claimed to have no expressive needs. She would tire of painting and stop for months, and then she'd tire of not painting and start again.

"You're so . . . happy," I commented.

"You say it as if you are completely surprised."

"I guess maybe I am." I reminded her that she used to be absolutely kinderphobic, unsettled by the prospect of being surrounded by a "living representation" of herself.

"What can I say? Sometimes clichés are true – people change."

"Why don't I change?"

"Maybe you will. Maybe once you're in the situation you'll find that it's easy, like walking. One step, two step, fall down, stand up. You'll discover that there is no great cosmic mystery."

"And what if I don't? What then?"

"Stop whining – oh, I don't care, whine if you must, I'm used to it. Maybe you should take a small tablet and enjoy life like all your fellow Americans."

Klara's recommendation notwithstanding, I wouldn't touch meds. It wasn't that I feared acknowledging to myself that I needed them. Instead, I was terrified by a single thought: *what if they don't work?* Then nothing would shield me from the abyss. The option of medicating myself was more comforting than the medication itself. So, for my daily headaches I made due with Advil. Some days I'd wake up with a pounding at the base of my skull, a dull hangover-like throb. On others, I'd feel fine until noon, then the screaming pressure would build over my right eye and slowly burrow down, tightening, like a fat screw in hard wood. A burning, radiant buzz saw heralded the weekly migraine; it chewed through my field of vision and ravaged my frontal lobe. Light harmed me. I lost weight, my pounds magically transferred to R., an efficient exchange. Pregnancy made her radiant. Her hair, the color of dark chocolate, had grown thick, as if a fresh unborn hair gestated within each strand. Her face was as smooth as the inside of an eggshell, and her breasts provocatively full. She had more than her share of nausea, fatigue, even pain and dizziness, but carried herself stoically, refusing to submit to the medical technology that transformed a woman's body into a sonar tracking of a nuclear sub. Even on her worst days, she remained cheerful, uncomplaining. By contrast, I became convinced that the pressures of fatherhood would precipitate a mental collapse. One day I opened the refrigerator and my heart began to pound furiously in a classic fight or flight response. *This really shouldn't happen from opening the fridge*, I thought. I read the biography of a famous abstract expressionist who developed schizophrenia after the birth of his child. Certain that a similar fate awaited me, I surveyed my hectic consciousness for the first signs of fraying: a ringing in my ear, a divine summons coming from our cat, a phantom voice issuing from my molars – anything that might herald the coming breakdown.

Gradually I lost the ability to distinguish between my original dread and my dread of my dread. My anxiety reflected back on itself, like an object trapped between two mirrors.

I began, then, to think about leaving R. At first the idea itself seemed crazy, less a measure to preserve sanity than a sign that I'd already lost it. Within days, however, I decided it was the only answer. R. came from a wealthy family, and so would be able to keep the house. I was prepared to hand over as much of my salary as she needed. Subsistence would suffice for me. The college maintained a row of barracks-like apartments that had been built in the 1940s for junior faculty returned from the war. The properties, long since fallen into disrepair, now housed terminal graduate students, visiting instructors, and other fringe figures on the academic stage. A nearby fraternity threw raucous parties, and the Amtrak Montrealer – known on campus as "The Sleep Wrecker" – thundered by at three-thirty every morning. But anything would be better than the hell of a psych ward.

On a gray November afternoon, when R. was in her fourth month, I toured a shabby one-bedroom. The apartment, supposedly vacant, appeared instead to have been the subject of an emergency evacuation. Assorted clothes – blouses, jeans, socks – still littered the floor. Books lay scattered about, covers tattered, pages creased. Two bras, one black and one purple, hung from a lamp. The place reeked of stale cigarettes. In the bathroom, a cereal bowl brimming with ashes sat on the edge of the gray tub. Taken as a whole, the place suggested the interior decorating flair of a heroin addict. I was fiddling with a leaky faucet when a woman appeared in the doorway.

"Can I help you?" she asked.

"I'm just looking at the apartment. I didn't realize it was still occupied – "

"Oh, it's not," she said. "I mean, it's not supposed to be." I recognized her as a colleague in the English Department. Her name was Rosalind Roth, a second- or third-year assistant professor. "I should have been out last week, but then my car broke down. It's something of a shit-can, but I'm very attached to it. Anyway, I promise I'll be gone by Sunday . . . Tuesday at the latest."

"There's no rush," I said, "Actually I'm just looking on behalf of a friend."

"Oh, that's generous of you." Her face reminded me of a Picasso portrait: huge startled eyes, chewed lips, a slightly off-center nose. She was dressed oddly, as for a rehearsal or a costume party, in a purple velvet doublet and green tights. I remembered a story I heard from a student: that Roth had once given a lecture on *My Ántonia* wearing a latex penis and cock ring.

She handed me a glass of water without my asking, and I drank from it before noticing the unidentifiable crud on the rim.

"It's an '84 Dodge Rampage," she said, breaking the silence. "You know, my car. It's really a hopeless piece of garbage, but I can't bring myself to put it out of its misery . . . I guess you're probably more interested in the apartment, though."

Her smile flickered briefly. She was cadaverously pale, her hair the color of dried leaves. Slight and willowy, she looked vulnerable to strong gusts. Yet somehow she wasn't unattractive. Her neck was elegantly swanlike, and her wrists, clustered with bracelets, suggested Audrey Hepburn's.

"Do you mind if I ask you why you're moving out?"

"It has nothing to do with the flat, if that's what you mean." She gestured toward the rooms, seemingly oblivious to the staggering mess. "Everything's in good working order. Only problem is I'm getting a dog, and the lease says no animals. So I'm moving into town."

"Really, what kind? Dog, I mean."

"A mutt."

"That's nice. They're supposed to be the healthiest." Or so R. had told me.

Rosalind nodded. Nervously she lit a cigarette.

"Mind if I have one?" I asked.

"Not at all." She handed me a cigarette and gave me a light. I hadn't smoked a cigarette since Klara and I broke up years ago. Klara had hand-rolled hers in protest against American tobacco companies. I had no idea why I wanted one now.

"Do you mind if I look around a little more?" I said.

"Be my guest. And tell your friend Tuesday at the latest."

"I'll let him know."

The rest of the apartment was much the same. Filthy windows, warped doors, broken showerhead, gurgling toilet. In a word – ideal. I wanted and deserved no better. I lost no time in contacting the college's director of rental properties. Using an account from my department, I sent a check for the security deposit and the first month's rent. The housing director, who knew R. and me from college functions, asked no questions.

In the evening, I cooked us dinner, then built a fire. Together we nestled on the couch in the living room, reading. Beyond the narrow arc of heat, the house was cold, and outside swirled the season's first tentative flurries. Sweetness, the anniversary cat, purred beneath the coffee table. Nibbling on a wedge of cheddar, R. turned to me, her nose quivering like a rabbit's.

"You smell of cigarettes."

"I had lunch with Jonathan Stein."

"I thought he'd quit."

"He had. But now he's at it again. He says it's his only pleasure."

"That's too bad. He's such a sad sack. I don't know how you stand him . . . Do you mind changing your shirt?"

"Not at all."

I brushed my teeth, gargled, changed, and rejoined R. on the couch. We lay in a quiet embrace, her head resting on my chest in the spot she simply called "Mine."

"You seem better," she said. "More relaxed."

Vacantly I smiled, all the while thinking about my dirty barrack with the leaking faucet.

That night I dreamt R. gave birth to a shrimp – not a runt; a shellfish. We were both profoundly shocked and disappointed. The only consolation in having a crustacean-child was that I could carry it in my breast pocket while running errands. Leaving the grocery store, I gently patted my pocket, but the shrimp was gone. Frantically I searched the aisles, up and down, looking everywhere. At last I discovered the baby in a grocery bag – it must have tumbled out of my pocket during checkout. I made sure it was all right and carefully slipped it back into my breast pocket. Our baby was safe. Perhaps we had expected something different, but the shrimp was our child and we would love it. I sobbed with relief.

The next morning I felt remarkably at peace. It was as if the strange dream had freed me from the dungeon of my dread. R. was still asleep, and the sky was the luminous gray that promises snow, the trees brittle and still in their bareness. I put out seed for the finches, then prepared R. an omelet and a mug of tea. As the eggs cooked, I monitored my feelings. In the past, my buds of hopefulness had quickly withered under the light of examination. But this time they showed sturdiness. I brought R. breakfast in bed, and cuddled beside her while she ate.

Spontaneously I said what I had neglected to for months, "I love you."

"And I love *you*."

I was about to describe the dream, but then decided to keep it to myself. Instead, I said, "How about Hannah? Or maybe Sophia?"

"Too popular." She had obviously been giving this topic some thought. "I like the biblical names."

"Abemilech?"

"Well . . . I was thinking more along the lines of Reuben or Tamara."

"They're both very nice," I said. "Our first can be Reuben, and our second Tamara."

"Excuse me, love, but in light of your recent behavior, maybe it would be wiser to take things one at a time – "

"And the third can be Abemilech."

For the first time that semester I taught a successful class, and that afternoon even managed to write a page of the conclusion of *Art and Atrocity*. I also read over some earlier sections, and they were a revelation. The book was good, devoted to an important subject. Once again I was eager to see it in print.

On my way out of the office, I remembered my insanity from the day before. I promptly dialed the housing director and told her that I wouldn't be needing the apartment after all.

"Well, that's a quick change of heart. Are you sure you don't want me to hold it for another week? Let you think it over? Nobody else has expressed any interest in it . . ."

I couldn't decide whether the director was being kind or meddle-some. "Positive, thanks. And can you be sure to send the check back to my office address – not to my home, please."

"Let me make a note of that," she said. "We wouldn't want to cause any needless embarrassment."

That evening I again cooked dinner and built a fire. R. went to sleep early. I read for a while with Sweetness at my feet, and graded a few papers. Then I, too, headed for bed.

A few hours later, I was awakened by a squelching sound, like boots stepping in mud. I reached out for R., but she wasn't there. She slept irregularly as of late, often nodding off after dinner, then waking up at 3 a.m. She'd paddle about, make herself soup or a sandwich, read, and return to bed close to dawn.

I traced the sound to the bathroom. "Trouble sleeping again?" I called out. "Hey, what are you doing in – "

All the lights were on, the overhead and the row of bulbs that terraced the mirror. What I saw first I can't say – R. or the blood. Blood was everywhere – streaked across the countertop and faucet, puddled on the floor. It was dark, the color of brackish water, and ran down the grouting of the tiles. R. was wearing a cotton nightgown. From the waist up it was floral and white. Below that it looked as if she had gone wading through a pool of hacked bodies.

"Oh, Jesus Christ," I muttered. "Jesus, Jesus, Jesus."

"Something's happened," said R. "I've been trying to clean up." In her hand she held the squeegee that we used to clean the mirror. She must have worked it on the tiles, spreading the gore.

"Stop whatever you're doing," I said. "Immediately."

"Yes, okay."

Somehow I misdialed 911. I hammered down the receiver in panic, then couldn't get a dial tone. After I got through, I pulled off R.'s drenched and sticky nightgown, and wrapped her in a blanket. A dark stain, like a Redon spider, spread across the pale wool.

"Jesus Christ," I said. "What's taking that ambulance?"

"Give it a minute, you just called." R.'s face was drained of all color. She was trembling and sweat beaded her forehead. With a damp towel, I sponged the tacky mess from her legs and toes, only the blood had burrowed into the pores of her shaven calves, a malignant scarlet design.

"C'mon, you stupid fucking ambulance. C'mon."

"Sssh," she said. "It's all my doing. This trouble and mess."

"That's the craziest thing I've ever heard you say. Jesus."

The ambulance pulled up to the house with no siren, just the lights flashing. Two paramedics looked at R. and surveyed the bathroom.

"Self-inflicted?" asked one. "Do we need the police?"

"For Christ's sake," I barked, "she's pregnant."

"What's her blood type?" asked the other.

My mind went blank. I had no idea – had I ever?

"A," my wife said softly, "Positive."

As they strapped her to the gurney, R. strained to rise. "Honey, please don't forget to take care of Sweetness."

As a child, I had frequently spoken to God. Every night, lying in bed, I'd turn to the Almighty, asking Him to spare me and my family the pain of bowel cancer or chronic lymphoblastic leukemia. These weren't exactly prayers – more like respectful conversations during which I'd imagine God's kind, paternal reassurances. As a teenager, I suspended these conversations, never having told a soul about them. Now, riding in the ambulance, I once again addressed God. I offered Him my life in exchange for hers. I agreed to the most gruesome death so that she might live.

Only it was obvious she was going to die. R. would die because I had not wanted the baby. Divine punishment thrived on irony and overstatement.

In the hospital, R. disappeared behind the proverbial swinging doors. The emergency room suggested a small failing business. It reeked of disinfectant and wilted flowers. An elderly janitor buffed the green linoleum floor. A fluorescent light flickered overhead. This was a hospital designed for runners with sprains, toddlers with ear infections; this wasn't the place to wage an early morning battle with death. The wall clock was the old school variety – the minute hand twitched toward five, an hour outside of time itself. The janitor finished his buffing, wound the cord around his arm, and shambled down the corridor. I stopped praying.

Sometime later, a doctor emerged from the swinging doors. He removed his surgical mask and wiped sleep from his eye. Before reaching me, he stopped by a water cooler and slowly filled a cup. He had to know that I knew he had attended R., yet he stood before me drinking. I loathed him.

Without introducing himself, he finally said, "I take it you know what an ectopic pregnancy is."

I stared at him less with fury than disbelief. "Perhaps you could begin by telling me whether my wife is alive."

"She is, but her condition is guarded – she's hardly out of the woods."

"What do you mean 'guarded'?" Critical, serious, guarded: I had never mastered the medical establishment's opaque argot of danger.

"She's lost a lot of blood, obviously, and as a result she's gone into shock. Shock is a tricky thing. It's the body's way of shutting itself down after a trauma. Unfortunately, it sometimes succeeds too well. If we can control the shock and make sure there isn't any fresh hemorrhaging, her prognosis should be pretty good. It's just a matter of surviving the next twenty-four hours."

"Jesus . . . and what are the chances?"

"Hard to say – I don't like placing odds on these matters. Maybe something like fifty-fifty. But I have to remind you that this kind of thing is awfully hard to predict. Everybody responds differently."

A nurse escorted me into the small ICU. The other three beds were empty; still, if she hadn't steered me to R., I would have walked straight past her. Her eyelids were purple, sunken in the sockets. Her nostrils, dark and cavernous, looked like subway tunnels. Tubes entered and exited, monitors twitched and pulsed, but the only sound was a faint hissing, like air leaking from a tire. The nurse assured me she was sleeping, but to me it looked more like a coma. Her hand was warm, though dried blood was crusted on her nails. Why hadn't they washed her? Wasn't that the least they could do? I held her hand, stroked her palm, and pressed her fingers to my lips.

"You can do this," I whispered, "You can beat even odds."

At times, we had imagined how each of us would respond to mortal peril – Nazi genocide provided the inevitable yardstick. R.'s father's family, successful financiers from Frankfurt, had managed an audacious escape during World War II, but R. was convinced she never would have made it. "I would have taken a pill or thrown myself against an electrified fence."

Now I reminded her of the untested regions of her tenacity. "You're tough," I whispered. "You freeze road-kill, tackle vines, fell trees."

Toward noon the doctor approached me in the waiting room. He had shaven and looked rested. In fact, he was quite good-looking, with rugged features that stirred my distrust.

"Good news," he said. "Hey, you look terrible."

"Is that the good news?" I asked dryly.

"No, no." He laughed, revealing sturdy equine teeth. "I'm glad you've kept your sense of humor through this ordeal. But it looks like your wife's already out of danger."

"Thank God."

"That's what fascinates me about the human body. How some bounce back from serious trouble, while others – those who really should recover – fade for no reason. Your wife, though, has a strong constitution, there's no denying that. I'll let you see her in a bit. But first let's talk about ectopic pregnancy." He held the mug in his hand toward me. "Can I get you some coffee?"

"No, but water would be nice."

"I should probably have water, too. The air in this hospital is incredibly dry, too dry, really. It makes you thoroughly dehydrated, and, as we all know, viruses thrive in warm dry conditions." But then it was as if he forgot his offer; he simply began his discourse. "Most people think ectopic means a pregnancy in the fallopian tubes, but really it just means 'out of place.' So an ectopic pregnancy could lodge anywhere, in the heart or liver, for example." He took a sip of coffee. "Though obviously that would be impossible."

"Obviously," I said, walking to the water cooler.

"In your wife's case, the ectopic location *was* the fallopian tube. This is a very dangerous condition. The embryo grows and grows, and sooner or later the fallopian tube ruptures. As we've seen, the embryo dies, and the mother hemorrhages, sometimes to death. In fact, before ultrasound, ectopic pregnancies were one of the three most common causes of maternal mortality in the United States . . . Your wife didn't have an ultrasound, did she?"

I shook my head. "Everything seemed to be going well . . . She's kind of into natural stuff."

"Well, I hope she doesn't have any political objections to emergency lifesaving surgery."

"I think not." I drank a second cup of water. I would have to remember to keep the doctor from talking with R. once she had awakened.

"Your wife was lucky. She came in with a completely ruptured fallopian. Obviously it was too late to use methotrexate or to do a salpingostomy. We weren't even sure if we could pull off an emergency laparoscopy."

The doctor was fast exhausting the debt of gratitude I owed him for saving R.'s life. "You know, I'm also a professional," I said. "And yet when I talk to a layperson, I make it my business to speak in understandable terms."

His eyes narrowed. At least our feelings were mutual. "I was *about* to explain. The laparoscope is a long hollow tube. We went in just under your wife's navel and removed the ectopic pregnancy. Are you following?"

"I think I am."

"Usually when the fallopian tube is completely ruptured you have to do a full surgical incision, but I managed to also get the tube with the laparoscope. Obviously we still have to monitor you wife's HCG levels to make sure we got all the fetal tissue. Assuming no additional bleeding and complications, we're looking at a stay at the hotel" – his first and only attempt at levity – "of about four days. And then about two weeks of rest at home. No sex during that period."

"I would assume not."

"Hey, I've learned to take nothing for granted around here. You wouldn't believe the things we see. But after that, you can get back to your normal, that is, pre-pregnancy, routine. In fact, we recommend it."

"And what does this means in terms of – "

"Women with one tube have about a forty percent loss of fertility, which isn't bad, considering. Of course, they also run a much higher risk of another ectopic pregnancy. So you have to monitor things closely. Ultimately it's your call."

When the nurse next brought me in, R. was sitting up in bed, nibbling at a spoonful of yogurt.

"You see," I said. "You *are* a survivor."

She gave a wan smile. "The doctor said I should have known that something was wrong. The dizziness was abnormal. And he reprimanded me for never having had an ultrasound."

"He reprimanded you?" I expressed the hope that medical competence and a good bedside manner were inversely related.

Her smile evaporated. "But even if I had noticed, they still would have had to remove it."

"Of course, they would have. There's nothing else that can be done. The doctor said that next time we just have to be more vigilant."

I couldn't tell where R. was fixing her gaze. It wasn't on the yogurt. And it wasn't on me.

"I don't want to go through that again," she said.

"God forbid. Next time everything will be completely different."

"I mean . . . I don't know if I want a next time."

"That's understandable. We'll have plenty of time to discuss it."

"And I'm not talking about me. It's the loss. I don't want that ever again."

"Of course. Knock wood, you're a fighter. Next time, we'll do things differently. We'll make sure everything's safe and okay."

"I already spoke to the doctor," she said, letting the spoon sink into the yogurt. "He said while I'm already here it would be easy to tie the other one."

"What? What are you talking about?"

"You know, having the other one done, getting 'fixed.' He said it would be a simple procedure."

In my shock, I looked around the room, as if searching among the monitors for a metaphor to capture the absurdity of the idea. I found none. "That's crazy. You're still upset. You need rest."

"But we could get it over and done with. It only requires a local anesthetic."

44

"For Christ's sake, you were just at death's door. Now's not the time to make any decisions."

Her eyes were heavy upon me. "I know you never wanted the baby, you don't have to pretend. You tried, I realize that, but you never did."

This again. The familiar pressure clamped my temples. "Please, please, please," I said. "Must we decide now? Shouldn't you rest?"

What angle of the lip's complex geometry introduces pity into a smile? "You too," she sighed. "You should go home and get some sleep."

"I can rest in the waiting room."

"No, go home. Get a decent night's sleep."

When I arrived home, the cat behaved strangely, avoiding me, keeping to the furniture. My legs almost gave out as I climbed the stairs. A light still burned in our bedroom. Also in the center hall and bathroom. In places the blood looked like dried wine; in others, like baked mud. Cracks had formed in its dried surface, like a fine raku. The smell was pungent, offal-like. I tried to open the window, but it was jammed, sealed shut by the recent paint job. The squeegee went straight into the garbage. Setting to work on the floor with a bucket and sponge, I saw a pattern of paw prints in the dried blood. Near this was an area that appeared to have been wiped by a thumb – Sweetness's tongue. My stomach tightened. I couldn't help but wonder where amid the blood was the human matter, the ruined collection of partially organized cells. Was it possible that the cat had eaten it? The thought made me recoil, gag.

The tiles cleaned easily. But the blood that had channeled down into the grout resisted even my most vigorous assaults with ammonia and a toothbrush, turning an indifferent shade of brownish-gray.

It was almost dawn when I climbed into bed. Only then did I think to check the sheets. A single dried medallion of blood had stained right through. I stripped the bed, but too exhausted to rise, lay splayed on the bare mattress and fell immediately to sleep.

A few hours later I awoke, feeling fully rested for the first time in months. The headache that had plagued me for weeks had magically vanished and my mind felt strangely clear. I would have started the day with a prayer if it hadn't seemed so blasphemous. It was as if my private pathology had scripted the whole episode.

PART 2

Five

The official letter, on Bundestag stationery, invited me to address an international forum on plans to build a vast Holocaust memorial in Berlin. That same month, a year to the day after R.'s miscarriage, the president of the college called. "Well, my friend," he said, "now you can stay till they carry you out." I had gotten tenure.

To celebrate, R. wanted to buy me a car. Most men would have been delighted, but frankly the only cars that had ever captivated me were of the Matchbox variety. Once, at a birthday party for R.'s former college roommate, the host/husband shepherded all the guests outside after the cake had been served. There on the driveway sat a new Toyota Corolla tied with an enormous pink ribbon. Afterward, R. and I agreed that it was a perverse display: the husband's smug look of patriarchal beneficence; his wife's silly celebratory jig; the guests' obliging applause when she turned the ignition – all for a white Corolla.

Seeing as we weren't going to have children, R. favored something sporty, perhaps a two-door coupe. Only it wasn't that simple. Trivial as it may sound, choosing a car poses special problems for professors. Most doctors or lawyers look forward to the day when they can drive a Jaguar, Mercedes, or Lexus. Not professors. Those dedicated to the life of the mind were expected to frown upon such ostentatious displays of the prerogatives of inherited wealth. For junior faculty, high-end automobiles were strictly off-limits. Years back, a young professor of engineering had tooled around campus in a red Alfa Romeo. After his tenure denial, assistant professors generally stuck with beat-up Subarus.

With tenure came the right to luxury cars, but only those on the margins. Volvo had once been the car of choice for senior faculty, but since being gobbled up by Ford and transformed into another faceless toady of global capitalism, its popularity had waned. Recently several colleagues had been sighted in low-end Audis and Acuras: transgressive, but still unlikely to court the disapprobation of former Marxists. After a few test drives, I decided to stick with my dependable, faithful Honda of nine years. I preferred something else – we decided to wait until the end of the fall term and then throw a party.

*

My promotion had turned out to be happily uneventful. After R.'s release from the hospital, I had anticipated long stretches devoted to nursing her back to health, but her recovery went so quickly and smoothly that I had plenty of time that spring to revise my manuscript. To my own surprise, I finished in two months. Having early on secured a contract with a leading academic press, I didn't need to shop the book around. And my editor, convinced of the book's topicality, expedited production. *Art and Atrocity* hit the shelves eight months later.

Around the time that humans, principally men, began systematically slaughtering each other, they started building monuments to their deeds. Many of the greatest buildings of classical antiquity – the Parthenon, the Great Altar at Pergamón – were built to celebrate military victory. These were monumental buildings in both senses of the word – commemorative and massive, products of an architecture of heroism and myth-making. As architectural styles changed, the basic function of the war memorial did not. Daunting in scale and lavish in expense, colossal structures such as the Arc de Triomphe and the Brandenburg Gate were designed to evoke and pay tribute to the great victories of conquering armies. Absent from these monuments was the slightest concern with the identity of the dead or the suffering of the fallen. That changed with the staggering carnage and world-historical futility of the First World War. Along with aerial warfare, tank warfare, trench warfare, and chemical warfare, the Great War also pioneered a new aesthetics of memorializing the very horrors that resulted from these innovations on the battlefield. The French introduced the Tomb of the Unknown Soldier, the somber marker of the Body without Name, while the English contributed the cenotaph, the Name without the Body. The grand arches over broad promenades, the garlanded kings on horseback, and the bronze mustached generals on towering pedestals quietly disappeared, replaced by granite obelisks and marble stelae, subdued ledgers that dotted the rolling countryside of all the former belligerents. This aesthetic worked well for a time, until the astonishing genocidal sweep of the Second World War posed fresh problems to the commemorative imagination. In the years directly following the war, many artists simply blanched before the challenge. Nathan Rappaport's Warsaw Ghetto Monument could do no better than to revive the impossibly antiquated and misplaced logic of the Parthenon friezes: outsized figures with classical features and buff bodies carved in stone, archetypes of heroism engaged in mythological acts of resistance and battle. It wasn't until decades later that a new, more subdued architecture of marking atrocity began to surface in Berlin. During my Fulbright year, I explored these monuments to the victims of the Nazi past. Many were transient, meant to pass like memory itself. In a quiet residential neighborhood of Charlottenburg, a mysterious street sign in the Gothic fraktur read Judengasse, the original name of the street from the days of the old ghetto, a gesture to the invisible quarter of what had once been the hub of Jewish Berlin. Painstakingly I documented an entire subculture of similarly obscure and subterranean monuments to the vanished world of Berlin's Jewry: discreet pillars that gradually sank, like disappearing tombstones, into the urban landscape; gashes in the ground that retraced the footprints of long-destroyed synagogues; and small metallic friezes, inscribed with random etchings that evoked indecipherable names of forgotten victims. In an article for a German art magazine, I described these works as "anti-monuments," deconstructions of the logic of the grand marble monstrosity that once typified public art. To my surprise, this essay attracted considerable attention in both scholarly and artistic circles. My name began to circulate.

Roughly at the time my book entered production, the German government designated six acres in the very heart of Berlin as the site for an enormous national Holocaust memorial. This sparked arguments about the design and purpose of such a gargantuan commemorative gesture, as well as a passionate meta-debate about Germany's traumatic history, and then a meta-meta-debate about Germany's obsession with debating its fraught past. Using material from my book, I wrote a long piece for *Die Zeit* arguing that the controversy concerning the monument was itself the most provocative memorial to the genocide. "Let there be," I wrote, "no Final Solution to the problem of honoring the memory of the exterminated." To my surprise, I was hailed by the press as the guru of Holocaust memorials. *Der Spiegel* reported on my work, and German radio interviewed me. Then, some months later, I received the invitation to address the international forum. The city's mayor and leading members of the Bundestag would be present.

A colleague once likened writing academic books to tossing rose petals into the Grand Canyon – they disappear soundlessly into the void. Now, suddenly, I was both tenured and on the fast track to academic celebrity. Only R.'s reaction diminished my excitement: she declined to come with me to Berlin. The forum was scheduled for the end of January, and R. claimed a heightened sensitivity to cold since the miscarriage. When I observed that Berlin never gets as frigid as New England, she said it wasn't the cold per se that bothered her, but the dampness. It was pointless to argue. The dreariness of winter in northern Europe, the legacy of the Third Reich, the associations with Klara: her decision was overdetermined.

Maybe envy also played a role. For just as my career was taking off, R.'s had stalled. After her recovery, R. complained of being tired of writing for *Smithsonian* and *Geo*. She too wanted to write a book. She sketched a proposal for a popular history of the coelacanth, the fish thought to have died out seventy million years ago until it began surfacing in fish markets in Indonesia. But after devoting a couple of months to concentrated reading, she abandoned the project. A rival science writer, she learned, was already completing a study of the bizarre creature, and it was doubtful that the market could support a second coelacanth book. Then she talked about trying her hand at personal essays, but the leather-bound diary that I bought her as encouragement remained untouched. She concluded she needed a break from writing altogether.

Paraphrasing Hegel, Marx remarked that history repeats itself, first as tragedy and then as farce. So it was with R.'s second attempt to establish a steady supply of fresh eggs. She planted wire deep into the ground around the coop, threaded netting over the top, and re-fitted the gate, measures designed to thwart tunneling foxes, dive-bombing owls, and dexterous raccoons. Still, disaster struck, this time from an unlikely source – the chickens themselves. Once mature, the putative hens (again three) began acting strangely. They laid no eggs, and instead crowed at daybreak. R. tried to ignore this anomalous behavior, but as the crowing became ever more boisterous, full-throated, and intolerable, she reluctantly contacted Chicken Carol, a local woman skilled in the slaughter of unwanted roosters. The chickens that R. had so dutifully raised found their resting place on a bed of couscous surrounded by steamed zucchini.

Next came the horses. A woman who had noticed the barn at the back of our property asked if she could board two retired harness-racers, a gelding and a mare. R. repaired the fence to our pasture, ordered bales of hay, and bought new padlocks. Soon the two horses were lazily grazing in the overgrown field, cutting handsome silhouettes at sunset. The woman promptly defaulted on her monthly boarding fee, and both animals suffered from asthma (the result of years of inhaling track dirt), but this didn't diminish R.'s pleasure. Every evening she'd feed them carrots and stroke their inflamed nostrils.

Frankly, I felt sorry for her – especially now that the issue of children was moot. R.'s recovery, as I've mentioned, went smoothly, and soon we were ready to return to our "routine." Under a full moon, R. climbed into bed wearing a black camisole with matching panties. I stroked her smooth, muscular back before reminding her that our procreative efforts had to wait until her cycle had returned to normal. "I suppose one of us should deal with the protection," I said.

"Not to worry," R. answered, all snuggly. "That's all been taken care of."

"What do you mean?"

She searched her night table for a stick of incense. "I mean I did it – I had the second procedure. Finito. Tube tied."

I tossed off the comforter. "You did *what?* Without even telling me? You just went ahead and did it?"

R. nodded.

"But *why*? That's the most outrageous thing I've ever heard. Why didn't you consult me?"

"What was the point?"

"The *point*? Aren't I your husband? Don't I have a say in this decision? And that fuckhead of a doctor went ahead and did it in the state you were in – this is absolutely insane."

"You made yourself perfectly clear. You don't want children. You should be thanking me."

"*Thanking* you? How do you know what I want? Since when are you so clairvoyant?"

"Stop whining. And yelling."

"No, really. Who gave you the right?"

"You don't want children – we learned that the hard way. But that's okay. Everything worked out for the best – for you."

"Christ! You make it sound like I'm glad that you lost it. I know I was struggling there for a while, but I was turning the corner. I really was."

R. just smiled at me. It was a very tense smile, like a rubber-band about to snap. "Stop."

"Stop what? Talking? Existing?"

R. slipped on her robe and crossed the room in silence, as if preparing to leave. From the top drawer of the dresser, she removed a piece of mail. She resettled herself at the edge of the bed, and handed me an envelope.

"You shouldn't leave your financial stuff lying around," she said, tightening her robe.

It was a letter from the college. Returning my deposit on the shabby apartment. The bitch of a housing director had sent it to my home address. Accidentally, intentionally – who could say?

All at once I was overwhelmed by fatigue. This was a toxic screw-up, the kind of thing that leaks into the water supply, spreading a slow poison that kills decades later.

"I know this looks bad," I said, fighting exhaustion. "But you have to believe me, I changed my mind *before* you had to go to the hospital. I swear, honestly. You see, I had this incredible dream that you had given birth to a shrimp – "

Massaging my shoulders, R. said, "It's okay. Not everyone was meant to have children."

"I tried," I offered feebly. "I wanted to want one. I was coming around, honestly . . . In the dream, I kept the shrimp in my breast pocket and took it shopping. I know that sounds crazy, but it really made me see things differently."

"I'm sure it did." She was a skilled masseuse.

"Couldn't you have at least consulted me? Why do you have to be so unilateral?"

"I know what you would have said. 'Let's wait. What's the rush? I don't know what I want.' All the usual stuff."

I glanced down at the stamp. I was astonished to see it was a coelacanth from a new series on prehistoric marine life. The cancellation date was clear: the letter had arrived a day or so after R. had returned from the hospital. This meant two additional things: that I, in my negligence, had brought her the offending letter, and that she had had the procedure *before* securing this final proof of my desperation. Yet now she enlisted the check as the ultimate justification for not consulting me. Wasn't that an abuse of evidence? Post hoc reasoning – my students used it all the time.

"But what about you?" I asked. "Are you going to be happy without, you know, a kid?"

"I wouldn't have done it if I didn't feel it was right for both of us."

I nodded. R.'s massage bore deeper, her fingers no longer intent on puzzling through the knots of my flesh. I often wondered where she had acquired this expertise. Had she taken a course? Learned on the back of a hard Arab youth during the year she lived in Paris? I felt myself growing aroused. It was an inopportune, even a ridiculous, time for sex. Or was it?

"C'mon," R. said. "Light a candle."

I was already reaching for the matches.

Six

On the surface, the months leading to my tenure party passed pleasantly. R. and I often worked together in shared solitude, reserving the weekends for travel. We bought mountain bikes, and on spring days we'd cycle to a former mill turned used bookstore. Close by was a café overlooking a waterfall, where we would lunch as a reward for our strenuous pedaling. On other weekends we drove north, exploring the antique stores of Vermont, sleeping in meticulously restored inns. We also worked on our house, replacing two windows in our bedroom and installing a granite-topped island in the kitchen.

There were a few squabbles, though. The first involved, of all things, a movie. It was shortly after I had mailed in my manuscript, and I decided to go to a matinee. R. was still researching the coelacanth project, so I went alone, settling for standard Hollywood fare, a chain of spectacular explosions linked by a preposterous plot. R. refused to see such movies, though typically enjoyed hearing about them. But when I started describing this film, she simply said, "Spare me." Except during a fight, I couldn't remember either of us so deliberately quashing communication.

The other episode that comes to mind occurred months later, at our anniversary dinner. Instead of our traditional spot, the Graylord,

R. wanted to dine at home. It was a mild fall evening, so we grilled and ate outside. During dessert, I mentioned the news I had heard that day at the college: Anastasia Jung, a colleague in my department, had just returned from China with a baby girl.

"I'm very happy for her," R. said.

"The little girl's name is Mirabella."

"That's a pretty name."

"You know, Anastasia once had an ectopic pregnancy."

"I didn't know that."

"They got the girl in Shanghai. The whole thing took less than a week."

R. sighed. "Why are you bringing this up now, Daniel? Why of all moments, now?"

"What do you mean? "

R. shook her head and stared off toward the asthmatic horses.

"Did I do something wrong?" I asked. "Is it a crime to talk about this?"

She didn't answer, and we didn't speak anymore that night. The next day, in my office, I wondered why I had brought up the topic. Was I simply behaving like a child who refuses to board the roller coaster, then cries the whole way home for missing the best ride? Or was I doing it for R. – reminding her that nothing was irrevocable? Whatever my motive, I certainly had meant no harm, and was disturbed by our failure to talk through the issue. I decided to delicately bring it up again at dinner.

That evening when I pulled into the driveway, I saw, in front of the barn, a pile of debris, smoldering like leftovers from a cookout. Circling the heap, I feared that Sweetness had been incinerated by a bolt of rogue lightening. Not until I prodded the smoking pile with my foot did I realize it was a painting: one of my favorites – a landscape that Klara had done in northern Portugal. I was too astonished to move. It was Klara whose rages had often ended with plates swept from a table, light bulbs pulverized in their sockets, and canvases slashed with a knife. R. was supposed to be the even-keeled one. Inside I expected to find her contrite, jittery, unnerved by her own loss of control, eager to make amends. Instead, she was munching a bar of dark chocolate.

"Feeling better?" I asked.

"Much," she said. "I never thought that painting looked good in the dining room."

*

In college, I discovered the writings of Emanuel Swedenborg, the eighteenth-century Swedish theologian. At the time I was reading a lot of Spinoza, Kierkegaard, Nietzsche, and Schopenhauer – the familiar seducers of the troubled undergraduate mind. A distinguished natural scientist and engineer, Swedenborg suffered a "spiritual crisis" in his mid-fifties. He abandoned his scientific studies, and devoted the last twenty-five years of his life to the adumbration of a new Christian teaching. Like many religious visionaries, Swedenborg clearly suffered a chemical imbalance: he insisted, for example, that his books were verbatim transcriptions of his lengthy and often contentious conversations with angels. Yet despite patches of derangement and opacity, I found his work luminous and deeply affecting, and, in the weeks before the party, returned to his book about marriage, *Conjugal Love*. Conventional Christian theology regards the platonic bond between God and worshiper as the archetype of love; Swedenborg, by contrast, taught that marriage, as the fusion of the spiritual and physical, was the purest form of union. He argued that adultery is a sin not because it violates God's sacrament, but because it "extinguishes the glimmer of life" – the precious trust at the heart of the marital bond.

R. and I were both the products of marriages that, if less than harmonious, had nonetheless endured. R.'s father had been born into a family of wealthy German-Jewish bankers transplanted to the Midwest. The father's grandparents had been founding members of the Standard Club, a famous institution of Jewish Chicago, its very name a tribute to assimilationist designs. R.'s mother was the proverbial beautiful *shiksa*, the eleventh child of a Catholic policeman from Milwaukee. When the father's parents, who, years earlier, had overruled their son's desire to have a Bar Mitzvah, unexpectedly objected to an interfaith marriage, the pliant bride agreed to convert. She had been agreeing ever since.

R.'s father was an odd combination of folksy, small-town businessman, big-time financier, and Asiatic despot. He was agreeable, generous, and fair to all people – save his wife, whom he treated like a frivolous and potentially volatile investment. Without any money of her own, the wife was kept on a strict monthly allowance, which could be exceeded only by borrowing against future installments. Husband and wife shared no interests. R.'s mother had never attended college, but had a passion for theater, opera, and art, and read widely and eclectically. The father, a product of boarding school and Princeton (where he was the only Jew in his eating club), waged a lifelong rebellion against higher culture, finding his most refined pleasure in duck hunting. The mother, a soft and sensuous woman, probably received little in the way of affection from her inflexible husband (except, perhaps, on their anniversary). But somehow their marriage worked. Their devotion to one another was fierce, and I remember the mother's stiff silence when I once ventured a humorous quip at her husband's expense.

With my parents, matters were more complicated. My parents fought openly and frequently, punishing each other with words, though their battles were usually limited to matters of money. When, early in their marriage, my mother supported my father through law school, her thrift and industry presumably had been a virtue. Later, when my father became a partner at a top Wall Street firm, her behavior appeared less reasonable, less attuned to reality. No matter how much Father earned, Mother couldn't buy a thing – not a can of tuna, not a box of cereal, not a pair of socks – unless it was on sale. She wasn't cheap; she could spend aggressively – in fact, she was the one who had pushed my father into the spacious Tudor in Larchmont where I grew up, but only because the previous owner had run afoul of securities law and had had to sell the house in a hurry and for a fraction of its market value. *Any moron can pay full price*, was her mantra and creed. Though she enjoyed decorating the house, her attitude toward the economy remained apocalyptic. She considered prosperity a fluke, a temporary aberration in the inevitable drift toward doom. The higher my father climbed, the further the family would fall. It was just a matter of time. By contrast, my father was always a stalwart optimist, his confidence in the American spirit and a balanced portfolio unshakable.

I long believed my parents' fights about money served as a screen for a deeper problem in their marriage, presumably sexual. Later I came to the opposite conclusion: that all their fights, even the most intimate, were really, at their heart, about finance. Of course, it wasn't hard to trace the origins of my mother's insecurities. She was fourteen when her younger sister died during a botched operation to repair a fused spine. Two years later, her mother, who had never recovered from the shock, committed suicide. Mother never talked about these tragedies. Even when I pressed her for details, she would simply respond, "Eugene O'Neill had nothing on my family" – this before I even had the slightest idea who Eugene O'Neill was.

On occasion, my mother would frankly acknowledge that she and my father were not made for each other. "Soulmate, no," she'd quip. "Cellmate, yes." She also often said, "What held us together was you." I never liked the idea of being the glue that cemented a bad marriage, and dismissed the implied counterfactual as absurd. (How could they possibly know what would have happened in my absence?) Gradually, though, I came to see my mother's words in a different light. For without a child, the only things left to keep a couple from drifting apart are love and will. And of the two, will is the more important. So I learned.

*

Even before my tenure party and my trip to Berlin, I was having a good semester, thanks largely to the talented students in my graduate seminar. Two in particular stood out – the young man who, a year earlier, had found me embracing the sycamore on the grounds of Hartfield Academy, and a drama student prophetically named Tamara Starr. Tamara had blazingly white teeth, long-lashed forest-green eyes, and an elegant jaw line – promising features for a fledgling actor interested in a life on stage. When she spoke her delicate nostrils flared with emotion, and even when silent, her mouth, round and full, kept working. Throughout the term I was aware of the weight of her gaze resting on me; on occasion we exchanged fraught eye contact. After class one day she handed me an invitation to an upcoming production of *Miss Julie*. "I play the lead," she said. "It would be great if you could come. And there's a cast party after Saturday's performance."

Before my promotion, I considered female students occupational hazards. If a young woman came to my office to discuss, say, Egon Schiele's erotic drawings, I'd wedge my door open and steer the conversation to a consideration of the works' formal properties. If she arrived in a white T-shirt without a bra, I'd stare at an imaginary point in the middle of her forehead. And, if, out of the clear blue, she began to sob, I'd comfort her with bland clichés while secretly dialing the number of the college's counseling center.

After the tenure decision, perhaps I lowered my guard a bit. In any case, I accepted the invitation. Admittedly my interest was piqued by the knowledge that Tamara was briefly to appear on stage naked. I arrived at the theater a good half hour before curtain, but it was already crowded, and as I found my seat, I felt oddly nervous, less excited than agitated, as if I had committed a crime simply by showing up. A colleague in another row tried to get my attention, but I pretended not to see him, and avoided making eye contact with the persons sitting on either side of me. The theater was so hot that I could barely follow the first scenes, which dragged on interminably. Then Tamara appeared without clothes. Her body was hardly the perfect youthful specimen I had expected. The weight of years hung more heavily on her than on R. Her breasts were pear-shaped, and even at a distance, I could discern pale stretch marks. Her hips fanned out with maternal ampleness. Yet Tamara presented her body with such honesty, in a gesture of such mature offering, that I found myself deeply moved and aroused. The local newspaper described the scene as "gratuitous student exhibitionism" (thereby guaranteeing a sold-out engagement), but I found it a tour de force of sensuous control. And as she stood naked on stage, Tamara seemed to stare directly at me. *Miss?! Call me Julie. There are no barriers between us now. Call me Julie!* I told myself that she had just chanced on my eyes, that this was merely a conceit of her performance, but still I could feel myself blush deeply in the darkened theater. Afterward, as I was leaving, I was still so preoccupied with the force of her gaze that I nearly walked directly into Rosalind Roth.

"Oh, hello," she said. "Remember me? You toured my apartment . . ."

"Yes, of course."

"So, what did you think of the performance?"

"A bit uneven," I said, "but kind of interesting. How about you?"

"I don't know. Maybe I would have medicated the female lead. I think it would have benefited from more frontal nudity."

"Yes, maybe," I said, at loss for a response.

Rosalind smiled nervously. Her lips had the same chewed appearance as the first time we met. She wore crushed velvet tights and something that looked like a bodice. She had an exceptionally tiny waist. I wondered where she shopped; maybe at an Elizabethan outlet store.

"How does your friend like the apartment?" she asked.

"Actually, he ended up not taking it."

"Oh . . . I hope he wasn't repelled by the filth."

"From what I know, I don't think that played a role."

"I see." She played with a cluster of bracelets that weighted her delicate wrist. "Would you like to get some coffee?" she asked.

"I don't drink coffee," I said.

"Oh. I hadn't pegged you as the boring anti-caffeine type."

"It makes my heart palpitate," I explained. "But I'll have tea."

We walked to a local café. She strode quickly on well-formed legs. Had I noticed those legs before? In the café, she smoked, but this time I declined to join her. Music was playing, drowning out her thin voice. She fidgeted with her bracelets. I think she was talking about theater, maybe Genet. Unable to hear a word, I kept nodding anyway.

Afterward, as we stood on the street, she said out of the blue, "Strange, but I only just noticed that ring."

She meant, I realized, my wedding band.

"I guess it signifies what it usually does," she said.

I nodded. It seemed she had suddenly developed a slight lisp.

"Just checking," she said. "I hate making a fool of myself, you know."

"Don't we all . . ."

"I guess, but for some of us, it comes all too naturally." She gave a fey wave of farewell.

"Hey," I called after her, touched by her orphaned expression. "You've got to come to my tenure party. It's going to be a real tah-dah. And you're already dressed for it." Here I gestured to her fuchsia tights.

"Will there be dancing?"

"Absolutely." I did a very brief and schematic Travolta move.

"Then I'm definitely not coming."

"I meant to say there'll be remarkably little in the way of dancing. Virtually none at all."

Her glassy eyes brightened. She looked to be formulating an idea, but all that came out was a whispered, "Bye."

I didn't see any more of Rosalind that term. But at the next meeting of my seminar, I felt Tamara's humid gaze again trained upon me. I feared I was blushing, and couldn't push from my mind an image of her large, dark nipples. After class, she waited until the other students had left before asking, rather insouciantly, "So?"

Blandly I complimented her performance and expressed my larger indifference to Strindberg.

"We missed you at the cast party."

"I wish I could have come – I was completely exhausted. Thanks for the invite, though."

When the seminar next met, I was relieved to see that she no longer pursued me with her eyes.

*

On the island in the kitchen the caterers laid out the appetizers: tiger prawns in coconut, quail eggs on toast, and several wheels of *Tête de Moine* cheese. In the dining room we spread a lavish buffet: Peking duck,

Chilean sea bass in green chutney, pheasant tangine with olives, and several smoked Scottish salmons, sliced razor-thin. The orgy would end with chocolate mousse, champagne truffles, and R.'s specialty, profiteroles with homemade whipped cream. A handful of students serviced the guests with martinis, manhattans, and margaritas, and twenty bottles of champagne rested on ice in the basement. The rooms were lit by a constellation of hand-dipped candles and oil lamps. The five slots of the CD player piped the house full with dance music, everything from Glenn Miller swing to RuPaul's disco chartbusters. R. wore a new zebra-striped miniskirt, and I donned a black cashmere jacket.

In all, about eighty people came to the party. Animated chatter filled the living and dining rooms. Forster, one of the few remaining members of a postwar philosophy department that had enjoyed an international reputation, was doing his much-touted Isaiah Berlin imitation: "I pleaded with Akhmatova, 'Darling you mustn't confuse the possibility of truth for the necessity of beauty . . .'" Rajeesh Mehta, a gay mathematician from Madras, fed papadums to his partner, a poet from the Bronx. In the den-turned-disco, Mellicent Sander, a performance artist, led a group of dancers consisting largely of the untenured in a funk romp.

Sebastian Winkie, a British historian and part of the Thatcher brain-drain that inundated the college in the 1980s, grabbed me by the wrist. "Best bloody food I've had in ages. Not the typical blue-chip-and-salsa bore."

Others said much the same. Arms strained to pluck a dumpling or shrimp from the buffet. Wine and vodka flowed freely. A scent familiar from bygone days unfurled across the living room: dope. An empty bottle exploded on the floor, always a sign of a party gaining momentum. Through the throng, R. and I passed each other, exchanging a delicate peck on the lips. "You look wonderful," I said.

"So do you, Professor."

Raymond Friedman, a local playwright who had recently enjoyed a substantial Off-Broadway success, staggered away from his wife and toward me. His shirt was batiked with red wine. "Very good party," he declared. "Could be Manhattan."

"I'm glad to hear it."

He took an uneven step closer and his voice dropped a register. "How about you and me go outside and I fuck you in the ass?"

"Excuse me?"

"You heard me – fuck you. In the ass. Outside. If it's too cold, we can find a more congenial spot."

"Thanks, but I think I'll have to decline."

"Shame . . . See that woman over there?" He gestured in the direction of Melanie Crenshaw, a friend of R.'s, his tone confidential. "She's carrying my baby in her anus."

"Really?"

"Why would I make up such a thing?" His eyes labored over the crowd before settling upon me again. I caught a whiff of his breath: frowsy and acidic. "Did I already offer to bugger you in the barn?"

"You did – I think I turned you down."

"I see." And he tottered off in a fresh direction.

Behind me, I heard colleagues in political science talking:

"Of course, they handed him the election. What makes you think we ever had an independent judiciary?"

"He'll play a little golf, trim the estate tax, and four years from now we'll be rid of him. Not to worry."

Just then I was cuffed on the arm by the college president. "So how does it feel, *Professor*?" The president was a freakishly well-preserved man of sixty, with a thick head of graying hair that bobbed when he energetically worked a crowd. A Quaker, vegetarian and former Olympic rower, he liked to talk principles with sleeves rolled up while liberally dispensing winks, backslaps, and shoulder-pummels. The faculty found him something of an embarrassment, but the alums adored him and it showed at giving time. "So where do you go from here?"

I wasn't sure if he was talking about the immediate future or the Big Picture. The latter was said to be a source of concern to the Board – while most colleagues remained productive after tenure, it was well known that Maxwell Scheffer in Religion had shaved his legs and joined a competitive cycling team, while Saddam Malik in Chemistry spent his days hunched over blackjack tables at Indian casinos. I decided on the safer route and told him about my impending trip to Berlin.

"Ah, yes. So I recall – that important memorial gig. Berlin – a helluva city, so vibrant and now so cosmopolitan. I'd give it the nod over Paris. Will the Bundeskanzler be in attendance?"

"I don't know. I wouldn't think so. It's more for the city planners. But the mayor should be there – "

"Did I ever tell you the story about the summit in the eighties with Reagan, Thatcher, and Kohl?" The president's brother had served as an undersecretary of state, plying him with a dependable, if antiquated, stock of anecdotes about world leaders. "So there they were, the Big Three, gathered at Camp David. After an afternoon of talks, Thatcher rose and announced, 'I could do with a brisk walk.' Reagan, who jumped at any excuse not to work, chimed in, 'Me, too.' And Kohl, eager to show off his mastery of English, merrily said, 'Me, *three*.'" The president's laugh was so explosive that I had to join in. Another cartilage-compressing handshake and he was gone.

Jonathan Stein made his way over. "Did he tell the Mitterrand story or the Gandhi joke?"

"It was the one about Helmut Kohl."

"Me, three?"

"Yeah."

"Well, here's to Joschka Fischer." We tapped beer bottles. Jonathan looked good. Instead of the obligatory Michigan sweatshirt, he wore a semipressed button-down shirt and jeans. The skin on his face also looked better – less green – and he was sporting a week-old goatee.

"So how's Mom?" I asked.

He shrugged. "She still spends most of her days buying up Mel Gibson memorabilia on the Web. She recently got one of his cigarette butts at auction. Fifty bucks. Can you believe it?"

"I've got to say, that sounds pretty strange. Isn't Gibson's father a Holocaust denier?"

"Is he?"

"I think I read that somewhere."

"I'll pass that on, not that it's going to make an iota of difference. She's been obsessed with him for years."

Someone asked me the way to the bathroom, and when I turned back to Jonathan, he was talking about a cannibal in Germany. A handful of colleagues had gathered around. "My sister in Frankfurt told me about it. This guy in Hamburg or Hanover ran an advertisement on the Internet looking for a well-built young male interested in being slaughtered and eaten. Some masochistic loser of course answered the ad, and the killer did just what he promised. First he sliced the guy's dick off, flambéed it, and the two ate that together. Then he hacked the guy to death and ate him."

"Christ, Jonathan."

"You should read the papers every now and then, it would help you to keep abreast of important world happenings. And sick as it sounds, the guy has an interesting case. He's claiming that he can't possibly be tried for murder because the victim consented. Apparently he videotaped the whole thing – killing, banquet, everything – and the victim is seen expressing his consent again and again."

"Before he gets eaten?"

"Presumably."

A colleague from the sociology department jumped in. "That's ridiculous – no one can consent to their own killing. That empties the idea of consent of all meaning."

"What about doctor-assisted suicide?"

"That's completely different!"

"Really? What's the distinction?"

I slipped away, bumping into R. by the desserts. "Jonathan Stein is talking about cannibalism."

"Here, have a bite of the mousse."

"It's amazing."

The untenured crowd was still dancing. Janet Xuan pulled me onto the dance floor with a hand wrapped in a carpel-tunnel brace. Small-breasted and compactly built, she danced with studied abandon, her boyish body moving with fluid energy. Together we danced several Motown classics, then I made a fanning motion, indicating a need for fresh air.

I scanned the crowd for Rosalind Roth, but could find her nowhere. My disappointment registered: keen.

Forster had taken a seat at the piano and was playing Handel for himself. Laughter erupted from the far corner of the room. The windows were thrown open to relieve the heat. Candles guttered in the winter air.

Again Sebastian Winkie clamped his hand around my wrist. His tongue flicked at flakes of chocolate lodged in the corners of his mouth. "Best goddamned profiterole I've ever tasted. I must get the recipe from you or your charming wife. Remind me."

Sometime after midnight the champagne was poured and R. tapped a glass for attention. When this didn't work, she cut loose an ear-splitting whistle. Promptly our guests fell silent.

"As you all know," she began, "my husband is the public speaker, not me – "

"Not I," Forster corrected.

R. gave the graying eminence the finger. Everyone howled in laughter. The last time she had toasted me, at our wedding, she had displayed the same unstudied poise and humor. "Anyway," she continued, "a few words are in order. After all, my husband's now an official member of a pretty exclusive club, even though you'd never know it looking at you people."

There followed more laughter. R. was a light drinker, and her face had a lovely flush. Once again I was reminded that I was married to an uncommonly attractive woman.

"Now I must admit that every time I discuss Daniel's work with my father he says, 'Holocaust art – certainly that's someone's idea of a sick joke.' But I, for one, want to express my admiration and to say, with complete objectivity, that the college has made the right decision." More laughter, and applause. In her low-key way, she knew how to work a crowd.

"I know you're all eager to sip the bubbly, but no celebration is complete without a little present. Though I'm not sure this gift will get Daniel all the way to Berlin, I hope it will help him steer his way through the inevitable post-tenure mid-life crisis." And with that she handed me a small wrapped box and planted a gentle kiss on my lips.

All eyes were upon me as I tore at the gift wrap. The box was fiendishly well sealed; only after a furious struggle was I able to prize it open. From the tissue paper I removed a set of keys. They were no ordinary keys – the black chain bore the sole word *VOLVO*.

Rajeesh broke the ice with lapidary force. "Whoa!"

That was all the others needed.

"Which model? Sedan or wagon?"

"I *told* you she had a trust fund!"

"When I got tenure, my husband got me a book – a book I already had."

I remained stupefied.

"Well, aren't you curious?" R. said, "It's in the barn."

Expectant stares followed me out of the house. The whole thing was bizarre, particularly in light of the distaste we had both felt at the "Toyota party." Now would I, too, have to inch the car down the driveway to the forced applause of our guests? I was flummoxed and mortified, but excited, too. But why the Volvo when I clearly had favored the Saab in our test drives? I hoped she at least got the color right – black.

I swung open the door to the barn, which we used as a garage only during fierce winter storms. Inside, the barn was dark save for a single spotlight shining down on the space for a car. Only there wasn't one. Until I looked closer and saw it. The car occupied the very center of the spot – a Volvo four-door sedan, and yes, black. I bent over, lifted it, and turned it over. Matchbox, made in China.

"I don't get it."

The voice could have issued from the speech center of my own puzzled brain, only it came from behind me. Rosalind Roth stood framed in the barn's open door.

"I'm not sure I do, either," I said. "But as a kid I loved Matchboxes." My mind worked slowly and poorly to make sense of the hoax. I couldn't decide if I was relieved or crushed.

"May I see it?" Rosalind asked. She wore a Napoleonic hat, a sleeveless crushed velvet vest that barely covered her upper thighs, black tights, and that was it. Her lips were chapped and purple with cold. A shiver rippled through her body. "It's very cute, though personally I would have preferred something sportier."

"Yeah, same with me. You know, your knees are shaking."

"That's because I'm freezing to death."

"Let's go back inside."

"No, I prefer it out here. I'm sorry – I told you parties aren't my thing. I mean, I was inside, briefly. But it's so peaceful out here, like outer space . . . Though frankly, there's been some nickering."

"We board two horses."

"Really? I used to ride as a girl. I won lots of ribbons. Red, white, blue – all the classic colors." She lit a cigarette with trembling hands. "So have you enjoyed your party? You know, you're pretty pale yourself."

"I just started feeling a bit queasy. I'm not much of a drinker. But otherwise, yeah, I've had a good time – I danced, chatted. Raymond Friedman asked me to have anal sex."

"That was sweet of him."

"Umm." I thought about the little Volvo, trying to decide whether the joke was hilarious or humiliating. Maybe both?

"You're probably eager to take a test drive, so I'm going to leave now. But I just wanted to thank you for inviting me. It seemed like a lot of fun. If I liked parties, I'm sure I would have had a great time. And your wife is very beautiful."

"Thanks. I'm glad you approve."

"I didn't say I approved. I just said she's beautiful." Rosalind smoked in quick, distracted puffs. "You've been married before, haven't you?"

"How did you learn that?"

"Sources . . . What went wrong the first time? – if you don't mind my asking."

"It's kind of a long story . . . Somehow we just never got along all that well."

"Sounds like a pretty short story, actually." Rosalind extinguished her cigarette on the driveway. I felt a prick of irritation – who asked her to comment on my first marriage and litter the asphalt?

"I don't mean to be grossly out of line," she said, "But I've been thinking – if you'd like to have an affair, you should give me a call. Seriously. Now that you're tenured, it's what comes next."

"Are you drunk?" I asked.

"Of course. But I usually know what I'm doing. At least, I think I do." And with an awkwardly placed kiss on my lips, she steered her goose bumps to her Rampage.

A lively hubbub erupted when I reentered the living room.

"Hey, whaddya do, drive to Vermont?"

"When do we get to see it?"

"Standard or automatic?"

Like a maestro commanding his orchestra to silence, I sliced my hand through the air. "Now presenting, straight off the assembly line, the spanking new Volvo S-80 . . ." And held out the Matchbox car.

A delay followed, as if the announcement had traveled via transatlantic cable. Then the commotion started.

"C'mon, is *that* it?"

"That key looked awfully real to me!"

"What is this, *Honey, I Shrunk the Swedish Car*?"

In very short order a consensus emerged. Most agreed it was a brilliant hoax, one to fix the party in collective memory. R. was in the center of the room, happily explaining how she had convinced a Volvo salesman to give her an old set of keys, and how I had once threatened to sue my mother over the loss of my Matchbox collection. Then she turned to me, as if she knew just where to find my eyes. Her riddler's smile seemed to ask, "Get it?" Amid the laughter I heard a voice say – and it wasn't mine – "There's got to be something else going on here."

Seven

I've always feared the tyranny of freak events – microbursts, light-ning strikes, bricks falling from crumbling facades – things that change or extinguish life in a heartbeat. Which is perhaps why I sensed the true nature of the little Volvo as talisman, not plaything. My instinct was right, even if I had to wait some weeks to learn what precisely the car portended. At 35,000 feet, Berlin-bound, and sleepless, I had to accept its status as pure cipher.

It might all have been very different. At Logan Airport, inch-ing my way forward on the serpentine check-in line, I had been tapped on the shoulder by a fellow passenger, toting a herringbone overcoat folded over a suitcase of ballistic nylon. Maybe because I had a simi-lar suitcase, he must have assumed that I had accidentally joined the wrong queue. He pointed to the Business Class check-in, but when I shook my head, he just shrugged and moved on. It occurred to me that I hadn't even thought to ask the conference organizers to fly me Business. The world of academia offers precious few opportu-nities to travel well, and I had squandered my first. Once boarded, I shuffled past the businessman; he was already ensconced in his over-sized leather recliner, sipping champagne, looking all very comfy.

Taking my window seat, I still harbored the hope of a row to myself. Seconds later, a disheveled sixty-year-old heaved his bulk next to me. We exchanged no greeting, which was to my liking, as I can't stand chatty strangers. (R. habitually exchanged life stories with old women and single men on public transportation.) Safety belt fastened, the man removed from a worn briefcase a half dozen European newspapers, reading each with great thoroughness. Wordlessly I asked to glance through his discarded *Frankfurter Allgemeine*, where I found an article by Jonathan Stein's sister about German mercenaries in the Balkans. I skimmed the piece, then folded the paper into the pouch of the forward seat. I was too distracted to read. Part of the problem was the man. He wore a gray suit, as if chosen to match his complexion, and his skin was slack, mottled with age spots. His fingers were stained with newsprint, but this didn't stop him from licking them to turn the pages. Worse, he smelled, not of perspiration or dirty clothes, but of medicine: a cloying odor of vitamins and embalming solution. I contemplated escape, only the cabin was packed. Once airborne he began chewing noisily on figs and dates that he kept in a zip-lock bag seemingly preserved from the pioneering days of plastics. When the meal arrived, he picked, crow-like, at a hillock of congealed meat, while I stared at the vegetarian option. Mercifully he didn't try to draw me into conversation. Meal and newspapers finished, he pulled on an eye mask and promptly fell asleep.

Under the best of circumstances I find sleeping on a plane a challenge. For years I sampled various remedies, but stopped after a combination of Jack Daniels, Benadryl, and Valium led to my partial collapse on an escalator at Heathrow. This time, wedged against the icy fuselage, I told myself, "You must remain awake." It was a technique I used with some success to relieve my intermittent bouts of insomnia: the effort of resisting sleep would gradually exhaust me.

During the flight, however, I was so preoccupied that I took the command at face value. My eyes remained peeled open.

Cold despite having wrapped myself in two blankets, I wondered whether these hours on the jet would be my last. All week long my trepidations had been growing, until that morning I suddenly announced, "I'm not going."

"What?"

"I've been giving it some thought – I really think I should cancel."

R. stared at me, waiting for an explanation.

"I just don't feel like all the travel. The weather's going to suck, and I'll be jetlagged for the beginning of the term. I'd just as soon stay home with you."

"Daniel, this lecture is a very big deal. You can't just pull out at the last second. You're always like this before you have to travel. The flight will be fine, I promise. You're going to go and have a great time. You deserve it."

It's odd how humans let themselves be comforted by those without superior knowledge or control – I suppose it explains the success of therapists, priests, and brokers. R.'s assurances helped settle my nerves, at least until the cabin darkened and the sickbed snores began issuing from my flying companion with the eye mask. Then thoughts about the general improbability of flight started to nag at me. My mind produced a picture of a 747 taking off, the bloated bathtub suspended in its slow-motion aggression against the law of gravity. Next I was visited by visions of mid-flight catastrophes: an air-to-air missile fired from an errant F-18, shaving off a wing and plunging the wounded craft into a prolonged death spiral; a deranged pilot chanting Koranic proverbs catapulting the jet into a vertical free fall; a Semtex detonation blowing a hole in the fuselage, then filling the night sky with a terrific fireball of twisted airplane guts and deadly streamers of burning titanium. I puzzled over the meaning of "instantaneous." A nanosecond before the disaster does one glance up from one's magazine, frozen with premonition? And as everything tears apart, is one fleetingly aware, like Hamlet speaking from beyond the grave, of one's own death?

I wanted to know R.'s thoughts on these matters. As a medium, I turned to the little Volvo, removing it from my briefcase and placing it on the folding table. Yes, I had taken the Volvo along. The mocking metallic rabbit's foot. Just as I had studied it the night of my tenure party, puzzling over its meaning till the wee hours as I waited for the last guests to leave. Sometime earlier, I had developed a vicious headache and had excused myself. Upstairs, I lay on our comforter fully dressed, waiting for R. to shoo away the stragglers. I parked the Volvo on my night table, and scrutinized both it and my feelings. What was I to make of the Matchbox? Had R. intended to humiliate me, or was I just succumbing to the professional hazard of academics: overreading? And what, precisely, was the character of that humiliation? Could the choice of a family sedan be innocent? Wasn't it clearly intended as a provocation, an unpleasant reminder of the most delicate and vexed issue in our marriage? The thoughts circled, hamster-like, in my aching head. Then there was Rosalind Roth and her blunt proposition. I wondered which side of her person would predominate in bed: the timorous or the bold, the chapped quivering lips or the superior legs? The thoughts remained abstract, rendered vague by the numbing pain radiating from the occipital lobe. Below, the last guests were singing Broadway show tunes. *South Pacific*, *Oklahoma*, *The Sound of Music*. R. was on the piano. She could sight read terrifically. I could make out a few voices, including Jonathan Stein's. I had him pegged as the type who would stand around in self-conscious silence while others sang, but there he was belting out "Climb Every Mountain." And he was good, too. My headache gradually improved thanks to the Advil snack. I thought about going back down and joining the sing-along, but couldn't quite rouse myself. Eventually R. swept into our bedroom, sweaty and flushed.

"All gone?" I asked.

"At last. How's your head?"

"Better. Listening to you guys helped. You sounded great."

"Your friend Jonathan is one excellent singer."

"I heard."

"No, I mean, he can really sing." R. disappeared into the bathroom to wash and brush her teeth. From there she called out, "You should see someone about all your headaches. Maybe there's a new medication."

"I'll look into it." I lacked the will to get up. R. once told me she had never gone to bed in her life without first brushing and flossing. She knew how to take care of herself.

"So did you have a good time?" She returned to our bedroom in a black nightgown.

"Yes, of course. Except for the headache at the end, I had a great time. You did a brilliant job, thanks. And the car, that was very . . . funny."

"I knew you'd like that."

And that was that. She seemed utterly oblivious to the deeper meanings of the Volvo. I wasn't going to push. She had worked awfully hard on the party, and I didn't want to start something. But I thought about her obliviousness. How was that to be interpreted? Is humiliation necessarily a crime of intent, or can it be perpetrated unwittingly?

R. climbed into bed and pressed her flank against me. "Your head feel good enough to stick it in?"

"What time is it?"

"A good time."

I yawned. "What makes this night different from all other nights?"

"Don't complain," she said. "Here's your big chance. Just stick it in and poke it around. Well?"

"Okay, okay. Just give me a sec . . ."

And in it went.

*

My forebodings about the trip weren't entirely unfounded. As soon as I arrived at Tegel, things began to go wrong. Toward the end of the flight, I detected a slight but unmistakable pain on swallowing. (I immediately took 3000 milligrams of vitamin C and 500 milligrams of zinc from my medical travel pack.) Emerging from Customs, I easily located the driver of the car sent by the conference organizers, but before I could ask him if we'd beat the morning rush hour, he informed me that we had to pick up another prominent invitee, who had arrived on the same flight. What should have been a short wait dragged out. Any number of reasons could have explained the delay of the world's leading authority on the Armenian genocide – lost luggage, belligerent immigration officials, misplaced documents – but these didn't make the time in the dreary terminal pass any faster. The driver had just phoned the organizers for instructions when the dusty mausoleum, my companion from the flight, came shuffling toward us.

"Excuse me," he said, "I notice you standing here. May I ask you if you are waiting for a Professor Kostygian?"

"We are," I answered, the first words we had exchanged.

"Ah, it is I. What a coincidence. Have you been waiting terribly long? I saw you, but I thought – ah, never mind . . . Did you enjoy the flight? You must be eager to get on the way, but, please, do you mind if I first exchange money? It will be only a moment . . ."

By the time we left the airport, the traffic was at a crawl. The morning sky was leaden, defeatist, as if the sun had surrendered to a winter-induced depression and had given up on rising for the day. The car was an old Mercedes diesel with the gearshift on the steering column. Its heating was on the blink – I hugged myself against the cold's trespass. The driver was also Armenian, and he and the scholar spent the ride talking. "You do not find it rude I hope if we speak our mother tongue?" If anything, I welcomed the chance to keep silent. My eyes closed, I pretended to doze and monitored the pain in my throat.

When I next looked up, we had taken an exit far from the heart of the city. "Please, do you mind," said the driver, "if I stop for moment at my home?" The scholar was something of a celebrity in the Armenian community, and the driver was eager to introduce him to his family. He drew up in front of a tidy suburban convenience store. Once inside, the driver took pictures of the professor posed beside his beaming relatives. Then he thrust the camera into my hands, as the entire extended family embraced the genocide expert. Olives, a round of bread, and coffee followed. An hour later we piled back into the taxi.

The driver couldn't find a way to the hotel because of all the construction in the area. Streets had been rerouted, closed off, made one-way. "It is no matter. We are in no rush," cried Professor Kostygian. I tucked myself into glum silence. It was early afternoon when we finally pulled up to the awning. The sky had congealed into a dark cold soup. Rain beat down in stinging crystalline daggers. I was thoroughly exhausted, probably feverish, longing to take a hot shower and throw myself into bed, but after handing a key to Professor Kostygian, the concierge informed me that my room wasn't available. Having learned from previous experience, I had expressly requested a room for an early arrival. "This is completely unacceptable," I barked, waving a copy of my fax. The concierge examined the document, then, in a tone so polite as to be supercilious, explained that the hotel *had* set aside a room for me, but because of my tardy arrival, had given it to a more punctual guest. "Regretfully, the next room will not be available for some hours." When I fumed that the hotel had to be nearly empty, he calmly corrected me: in fact, it was completely booked, as it was hosting a reunion of British officers from World War II. (He handed me a pamphlet-history of the hotel, noting that it had served as headquarters of the British occupation force after Germany's capitulation.) Just then a group of elderly British gentlemen crossed the lobby. Each wore a beige trench coat, carried a wood-handled umbrella, and walked with vestigial ramrod posture. "Shall we take the Reichstag?" I heard one say. "Brilliant, off we go." The concierge nodded deferentially toward the group and turned back to me. "Your room will be ready at four in the afternoon, unfortunately no earlier. At present I can only offer you a suite. This, naturally, is considerably more expensive."

"I'll wait," I said, miserably.

In the lobby bathroom I shaved, brushed my teeth, and swallowed two more horse tablets of vitamin C. With a couple of hours to kill, I headed to the Ku'damm and hailed a cab. The driver had no idea where the Holocaust memorial site was – had never heard of it – so I directed him myself. From the befogged window of the cab, I stared out at the sprawling metropolis of flame-licked buildings and dismal cinderblock Neubaus.

The site was just south of the Brandenburg Gate. Half of the Gate was obscured by scaffolding, and workmen were sandblasting and resurfacing the Quadriga, the great monument to an earlier century's carnage, which itself had once been carried off as war booty by Napoleon before being variously bombed, mangled, and shot up during World War II. Turned around this way and that during the

Cold War, the Quadriga again faced the Tiergarten, seemingly oblivious to all it had witnessed and survived. To the north I could see the Reichstag, enveloped in a shroud, as if Christo had never left, its half-finished crystal dome illuminated by mercury vapor lamps. In the opposite direction, toward Potstdamerplatz, loomed an army of tower cranes, their thin, counterweighted arms swinging in disjointed concert over a gridwork of rising buildings. And from all directions reverberated the din of construction equipment, the heartbeat of the new city, a metropolis turned art installation. All at once I felt exhilarated. To be back in Berlin, exhausted, freezing and grippy – it all seemed right. I traversed the future Holocaust memorial, two huge city blocks of as yet undisturbed barrenness and desolation. An inconspicuous sign marked the flat expanse for its eventual purpose, but otherwise I was surrounded by a comfortless urban landscape of brown weeds flecked with global garbage: broken glass, shredded newspapers, McDonalds wrappers, plastic bags, bottle-tops, and cigarette butts. An old woman mumbled to herself while her dog, a wire-haired Schnauzer in a worsted plaid canine coat, urinated on land set aside for a sacral end. It was all too easy to fashion biographies for such women – the husband fallen at Stalingrad or in the Kursk, the years of bitter compliance with the Stasi, the strange fears of the influx of capital, the half-demented nostalgia for Hitler and the old days. Farther afield, two boys, probably children of *Gastarbeiter*, were kicking a beat-up soccer ball. I tried to imagine the melancholic acreage transformed into a sprawling memorial, a space to which tourists, but not Berliners, would flock. It seemed somehow fitting that carved into the heart of the city would be a place where its residents would feel like trespassers.

The rain had tapered to a fine mist, trapping the light of street lamps in isolated orbs. A chill ran down the small of my back. Stepping over fragments of a Coke bottle, I tried to visualize the various plans that had been mentioned for the site: the limestone pit shaped like an inverted pyramid meant to draw connections between the Holocaust and the earliest practices of anti-Semitism (this notwithstanding the fact that many scholars now disputed that Cheop's pyramid had been built with Israelite slave labor); the massive tilted slab of stone engraved with the names of all the identified victims of the Holocaust – 4.2 million to date, engraved microscopically in order to fit on the five-acre ledger; the transportation hub, shuttling would-be visitors to various concentration camps in specially designated buses that would run day and night all year long; the sea of flags, fifteen thousand in all, each bearing a simple question, "Why?" in all the languages and dialects of the world; the viewing stand assembled for a onetime only event: the exploding of the Brandenburg Gate; the bed of yellow tulips planted in the shape of a Jewish star; the disarticulated star made of broken monoliths; the huge tear drop; the gigantic frown; the shallow grave; the twisted spire. As I stood on the field imagining the designs, I noticed, among the debris, a single purposeful object, a Yahrzeit candle, like the one my mother lighted every year for her mother. Crouching, I examined it. It was only partially burned down, the flame presumably extinguished by the wet. On the glass of the candle-holder were engraved the words, *Meinem Kind, Moses Wechsler, geb. Berlin 10.3.38, gest. Auschwitz?* For my child, Moses Wechsler, born Berlin 10. 3. 38., died Auschwitz? Somewhere in the city an old man or woman still mourned the passing of a child who, had he lived, would now be over sixty. All at once, I thought about the lost bit of human matter that had fallen from R., the tiny assemblage which, had it lodged properly and followed its biological script, would now be our child. It was an impossible thought, the worst form of "what if" reasoning, but it still filled me with a peculiar melancholy. In its wake I was struck by the conviction that the single Yahrzeit candle for Moses Wechsler was the only authentic memorial to the Shoah. The site had to remain in its present state: an empty garbage-strewn lot, host to a single extinguished candle laid to the memory of a long-dead child. I would scrap my prepared speech, and instead would defend the radical simplicity of the neglected wasteland.

The woman with the Schnauzer shuffled away. The two boys also left. There was no wind. The cold seemed to rise from the earth itself, a dense penetrating vapor. My throat had grown more painful. I probably should have returned to the hotel, but reckoned the virus had advanced too far to be warded off with mere bed rest. I swallowed three Advil and turned south onto Wilhelmstraße.

My feet moved of their own accord. Around me spread a netherworld of foundation pits and skeletal buildings, an unfinished outpost on a distant planet. Past the Topography of Terror – half open-air Gestapo museum, half archaeological site – I came across a lonely free-standing section of the former Wall covered with a rich collage of images and graffiti: a pair of implacable brooding T. J. Eckleburg eyes, a cartoon devil wearing a sly grin and holding a trident, a simple spray-painted equation: *Stalinism* = *Nazism* = *Apartheid* = *Zionism*. Crossing the Mehring bridge, I realized that I was heading in the direction of Klara's old neighborhood – *our* old neighborhood. At the time it had provided decrepit but cheap housing to students and Turkish *Gastarbeiter* imported to do the city's menial jobs. Our apartment had consisted of three tiny dank rooms in a prewar building that had survived Allied bombing but not the neglect of rapacious landlords. For heating we relied on two ancient coal stoves; at night we'd wrap the bricks of coal in dampened newspaper to slow their burn. Our bedroom could have served as a set for a Beckett play, its sole window commanding an unobstructed view of a cinderblock wall not ten feet away. The apartment had no bathroom. A bathtub unfolded like a Murphy bed from the kitchen wall. An unheated closet on the landing had been converted into a toilet, which we shared with two other tenants, a Turkish couple with a five-year-old daughter, and a forty-five-year-old graduate student preparing a multivolume German-Aramaic dictionary. Not long after I moved in, the wooden toilet seat cracked off its hinges. The landlord, a young doctor, formerly an anarchist, refused to do small repairs. He planned to sell the property to a developer once the neighborhood gentrified.

So much for gentrification. From halfway down the block, I could see that the entire building had been boarded up. Our friends had long since moved away, and others had warned me of the deterioration as eager speculators drove out tenants and drove up prices, trading properties back and forth, scaring away even the builders. The street, once home to second-hand bookstores, experimental galleries, funky clubs, and Turkish cafés, now looked much like the vacant memorial site. Storefronts stood empty and gutted. Graffiti decorated a smashed telephone booth: *"Autos Brennen Bullen Sterben." Cars Burn Cops Die.* The skeleton of a bicycle lay twisted around a defunct parking meter. It looked all very inner-city USA. I used to walk these streets at all hours without a worry; now, as I reached the vacant hulk that had been our apartment, I didn't linger. I turned onto Bergmannstraße, but it too was just as ghostly, and to my dismay I couldn't remember the way to the nearest U-bahn station. I hadn't bothered to bring a map, not that it would have mattered. This wasn't the place to stand around gazing at a street guide.

Only I *was* lost. No sooner had this sunk in than I noticed two young guys walking behind me. I quickened my step to simulate that of a harried businessman, not a flummoxed tourist. At the next corner, I turned abruptly, bringing me to the gates of Viktoriapark, a once-popular ground for picnicking *Gastarbeiter*. Every suburban New Yorker instinct howled at the idea of entering a dark, deserted city park, but when I glanced behind me, the youths had vanished. The west side of the enclosure, I recalled, had opened onto a better neighborhood. I set off on the poorly lit path at a mild trot. In the thick of the park I slowed to a quick walk, my shoes chewing the gravel. The path was lined with huge bare oaks. Tattered tabloids clung to their roots, benches were curved to disrupt the sleep of the homeless. But then I saw something that wobbled my intestines. It was the same two youths, this time heading in my direction. They were dressed in hooded sweatshirts, donkey coats, and knit caps: the transnational uniform of the thug. Perhaps seventy yards off, on another path, I noticed vague shapes, a second pair of men dimly illumined by a flickering street lamp. There was an open moment when I could have sprinted toward this second pair, shouting. Instead I continued walking briskly toward my would-be assailants. Why? – The fear they'd run me down and beat me for attempting to flee? The possibility that I'd be exposed as a racist for taking flight? (The two appeared to be Arab.) There was little time to sort out the logic, before they were upon me. "*Sie Haben Uhr Zeit?*" asked the taller one in broken German. "You have clock time?" – the classic come-on line of the would-be mugger.

"Can't help you there," I half-shouted in English, not slowing for a second. "Forgot to wear my watch, sorry."

The answer failed to satisfy. They grabbed me by the arms and backed me against a tree. The shorter one produced a knife, which he pressed to my throat.

"Money," he hissed.

"Okay, okay." I recalled the lesson drilled into every suburban New Yorker: politely comply, or resist and die. "Relax. Here, take it."

He snatched the wallet from me and handed it to his friend, who grabbed the cash, about two hundred marks, and clumsily fingered the other slots. Gaze askance (staring might have seemed defiant, provoked violence), I examined this assailant. He had lusterless dark eyes and a thin wisp of pubescent moustache. Stitched onto his black cap was a BMW logo, and his sweatshirt bore the classic image of Che. It was a brilliant display of iconic dissonance, a clash of meaning that would have made any contemporary artist smile.

"Just credit cards," I said. "Now can I please have my wallet back?"

"Hey, shut mouth!" he commanded, tossing the wallet on the ground. The little thug still held the knife to my throat, the long cold blade squeezing against startled flesh. His partner grabbed at my sleeve, and quickly sized up my watch. So I had lied; still he showed no interest – the moron couldn't even tell a thousand-dollar Cartier, R.'s engagement present, when it was staring him in the face. But then he tugged at my wedding band. "Let me do it," I said calmly, lest he remove my finger. He grabbed the proffered ring, then yelled, "Okay – *Hau ab!*" Beat it. As I bent to retrieve my wallet, one of them kicked me in the rear, sending me sprawling onto the muddy gravel path. They faked another kick, making me cower. "Fucking faggot," one snarled in English. Laughing, they ran off.

My palms were scraped, but not exactly bleeding. I removed my coat, and, examining it in the lamplight, wiped off the gravel and wet dirt. My pant leg was also muddied. I dabbed at my throat, but there was no sign of blood. Then I continued my walk through the park, this time at a leisurely pace, glumly confident I wouldn't be assailed a second time.

Emerging from the park, I turned onto a street with all the improbable glitter of a movie set: freshly renovated buildings and handsome boutiques and cafés, still festooned with Christmas lights and New Years decorations: "*Herzliche Glückwünsche zu Silvester 2001.*" I had eaten virtually nothing all day. Without even glancing at the menu, I tumbled into the first restaurant I saw. It took plastic – that was all that mattered.

Eight

It was still early by German dining standards. The restaurant was half-empty, the decor austerely contemporary. At the next table sat a young man nervously checking his watch. He glanced at me before quickly looking away. Only then did I realize that blood was oozing from the abrasions on my hands. I promptly drained a schnapps and headed for the bathroom, where I cleaned the cuts and examined myself in the mirror. Considering the virus, absence of sleep, and recent attack, I thought I looked pretty good. The Advil in tandem with the recent burst of adrenaline had restored me, and my larynx felt better than it had all day. I returned to my table with a bounce in my step. The young man had been joined by a woman, who was blandly apologizing for her tardiness, no doubt an intentional rebuff. He was too preoccupied with her to notice my smile of sympathy.

I ordered broiled trout and a half bottle of Thüringer wine. In no time the half bottle stood empty. My spirits were high. In fact, I felt very happy. My previous encounters with grave danger had not ended well. I could still taste the panic of the night that I had discovered R. in the bathroom, the terror that rendered me helium-headed and weak-kneed. This time, I thought I had acquitted myself admirably. Granted, strolling through a vacant neighborhood to indulge a spirit of misplaced nostalgia had been unwise, as was the failure to run when I had the chance. That said, I couldn't knock my conduct during the attack itself. The knife at my throat hadn't unhinged me. I had had the presence of mind to ask for my wallet back without sounding either overly pushy or pathetically obsequious. Only the kicking business continued to bother me, the ribbon of dread that after the clean transaction, the two would deliver a gratuitous beating. My lower back still ached from the blow, but otherwise I felt good, vigorously alive.

The restaurant's business card doubled as a postcard, and, having finished my meal, I neatly addressed a card to R., but after staring at the unmasterable blankness, I started a second one to Rosalind Roth. In the days between the party and my departure, we had exchanged several playful e-mails, though her drunken proposition hadn't come up again. Now, without a word of salutation, I wrote:

> *Greetings from Berlin. Just mugged at knifepoint. Peculiar feeling, the sensation of razor-sharp steel caressing exposed neck flesh. Otherwise, freezing, exhausted, and sick – in a word, exhilarated!*
> *Tschüß*

I treated myself to a cognac. Sipping the drink, I listened in on the pair at the next table. To my surprise, they were business associates, not lovers. The balding young man had just received a dismal evaluation at work and was asking his colleague for advice. The woman was doing her best to cheer him up. "You can think of it in one of two ways," she said, brightly. "The cup is either nine-tenths empty, or one-tenth full." I stole a glance as this rarity, a German with a sense of humor. The woman had gigantic eyes, swimming pools of aqua, barely contained within the black rectangles of her glasses. Her lips were full, and her frequent laughs bared a set of very white, large teeth. Her nose was long, ending in a doughy bulb. An abundance of shiny chestnut hair fell haphazardly about her shoulders. The net effect of such exaggerated features wasn't exactly a beautiful face, but one that was open and terrifically expressive. It was a face delightful to watch.

"Think of it this way," she said. "If you are fired, you can collect workers' compensation for six months, eat pizza, play ping-pong, and look for other work. That doesn't sound so tragic to me."

"So you think they will fire me . . ."

"Not at all. I'm just saying, *if*. I told you, they always give harsh evaluations."

"Did you receive one?"

"Maybe I was the exception. But, yes, I think mine too was critical. This is simply the way they deal with beginners – "

"But this is my fourth year."

"Fourth – really? But you've just been relocated to Berlin."

"Six months ago."

"You see, that must be it. Just a period of adjustment. And at least you can be thankful that you are now in such an extremely fantastic city."

"To be entirely honest, I'm not sure I like Berlin."

"Really? Give it time. It takes a while to fall in love with the greatest city in the whole world."

"You've got to be kidding. Obviously you haven't spent any time in New York." This latter challenge did not issue from the morose colleague, but from me. I've said that I rarely strike up conversations with strangers, least of all in restaurants when any remark inevitably betrays the extent of one's eavesdropping. But the assault, alcohol, and desire to practice my German had made me voluble. That and the woman's pleasing face.

"Ah, a New Yorker," she said, turning to me. "What part of the city?"

"Do you know Manhattan? I'm from Central Park West." Having butted in, I saw no reason to exile myself to the Westchester suburb where I actually grew up.

"Near the Natural History Museum?"

"Two blocks north."

"Oh, I love that area. Breakfast at Sarabeth's."

"Now where can you get French toast like that in Berlin?" I demanded.

"Yes, on this score I must admit defeat."

"For three months I studied at Fordham," the sad-sack offered.

The two paid and rose to leave. Following their cue, I pulled on my coat. "I hope I didn't interrupt your conversation," I said. "But given your enthusiasm for Berlin, perhaps you could give a jet-lagged American some recommendations." That I knew the city well seemed, for the moment, beside the point.

Together we left the restaurant and lingered in the street. The temperature had dropped, but the sky had partially cleared. Purple clouds scudded by; behind them flickered dim stars.

"Till when are you here?" the woman asked.

"Sunday."

"So short! It's a shame you are so jet-lagged, otherwise I could show you around right now."

"I said 'jet-lagged,' not '*too* jet-lagged.'"

"Then it's settled. I'll give you a little tour . . . Good night, Thomas. Please try not to worry. Have an enjoyable weekend!"

"Yes, okay," he said. "But maybe we could go to a café."

"Ordinarily, of course," the woman said. "But now I have this jet-lagged American to deal with. Good night."

"Good night," said Thomas, astonished and beaten.

"Poor Thomas," she said after a few strides. "I hope I wasn't too rude."

"It sounds like he's having trouble at work."

"He's an intelligent fellow, but always so negative. He's so convinced that people disapprove of his work that it makes it so. I hope the situation improves, but I'm pessimistic . . . Enough about that – I'm Bettina."

We shook hands with exaggerated ceremony. "And my name's Daniel."

"Hello, Daniel. But look – you have hurt your hand."

"It's nothing. I slipped earlier."

"It's this cold rain! So tell me, are you named after anyone, Daniel?"

"Not that I know of. My parents just liked it, I think."

"That's very American, isn't it? – not having a name mean anything. I was named after my grandmother. She was wonderful, though a bit crazy . . . She moved to Portugal when she was ninety."

As we walked, I wondered if the sidewalk was peculiarly sloped, or if Bettina was moving on an invisible berm. Then I realized how tall she was. She was an inch, at least, over six feet, and full-figured, too. She was simply outsized in every respect.

"So what is your business?" she asked, dispensing with German's formal mode of address.

"Actually, I'm a professor. My field is art history." Just then we passed a kiosk plastered with public announcements. In several spots was a placard for the memorial conference. I thought this very serendipitous and pointed to my name. "See, that's me."

"Really? Excellent. And look – it's tomorrow night. A shame, I'm going to the theater, otherwise I would come. And quite a topic – 'The Holocaust in Contemporary Public Art: Challenging the Dogma.' Who told you to speak about this?"

"Uh, nobody told me. I was invited."

"Are you famous?"

"Hardly. But as far as this topic goes, I suppose I'm pretty well known."

"But why would you choose to write about such a sad subject?"

"Contemporary art?"

"No, comedian. The Holocaust."

I tried to answer delicately. "I suppose I think of it as horrific and shocking and emblematic, but I don't think of it as sad, no."

She didn't immediately respond. The Holocaust was doing little to advance our fledgling friendship.

"And what do you do?" I asked.

"Gainfully, I'm a consultant. I work for Accenture, you know, the American firm. I help mega-gigantic telecommunications companies decide if they want to merge with megagigantic telecommunications companies."

On the S-bahn, hurtling toward a destination that only she knew, I studied her eyes, trying to resolve the issue of color. As the light shifted they were by turns lapis and turquoise. Despite the outrageous largeness of all her features, they worked together harmoniously. When she smiled, there was something radiant, even beautiful, about the face.

"Ungainfully," she said, "I paint."

"Excuse me?"

"When I am not working as a corporate slave, I paint. Oil on canvas. You're a famous art historian, you know about such things."

For the rest of the ride, we talked about painting. It seemed improbable that a telecommunications consultant would have a passionate interest in art, but her knowledge was impressive, and, better yet, our tastes largely agreed. She loved Edward Hopper and Lucian Freud, two of my favorites.

"And the Impressionists?" I queried.

"Like Renoir? I'm afraid I cannot stand them."

"Good, neither can I. And Manet?"

"Oh, he's completely different. He's extremely fantastic, maybe the best."

"What about Giotto and Titian?"

"You are right. Giotto is a true God. Titian, too – an extremely fantastic, godlike painter."

She brought me to a bar in the renovated Hackesche Höfe, a darkly lit architectural mishmash, retro-futuristic. To reach the counter, a raised platform of burnished steel, one had to climb bar stools designed like scaffolding. The scale of every object was skewed: atop the sleek metallic counter squatted tiny candy-colored salt and pepper shakers, no larger than thimbles. Bettina ordered fresh-squeezed peach juice and Bacardi. I tried to think of something equally exotic, but settled on a Vodka martini.

Perched on her stool, Bettina stretched languidly. Her legs, in black slacks, were of vertiginous length. Her waist was trim, and her breasts swelled voluptuously beneath a dark knit turtleneck. She was something of a warrior-princess. It was possible that she weighed more than me.

"It's wonderful, isn't it?" she said, gesturing toward the space.

"Yes, it's like a postmodern version of Alice in Wonderland."

"Exactly! I must remember that. You're very clever, aren't you? And where did you learn to speak such extremely fantastic German? Your countrymen are not exactly known for their foreign-language skills."

"I had a Fulbright to study here – I mean, Germany. I was in Heidelberg."

"Ah, Heidelberg. It's a pretty town, but rather boring, no?"

"I probably would have transferred, but that's where my girl-friend was studying . . . Actually we got married, but it didn't last." I provided a condensed version of the Klara story. It was all basically accurate, though I might have left the impression that I was presently a divorcé. The theft of my wedding ring seemed dangerously serendipitous. With a touch of strategic brilliance, I waited for Bettina to ask me more about Klara.

"She never really had a steady job. You see, she's a painter."

"Really?" She was obviously excited by the coincidence.

"Yeah, very talented. But I could never get her to respect Manet."

"*Schade* . . . No wonder you divorced – I'm sorry, that must have sounded very insensitive . . . Come, it's time for the next destination. Unless you are suffering too greatly from jet-lag . . ."

"Nonsense."

In the bathroom I washed down two zincs and three more Advil, and out we went.

The sky was clear, and the retreating clouds had left the air still and cold. We walked the length of the Oranienburgerstraße, past the reconstructed New Synagogue, where a reception for the conference speakers was scheduled for the following night. Next door was a kosher restaurant packed with chicly attired Berliners tapping their feet to a live Klezmer band. A detail of helmeted policemen in black assault uniforms toting automatic weapons stood on either corner of the block; they nodded to us as we passed. I kept to the inside of the sidewalk to appear roughly the same height as Bettina. She shivered dramatically.

"You haven't dressed properly," I said, wrapping my scarf around her neck. The scarf probably carried my germs, but demonstrating gallantry was my foremost concern.

She ushered us into the ruined shell of an unreconstructed prewar building. In it was a subterranean world of bars, galleries, and dance spots. We entered a huge crowded cavern, empty of all furniture save a decommissioned MiG fighter. Bettina ordered a shot of

Buffalo Grass vodka, and I tried my luck with a gimlet. We rested our drinks on the wing near a gun mount. Music vibrated through the floor, a monotonous, pile-driving sound.

Vaguely swaying to the beat, Bettina half-shouted, "I used to be married to an American."

"Really? For how long?"

"Almost six years. The divorce came through this Christmas." Adjusting for the dim lighting, I calculated she was thirty-two or -three. At least I understood why she had nothing better to do on a Friday night than to shepherd an exhausted professor around the city.

"He was very talented – a Jew."

"Me, too."

"Yes, I already figured as much."

"Really? How so?"

"Oh, there is just something about you. And you work on the Holocaust."

"Non-Jews study it, too."

"I suppose . . ."

She ordered another drink while I nursed my gimlet. She certainly had a taste for alcohol.

"So what went wrong with your American husband? If you don't mind me asking . . ."

"What can I say? People, even excellent people, can be simply terrible. My father left my mother for a younger woman, and my husband left me for an older one. He also works at Accenture – he was the one who hired me. He was very clever and handsome, and also loved art. I thought we had a perfect life. But then he began to carry on with a colleague at work. She was the one who told me – she had this crazy idea that we could all be friends. And Robert thought so, too. He thought we could carry on just as before, even sexually, and found it very unfair when I demanded that he choose. He considered himself the great victim. It was total insanity. You don't look like a monster – you're not, are you?"

"Me? I'm very unmonsterlike."

"Good, though Robert wasn't really a monster – a big spoiled baby is more like it. At least now it's officially over. I am again a free woman, so to speak. Unfortunately, I *do* see them every day at work. Can you imagine?"

"That must be awful."

"Yes, it's quite bad."

All at once I felt as if I had run into a wall. My throat burned, and my bladder declared its unwillingness to tolerate more alcohol. I found the bathroom. Beside the urinal hung a condom dispenser covered with anarchist and neo-Nazi graffiti. Without probing my intentions, I dropped a coin into the slot and choose a Vitalis mint-flavored ultra-lite and slipped it into my back pocket. When I returned, Bettina flashed me a lovely tender smile.

"Still alive?"

"Barely."

"Should I take you home, or do you want one more stop on your comprehensive tour of Berlin?"

"One more."

"Are you sure?"

"Definitely."

By cab we traveled to Prenzlauerberg. There followed a brief scuffle as to who would pay the fare.

"Please, I'm a rich capitalist. You're a poor professor."

"But from a rich family." Or rather, had married into one, but again I saw no point in such precision.

"In that case, you pay for me when I visit in New York."

"It's a deal."

We emerged onto an intimate square surrounded by prewar houses still pockmarked from shrapnel.

"Do you like Käthe Kollwitz?" she asked.

"Kind of . . . To be perfectly honest, not really."

"We're so similar! Neither do I! Her art is so . . . earnest. All those sad mothers with their sad colorless children. But this is where she was born. The square is named after her."

"It's very lovely."

"Isn't it? There's also a very nice Jewish cemetery down the block. Would you like to see it?"

"Is that why we came?"

"Of course not. There's an adorable bar directly across the square."

So we skipped the cemetery. Bettina drank Irish coffee with an extra shot of whiskey, while I sipped chamomile tea. Just then I realized who she reminded me of. It was R. Not physically, of course. And not the R. of the present, the woman who bestowed on me passive-aggressive presents and consented to indifferent intercourse. No, it was the R. of the early days of our relationship, the woman who had given me the rare gift of affection unencumbered by am-bivalence. There was something about Bettina's self-confidence, her intelligence untainted by psychological woe, that summoned up the R. I had fallen in love with.

"Are you tired?" she asked.

"Tired? I was tired twenty hours ago. Now I'm floating in space."

"Let's take you back."

As it turned out, Bettina's apartment was only a few blocks from the hotel. "I know you're half-dead," she said, "but I cannot permit you to go back to your room without first showing you my paintings. You don't mind, do you?"

It was shortly after 2 a.m. when we arrived at her apartment. It was a gigantic flat with towering ceilings and sparsely furnished rooms. I followed her into the space that served as her studio, inhaling the familiar narcotic of paint, turpentine, and linseed oil. On the walls hung a handful of completed paintings, unframed, and several postcards. An unfinished canvas stood on an easel, and others leaned against the wall.

Frankly, I dreaded seeing Bettina's work, if only because painting is so unforgiving of a want of talent and technique. To my relief her work was rendered with decent facility and something of an eye. Except for one unpromising abstract effort, the paintings were portraits, not exactly of people, but of figures made to look peculiarly stiff, as if frozen or made of wood. The work wasn't even close to being in Klara's league, but what did that matter?

"So what do you think? I'm very anxious to know the opinion of the world-famous expert."

"I'm really quite impressed. They're very good, honestly . . . But I'm also a little surprised. They're rather dark, golem-like figures. Not what I would have expected from you."

"Oh, really? And what did you expect, now that we've spent a few hours together?"

"Happier, brighter images, I suppose. With more of a sense of humor."

"Really? How mortifying."

"It's not an insult, you know. I'm all for happiness. Frankly, I'm tired of misery and insanity and that kind of thing."

"Yes, I know what you mean. And you're correct, of course. I am a happy person. But one can still have a dark and edgy side, too, can't one? In any case, that's my ambition."

While she prepared a pot of tea, I examined the living room. She had an impressive collection of art books and museum catalogues that lined an entire wall. Propped on the bookcase were a number of photographs: Bettina with an older couple, presumably her parents; Bettina with a little boy; Bettina with friends or maybe siblings; another shot of the boy. There was also a photo of a man in profile, hunched fiercely over a desk, hand raking a bale of curly hair, seemingly wrestling with a thorny problem of particle physics.

Bettina returned, carrying a tray. In her stockinged feet we were now roughly the same height.

"You still keep a picture of him up?"

"Oh, that . . . I don't know – it helps me to focus my rage. But of course you are right, I should take it down."

She put on a CD of Billie Holiday. Had I noted the title of the first track, I would now record the lyrics in dreamy italics. I remember only that the song prominently featured the word "love."

From a shelf she removed a book about Manet. We sat on a couch and looked through it together.

"I want to show you my favorite still life of all time," she said. "Look – isn't it extremely fantastic? And doesn't the melon look like a man's head? I feel I can almost run my fingers through his thick hair. I would not think a piece of fruit could be so incredibly sexy."

The song ended. I asked the way to the bathroom.

"Straight down the hall. Door on the left."

It was all pretext. I washed my hands and face, and, removing a tube of toothpaste from Bettina's medicine cabinet, spread a patch across my teeth. The cabinet contained various pills and lotions, as well as a large bottle of Joop! perfume. Sniffing this, I discovered the secret to Bettina's odor of kissability, a delicate spicy scent that reminded me of cinnamon toast. I remembered the first night that I had spent in R.'s apartment. The following morning while showering, I discovered that R. used a medicated shampoo. The knowledge that this beautiful woman suffered from dandruff had quickened my love. The love I was about to violate.

In his book on conjugal relations, Swedenborg describes three degrees of adultery. Adultery in the first degree is committed by persons who marry young and stray because they're too immature to know better. Swedenborg considers this a mild offense. Adultery in the second degree is caused by lust. It is committed by people who are drunk or otherwise temporarily unable to control their sexual appetite. This is a more serious offense, inasmuch as it represents a failure of self-control. But most serious of all is adultery in the third degree. This is adultery "approved by reason, committed by those who convince themselves that it is not a sinful act."

Certainly I was exhausted and had consumed a fair share of alcohol, but I knew precisely what I was doing – or about to do. More, I felt justified. If anyone was to blame, it was R. When was the last time she had shown me humor and tenderness that didn't have a hard edge? That didn't carry a quiet but sharp undertone of hostility? I combed my hair, patted the Vitalis peppermint ultra-lite in my back pocket, and returned to the living room.

Billie Holiday was singing a new song about love. Bettina was curled on her side, looking at me, smiling dreamily. She closed the book on Manet.

"Hi." It was her first word of English. She shifted to make room for me. "Come, sit down."

Settling beside her, I said, "Hey, would you like to see a photograph of my wife?"

"The German painter?"

"No, I told you – we divorced years ago. I mean my present wife."

"I don't understand. I thought – "

"Here let me show you a picture of her."

"This is your *wife*?"

"Uh-huh, here." I fished for the photo, unscathed from the mugging, and handed it to Bettina. And there was R., lying on her side in our yard, curled in much the same position as I now found my new German friend.

"She's very beautiful," said Bettina mechanically. "Somehow I didn't realize that you are remarried."

"Sorry for the confusion." I studied the picture and slipped it back into my wallet.

"Is she also a painter?"

I shook my head. "A writer."

Bettina sighed. "Well, it is awfully late. I suppose you should be going."

"Yes, I suppose."

"Come, I'll walk you down and give you directions." Her steps were heavy as we descended the worn stone stairs.

Standing in the deserted street, I again invited her to my lecture.

"I'm afraid that's impossible. I'm busy all of tomorrow."

"How about Sunday? My flight doesn't leave until early evening. Can't we have brunch? – I *have* to see you again."

"Well, yes, maybe . . . Ring me on Sunday morning."

"Good night. You're a terrific tour guide."

"Yes, okay. Good night."

Nine

In the hotel lobby, the night porter nodded at me in a manner at once deferential and conspiratorial.

"*Gute Nacht*," he said.

"*Gute Nacht*."

"Sleep will do you well," he added cryptically.

Without bothering to wash, I peeled off my clothes and tumbled into bed. My legs twitched with exhaustion, but I couldn't shut my eyes, much less sleep. Light from the street filtered into the room. An occasional car sped by. The wail of a siren. Mute laughter. Silence.

All at once, I kicked off the blanket and sat up. Why on earth had I shown Bettina the photo of R.? Had I suffered a pang of conscience? Gotten cold feet? Too agitated to think this through, I flicked on the light and studied the phone number she'd scribbled down. I had to act immediately, before she went to sleep. I rehearsed the conversation, distilling a tangle of fevered thoughts into a single potent sentence: *Bettina, I'm coming back.*

Twice I dialed, both times hanging up before the first ring. I mauled my forehead, flung the condom across the room. Fool! She herself had been hurt by unfaithful men – her father, her husband.

Certainly she would refuse to sleep with a married man if it meant inflicting pain upon another woman. Now I was like all the others, a moral monster willing to deceive for erotic adventure. But wasn't that what I was?

A third time I dialed and hung up. I flipped on the television. As if projected from my mind, a pair of exquisitely formed breasts swelled across the screen. The camera moved back to reveal a naked woman, her body glistening with oil. It was a program on the art of sensual massage hosted by an official from the Ministry of Cultural Exchange. The masseur was Indian, a wiry, ponytailed swami in a loincloth. The swami anointed her breasts, treating them like pampered deities, while the official narrated in *hochdeutsch*. The camera focused on a drop of oil beaded on a perfectly pink nipple. The oil clung to the pinnacle, then slid down the voluptuous curve.

I tore off my underwear and grabbed a towel from the bathroom, but then thought better of it, instead swigging down a colorful menagerie of Advil, melatonin, and Benadryl with bourbon raided from the mini-bar. Back in bed I channel-surfed. A woman in a gardening smock and rubber clogs reported on Bavarian horticulture; Rudi Völler discussed the state of the *Nationalelf*; Hitler clawed air in an old newsreel; then back to the masseur who had moved on to the woman's pale buttocks. Gradually the concoction began to work. But as I grew drowsy, something stunned me back to wakefulness, a sound, a soft knocking! It's coming from the door, a rapping that grows louder, more insistent! Surely I am hallucinating, but no matter. I struggle into a pair of jeans, but the knob is already turning on its own. It's Bettina, bundled in a trench coat, arms folded for warmth. When she reaches to embrace me, the coat falls open. She's wearing black knee socks, a black camisole, and nothing more. "Come to my bed," I whisper, but why am I speaking with this strange Indian accent? She shakes her head. "No, right here," she whispers, gently falling to her knees. "I want to blow you to Kingdom Cum . . ."

At six I abandoned all hope of sleep. Woozy from the drugs, I drew a bath, reached for the phone by the tub, and punched in the familiar number.

"Hello," I said.

"Oh, hello," R. answered. "I was just climbing into bed. It's late. Why didn't you call earlier?"

"Yesterday was a bit of a mess. But you were right – I did survive the flight."

"See."

"Though I *was* mugged."

"What do you mean?"

"Just that. I was mugged. It was stupid of me, totally my fault. I was walking around this lousy neighborhood where you-know-who and I used to live, and these two kids pulled a knife on me."

"Oh, my God!"

"It sounds very dramatic but I'm absolutely fine, honestly." I described the mugging as nonchalantly as possible, omitting mention of the kick. In fact, my lower back had begun to stiffen and the bathwater felt good. "Except for holding a knife to my throat, they were really quite polite. They gave me my wallet back, though they did take my wedding band."

"Oh no! You poor puppy. You must be shaken up."

"Actually, it's strange – I feel completely fine. I mean, except for the wedding band."

"We'll get you a new one when you get home. An even nicer one."

"No, I just want the same one."

"Okay." R. sighed. "Any other excitement?"

"I'm taking a bath," I said.

"That's good. Baths always help me relax. I took one the night you left. I almost turned into a prune reading about panspermia." As I closed my eyes and leaned back in the tub, R. explained that panspermia is the idea that life came to earth from outer space through microbes and viruses on meteors. The chief virtue of the theory is that it explains why life on earth was able to develop so quickly in geobiological terms. "A lot of leading cosmologists now support it. Francis Crick, as in Watson and Crick – you know, the double-helix guys – even believes that the earth was intentionally seeded with life by aliens."

"Good thing he waited until after the Nobel to go on record with that."

"I guess so."

"And Sweetness?"

"She's taking care of me. Today she ate two mice."

"Did she leave the heads?"

"Of course."

I felt my chest rise and fall in the warm water. Life tumbling from the heavens – was it any less plausible than life developing ex nihilo from an ammonia swamp struck by lightning? Creatures forged of stardust, supernovas as overheated incubators of life: cosmological thinking made my mind feel dreamy.

R. yawned. "I'm sleepy . . ."

"Yeah," I said. "Me, too."

"Well, why are you up so early? Why don't you go back to bed?"

"Actually, I haven't been to sleep at all."

"Poor animal . . . See, you *are* upset about the mugging."

"Actually, that's not it."

"Jet-lag?"

"No."

"What, did you pick up some young German Fräulein?"

"How'd you guess?" I said with a laugh.

"Seriously?"

"Yeah, sort of . . ."

There came a very demonstrative sigh. "So you've been away for one day, and manage to get yourself almost murdered and then have a one-night stand. Acting out, dear?"

"Absolutely nothing happened. You'd have been proud of me – I actually struck up a conversation with a stranger in a restaurant. Anyway, this woman offered to take me on a little tour of the city, and then we went to her apartment to see her paintings."

"You went to her apartment?"

"Just for a minute."

"And Christ, not another painter?"

"Only on the side. She's actually a corporate type, a consultant."

"I'm sure. Is she also blonde and bovine and insane?" R. had never really taken to Klara.

"Not at all. In fact, she reminds me of you. I mean, she's not nearly as attractive. For one thing, she's a veritable giraffe; she must be nearly 6' 1". But there's something about her that really is very much like you. Kind of a charm and energy uninflected by neurosis."

"Don't use your professor voice . . . And you behaved?"

"Of course, don't be silly."

"But you made out, just a little bit, right?"

"Never so much as touched her, no goodnight kiss, nothing."

I hung up warm and relaxed. It was still dark and breakfast would not begin for another half hour, so I lay back in bed, agreeably drowsy.

Some time later I woke up with a start. In my dream I had stood in our bathroom in the middle of a puddle of bright blood, trying to figure out its source. R. was nowhere to be found, yet the puddle continued to spread. I checked and rechecked my arms and legs for wounds, but found none. Only after glancing in the mirror did I notice the razor-thin cut that ran around the entire circumference of my neck. Blood flowed from it like water over a fountain's brink. My head, I realized, was merely balancing on my neck; the slightest movement would send it tumbling. There was no pain – just the horrible certainty of doom.

Still jittery from the dream, I yanked open the drapes. A dusky gray penetrated the room. A grimy inch of colorless snow clung to the street below. There were no pedestrians and few cars. It was as if Berlin had been evacuated, emptied of ordered life, leaving the city in the hands of marauding thieves and hooligans. How close had I come to having my throat slashed the day before? Instinctively I checked myself in the mirror. I was pale, discomposed.

It was past eleven. The breakfast room had just closed. A waiter grudgingly brought me a pot of tea, a mournful Germanic croissant, and the house phone. "Yes," I said. "Could you please put me through to the police. I'd like to report a mugging."

*

The two men and one woman who strode lockstep into the lobby wore the leaf-green uniform of the Berlin municipal police, pathetic outfits designed to erase memories of leather jackboots, black shirts, and death's-head medallions. I felt for them – it was impossible to intimidate in a uniform like that. The officers had just introduced themselves when the elderly concierge shuffled to us, all smiles yet looking as if a pox had been brought upon his hotel. "Perhaps the gentleman and officers would be more comfortable in the bar," he said discreetly. "At present it is unoccupied." Once resettled, I gave an account of the mugging, then the three took turns asking questions.

"You say the attack took place shortly before seven last evening. Why did you wait until now to report it?"

I said that I had been too exhausted, jet-lagged.

"You just arrived in Berlin?"

"Yes, yesterday."

"For business or pleasure."

"Business." I explained that I had been invited to give a speech about the proposed Holocaust memorial.

"Are you Jewish?"

"Of what possible relevance can that be?" I asked, annoyed.

"You have said that your assailants were Arabs or youths from the Middle East. How do you know this?"

"I said I *thought* they looked Middle Eastern. They had dark complexions – they certainly weren't Germans."

"Is it possible that the attack was ethnically motivated?"

"They didn't target me, they *mugged* me. They had no idea who I was. Anyway I'm only half-Jewish, a *Mischling* to use the old parlance." Why had I thrown this absurd lie at the well-meaning officers?

The female officer wrote something in her notebook, then said, "You understand why we must ask these questions. We are very concerned with the spread of xenophobia and extremism in our city. Of course, the two go together. As members of the police, we unfortunately have insufficient scientific resources at our disposal to fight the root causes of these social problems."

I nodded. It was difficult to imagine a New York cop talking this way.

"Now, you say the attack took place in the Viktoriapark?"

"That's right."

"And what were you doing there?"

"I told you. I got lost visiting a neighborhood where I had once lived."

One of the male officers whispered to his colleagues, "*Vielleicht ist der Schwüle.*"

I glared at them. "I'm most certainly not gay. Perhaps someone can tell me *what* is going on here."

The female officer made another notation. "You must excuse us. It's just that the Viktoriapark is a notorious meeting place for homosexuals. This is particularly so on Friday nights."

"How could I possible know that? I said I was lost."

"Yet you say you knew the neighborhood well."

I began to regret having reported the incident. Had the park had that reputation fifteen years ago? I couldn't possibly say. And what about the second pair of men I had glimpsed – hadn't I sensed something odd about their mulling about? Perhaps, or perhaps not.

"Homosexuals are treated with full equality in German law," she continued. "Not like in America."

"However," added her colleague, "solicitation remains a crime. Of course, this applies to heterosexuals as well."

They were all staring at me, as if waiting for my confession. Vehement outrage was called for, but suspicion always unnerves me: I wither under accusation's steady gaze. Idiotically I stuttered, "The fact is, I'm married. I called my wife from the bathtub after the mugging. You can check the phone records . . ."

"I have no further questions," announced the female officer. "Regrettably, the odds of catching the assailants are very low. We'll contact you at the present address if we find anything. You will be reachable here until – "

"Tomorrow evening."

"Well, then. Good luck with your lecture."

They rose, their expressions betraying lingering doubt. I felt hollow and forsaken, eager to vindicate my complete blamelessness. "So whatever happened," I asked, trying to end matters on a friendly note, "to the guy accused of cannibalism, the one who claimed his victim consented to be eaten?"

Three pairs of wintry blue eyes regarded me curiously.

"Why do you ask?"

"I'm just interested . . . The case has got a lot of press back home."

"I must say I haven't followed it," said one officer. "I believe the trial is still pending."

"The killer is clearly a very sick man," said the woman. "I fear Germany is becoming in this regard more like the States every day."

They exchanged glances and left. Obviously they thought I was deranged.

The concierge smiled wanly. "I hope everything has been settled satisfactorily."

"Most satisfactorily, thank you." *Fucking Nazi sycophant.*

In my room, I reviewed my speech. My decision of the day before, to scrap it entirely, now seemed rash. I had the lecture mostly memorized, and hardly had the time to draft a new one.

The remainder of the afternoon I spent shopping. The bit of snow had succumbed to a pale sun. People had quietly returned to the streets. First I bought Bettina a lavishly illustrated book about Lucian Freud from *Bücherbogen* on Savignyplatz. Next, indulging nostalgia for my uneventful childhood and embracing the stereotype of the childless man with precious hobbies, I bought myself a die-cast Schuco Mercedes, a virtual replica of the micro-racer my father had bought me for my tenth birthday. The little Volvo now had company.

Last came R.'s gift. The perverse idea had come to me during our phone call. In an elegant Parfumerei on the Ku'damm I found a bottle of Joop! identical to Bettina's. The scent was conveniently called *Berlin*. Oddly, though, when a saleswoman offered me a sample,

I could barely recognize the alluring fragrance from the night before. Maybe that's the genius of perfume, its power to mix differently with every woman's intimate chemistry. The difference was so profound that I balked at making the purchase, and instead sampled other fragrances. I noticed that the saleswoman had left the bottle of Joop! on the counter. After trying several more, I thanked her for her patience and left the store. But not before I had slipped the Joop! into the pocket of my overcoat.

What prompted this act of madness I cannot say. As a child I had rarely if ever shoplifted. In college, during a brief flirtation with Marxism, I had convinced myself that all books should be free, a principle I briefly implemented at the Yale Co-op. More recently though, I had watched a student pinch a bag of M&Ms from the college's convenience store with utter disgust. "Can you really not afford the fifty cents?" I had whispered to the startled thief. How then could I explain my behavior? It was beyond comprehension. And what would I have said if caught? The results would have been catastrophic, particularly in light of my bizarre conversation with the police. Perhaps in a convoluted way, I was trying to punish them for the humiliating interrogation. Or maybe the theft had to do with Bettina – I had entered a zone ungoverned by conventional rules.

I resolved to throw out the bottle the instant I returned to the hotel.

*

A standard academic conference in the States is lucky to attract an audience larger than the number of speakers. More than six hundred people packed the Center for Contemporary Culture off Friedrichstraße. Bulbs flashed as I chatted briefly with the mayor and hobnobbed with colleagues I knew from the atrocity lecture and conference circuit. Christian Knuffle was there, whose award-winning *Schlock and Genocide* had examined why so many failed artists – Hitler, the kitsch water-colorist; Stalin, the weak pianist; Karadzic, the writer of maudlin lyric – had turned into mass murderers. Also on hand was Bertrand Schnitzler, who in his youth was a member of the Baader-Meinhof gang and now served as the director of Blitzschlag, Berlin's leading contemporary art gallery. There were also a fair share of Bundestag delegates present, along with many officials from the Ministry of the Interior, including the recently appointed *Bundesbeauftragte für Gedächtnisschutz*, the Special Federal Emissary for the Protection of Memory; the president of the *Zentrum für NS-Erinnerungsverarbeitung*, the Center for the Working Through of Memories of the Nazi Era; the Commissioner of the *Sonderauschuß für NS-Opfer Denk- und Mahnmalpflege*, the Special Committee for the Maintenance of Monuments to Victims of National Socialism; and, of course, the Director of the Holocaust Memorial Commission. The speakers were introduced by the Minister President of Brandenburg, an imposing figure in a silver suit and silver tie graced with the ability to deliver pleasing banalities as sonorous nostrums.

The schedule called for Professor Kostygian to precede me. He shambled to the lectern, pale and cadaverous, dressed in the same musty gray suit that he had worn on the flight. He coughed twice, took an unsteady sip of water, then, all at once, a stunning transformation took place. My threadbare traveling companion vanished, and in his place stood a vigorous orator. The professor's eyes glowed with fierce intelligence, and his voice was firm, oracular. Waving an arthritic fist, he powerfully described the Turkish government's continuing disavowal of the crimes committed against the Armenians in the second decade of the twentieth century. "It is worse than denial," he cried. "To this day, the Turkish government *honors* the architects of genocide!

"Do you remember Talaat Pasha? It is a name that must be familiar to all who study the history of human infamy. He is the Turkish Himmler, the man who drove hundreds of thousands of my people to their violent deaths. The Germans in today's audience naturally know that Talaat was assassinated just blocks from here in Berlin in 1921 by an Armenian freedom fighter. Yet in 1943 the Nazis transferred Talaat's remains back to Istanbul. Why? So he could be given a state burial with full honors! Travel today to bucolic Caglayan and you will find built on the side of lovely Liberty Hill a green marble mausoleum with a handsome dome – this is Talaat's memorial. Can you imagine a similar memorial to Himmler in Potsdam at Wannsee? *Wahnsinn!* It is impossible! It would scandalize the nation, the world! And yet in Turkey, Talaat is still a hero, revered as a great Turkish patriot.

"So where in Turkey does a traveler find the great monuments to the Armenian genocide, in what corner of the country, in what town or hamlet? But of course, the answer is nowhere! To find the memorials you must travel to Yerevan in Russia, to São Paulo in Brazil, to Montebello in California. Like the Jews, we are a diasporic people and our monuments are found only in diaspora.

"But we are here to talk about Berlin and the memorial planned for the lost Jews of Europe. Fortunately the Jews are a people of generous memory. I believe it is fair to say that they are the people of memory *par excellence*. Doesn't the long history of the suffering of the Jews contain the suffering of all peoples? Shouldn't their memorial serve to remember all acts of mass killing – the genocide of my people, Stalin's purges, Pol Pot's killing fields, Milosevic's ethnic cleansing, the Rwandan frenzy? Suffering is not parochial, it knows no ethnicity. Let the monument pay homage to *all* victims. Let it stand as a reminder of the universality of atrocity."

The crowd erupted in enthusiastic applause. The professor had touched the Germans' fervor for moral reckoning. Only he hadn't finished.

"In 1943 a Polish Jew named Raphael Lemkin coined the word 'genocide' to describe the ongoing annihilation of the Jews of Europe. The world did not listen. Two decades earlier, the same Lemkin, this great man, had struggled to teach the nations of the world about the slaughter of the Armenians. No one was interested. Years later, Adolf Hitler found this indifference instructive. 'Who remembers the Armenians?' he is said to have quipped as he hatched his own genocidal designs.

"But it is more than genocide that unites the Armenian and Jewish peoples. The Jews were the first monotheists, and we Armenians the first Christians – *die Urchristen, wenn Sie Wollen*. We are both peoples of peace who continue to be singled out for attack. Who is our attacker? Nobody would deny that Islam is a great religion, but likewise we cannot deny that today it has been hijacked by fanatics who praise and find inspiration in the crimes of Hitler and Talaat . . ."

He continued on. We had each been allotted half an hour, but he clearly thought his message was more important than a time limit. I glanced at my watch, took a sip of water, and riffled through the text of my speech. I gazed at the audience. A few had nodded off, some were staring off into space, but most appeared attentive. I wondered how many were Jewish – by looks, not many, though who could say? During my fellowship year, German students often expressed surprise when they discovered I was Jewish. *'Really? I would have never guessed.' 'Is that so? Tell me – what does a Jew look like?'* I suppose it was an unfair question designed to spread discomfort. Yet the fact remained that most young Germans had never met a Jew before. Their mental image was based on the Nazi propaganda they had studied in school.

There was more talk and more clapping. Finally, it was my turn.

"That's a difficult speech to follow," I began, almost stumbling as I approached the lectern. Several members of the audience smiled sympathetically. Some even laughed, as if I had told a joke. "But before I turn to my own prepared remarks, I would like briefly to respond to my distinguished colleague's powerful lecture. Specifically, I think it's important to observe the critical difference between a memorial created by a diasporic community in São Paulo, and an omnibus memorial in Berlin – which is what I heard Professor Kostygian advocating." This earned a fair share of applause – obviously some were treating this less like a conference and more like a political rally. I reminded the audience that the memorial site, a mere stone's throw from Hitler's bunker, still bore the traces of the Nazi past. An all-purpose Mecca for victims of atrocity would signal a failure on Germany's part to accept full responsibility for the most singular crime in human history. "Remember that the memorial is as much for Germany as for the Jews of Europe. It is meant as a gesture of reckoning, of confronting the fraught legacy of an ever-receding past. What kind of precedent would an omnibus memorial establish? Every country could erect one and so escape any reflection on its own specific history. Far from unsettling, these memorials would be smug, arrogant structures of reassurance. Imagine – Paris could combine a monument to Algerian victims of French colonialism with one honoring the slaves and native Indians killed by American farmers and settlers. Brussels could have a memorial for those killed by King Leopold and Pol Pot. London could memorialize the English suppression of India along with the Soviet suppression of Eastern Europe. Please don't misunderstand me; every group of victims deserves its memorial – only not in a commemorative omnibus, least of all here in Berlin. Let's not turn a brave, necessary gesture into political pap." It often crossed my mind while addressing an academic audience that my position was entirely specious

– that I could just as easily have been arguing the opposite view. This time my comments felt authentic, free of the nagging sense of fraudulence, undisturbed by the fear of impending exposure. I believed in my words. My early morning pharmaceutical experiment had smoothed my jitters, if not buoyed my belief in self. When it came to my prepared remarks, I delivered them with hardly a glance at my text. My speech ended to sustained ovation.

At the reception, Kostygian gave me a polite, bony handshake.

"A masterful delivery," he said.

"Yours was the true tour de force."

"You're very kind . . . Have you by chance seen the Dog Memorial in Washington, D.C.? No? You really should – it's extraordinary. It was built to memorialize the four thousand Army dogs that were killed in Vietnam. It's less than a kilometer away from Maya Lin's structure. It shows what can be built with a powerful constituency. Americans have always loved their dogs."

I nodded, unsure where this was going.

"Of course, your position will prevail," he continued. "I must confess I resent a little the success of you Jewish people in getting your memorials built."

You Jewish people? Did the expression "you Armenian people" even exist? But his eyes were moist and warm.

"If you think of it as a giant tombstone," I said, "there's little room for envy."

"Perhaps, but at least you have a place to mourn your dead. If you don't mind me asking, is your involvement at all personal? I'm always curious what draws us to these subjects. You see, I lost most of my family in the genocide – both grandfathers, a grandmother and most of my aunts and uncles. I was born fifteen years after the killing, but I knew it intimately from the scars on my parents."

I heard myself tell him that both my parents were survivors, too.

"Yes, I suspected as much – I could tell by the passion of your words. We may disagree, but let us never forget – we are kin of sorts."

All at once, we exchanged an emotional embrace. The professor's skeletal arms held me with unaccountable strength, leaving me revolted and moved. Mixed in with the medicinal odor was something unexpectedly pleasing, a bracing scent of expensive aftershave. As we separated, a reporter from the *Berliner Morgenpost* approached me. She had caught bits of my conversation with Kostygian, and was eager to hear more about my past. I explained that my original interest in the memorial had been largely formal. "As an art historian," I said, staring into her clear blue eyes, "I've long been fascinated by the power of public art to serve the interests of history and memory. This goes all the way back to my college thesis on Richard Serra's *Tilted Arch*." As for the personal side, I should have immediately corrected the record. Instead, I might have let stand the story that my parents were Polish survivors. Though less than accurate in its specific details, the story felt true to my experience. (I had long been struck by certain similarities between my mother and the mother of Daniel F., a childhood friend, as regarded fiscal austerity. Daniel's mother, the sole surviving member of one of Vienna's wealthiest Jewish families, had hoarded vast quantities of junk, maintaining useless stockpiles of desiccated rubber bands, bent twisties, McDonald's ketchup packets, miniature pencils from golf courses, and tea bags from Chinese restaurants.) So it did not seem altogether wrong to repeat the story – to a journalist from *Die Zeit*, to the Minister President, and finally to the director of the Berlin Holocaust Commission. By the end of the evening, it was clear that I occupied a position of peculiar privilege in the controversy. As an American expert on memorials and a child of survivors, I was both outsider and insider, a professional with a valuable combination of scholarly and moral authority. Taking me by the elbow, the director of the commission asked me if I would serve as a special consultant to his group, and help them choose a design they could "sell" to the German nation. I accepted on the spot.

Back in my hotel room, I called Bettina to share the news. When she didn't answer, I tried R., but she, too, was out. Though barely midnight, I threw myself into bed, and despite my excitement, immediately dropped off.

I woke up early. My sore throat had vanished. Having never before successfully fought off a virus, I considered this something of a miracle. I showered, shaved, and read the Sunday papers at breakfast. Back home, if the *New York Times* or the *New Yorker* reports on an academic conference, it's usually a satiric exposé of the insular, jargony claptrap that passes for scholarship these days. Here, every major German paper ran a piece on the event, mentioning me by name. The *Morgenpost* featured the interview with me in a sidebar. Meticulously I collected all the articles. My fifteen minutes were ticking.

At ten o'clock, unable to contain myself, I called Bettina, instinctively examining my appearance in the mirror before she picked up.

"Good morning," I said, cheerfully. "It's me. I hope I didn't wake you . . ."

"Who's 'me'? Oh, yes, of course. Good morning. How did your lecture go?"

"Very well, thanks." I tried to conceal my dismay that she hadn't immediately recognized my voice. "You can actually read about it in the papers."

"Oh, really? Yes, I will."

"Will I see you today?" I asked.

"Today? Hmm . . . I have an aerobics class, after that . . . well, okay. Why don't you come here around noon? Or must you already leave for the airport?"

"No, noon will be great."

Not promising, her unwillingness to skip aerobics on my behalf. I recalled the lines from Shakespeare, committed to memory in high school but now recalled only in their general sense: that there is a tide in human affairs which if caught at its crest carries one forward to great and unexpected successes, but if missed, leaves one stranded on the beach. I could already smell the seaweed.

I arrived at her building at noon – a few minutes past, lest I appear too ardent. The buzzer admitted me, and the apartment door swung open at my approach. On the threshold stood a little boy.

"I guess you're the American professor," he said. "C'mon in." He addressed me in English, without a trace of a German accent. "My mom's in the shower. She'll be out real soon."

"Your . . . ? I *see*." I recognized the boy from the picture on the bookcase, the putative nephew or the son of friends.

He ushered me into a room that Bettina had left off the home tour. It was filled with standard kid's fare, except in greater size and abundance – masses of huge stuffed animals, stacks of picture books, and dozens of bobble-headed soccer players. On the wall hung a portrait that Bettina had ventured of the boy.

"Do you want to see my trucks?" he asked.

"Alright, sure."

"Look at this one." He handed me a heavy and meticulously detailed diecast metallic construction vehicle with a shovel and plow. It looked awfully complicated for a toy. "Is this a backhoe?" he asked. "Well . . . is it?"

"Yes, that's a very lovely backhoe."

"Wrong! It's a front loader!" He smiled mischievously. "Do you know what these parts are called?"

"Metal bars."

"No, silly! They're hydraulic stabilizers!"

I glanced at my watch. "How old are you anyway?"

He held up four fingers and announced redundantly, "Four!" I realized that since my own childhood I had spent virtually no time with children.

"You have a pretty formidable vocabulary for a four-year-old, don't you?"

I thought this would trip him up, but he answered matter-of-factly, "Yes, I have a good brain . . . I'm also quite tall for my age." That presumably came from Bettina. Otherwise, it was difficult to find any trace of her genetic legacy. The boy had alert brown eyes, long dark eyelashes, and a tumult of biscuit-colored hair. In the dead of winter, his skin looked golden, tanned. Curiously, he bore a far stronger resemblance to R. than to Bettina.

"And do you have a name?"

"It's Alexander. My dad calls me Alex. My mom calls me Xander."

"And I'm Daniel." We exchanged an official though limp handshake. I glanced out the window where a reluctant sun was threatening to break through a paste of clouds.

"Let's talk," the boy commanded, "about space!"

"Fine. An excellent subject, one of my areas of uncommon expertise. Go ahead, ask me anything."

"Is Mars hotter than Earth?"

I felt another trap being laid, though felt confident I could avoid this one. "No, Mars is colder."

"But it's red!"

"True. But it's further from the sun than the earth. Therefore, it's colder."

The boy shook his head. "I'm *pretty* sure Mars is hotter than Earth."

"Well, Xander, it doesn't really matter what you think, 'cause you're wrong. Now, enough about Mars. Ask me another question. Anything."

"Hmm . . . Is space high?"

"Yeah, it's *really* high."

"Wow. Like a million?"

"Yeah, exactly." I glanced again at my watch. How long could a shower take? It occurred to me that perhaps she was in her bedroom with a man, an outlandish thought.

"When I'm five, I'm getting a rocket."

"Excellent. Then you can journey into deep space. Vrrooom."

"No, silly, it's just a toy."

"A toy? Why settle for a toy? Listen to an expert – you should go for the real thing. A multistage booster."

"Maybe when I'm . . . eight. Then I'll go and visit my dad."

"Is your dad on cold red Mars?"

"No, he lives in New York. It's bigger than Berlin."

"Hey, you know who else is from New York?" I pointed at my chest.

"Honestly? Wow . . ."

"That reminds me," I said, reaching over to my coat and fishing into my pocket. "I almost forgot to give you your present."

"You got me a present? Really? Oh, it's a car. Wow, it's metallic. I love metallic vehicles. Thank you."

He sat staring at the Schuco Mercedes micro-racer, which, I suppose, is all one can really do – that, or push it across the floor and simulate the sounds of internal combustion. Then he got up and plumped himself down on my lap. "Read me a book!" I was relieved that he hadn't yet mastered reading, and in short order we made our way through *Airplanes and Other Flying Machines*, *Mrs. Tittlemouse*, and *The Berenstain Bears Go to The Dentist*. The boy held the car in one hand, and rested his other on my forearm, which he began to stroke gently. His unruly mop smelled of shampoo and something else delicious, like warm milk spiced with cinnamon. Could I recall a moment of comparable pleasure? Halfway through *An Anteater Named Arthur* the child fell asleep, his hands balled into stressless fists, his fingers still curled around the car. My leg was falling asleep and his elbow was pressing into my pancreas, but I didn't move. The weight of his body upon mine filled me with a rare and unexpected happiness. Had I ever held a sleeping child in my entire life? The pleasure was profound and wordless, the work of deep biology.

Presently Bettina appeared. It was one of those heart-warming cinematic moments. A beatific child slumbering in peace; a man surveying the boy with dreamy contentment; and a woman, framed in a doorway, hair clean and fluffy, barefoot in jeans and a cashmere top, looking on, smiling tenderly. All was right in the universe. We were a small happy family.

"Where did this come from?" I whispered, pointing at the napping child.

"That was wrong – criminal – not to say anything about my little hedgehog," Bettina said. "I'm sorry not only to you, but more to Xander. He's my joy, not my burden." She came over and brushed the hair from his forehead. "At least, *usually*. Anyway, you also were not totally candid, not until the end. Like you, I guess I wanted to be free, so to speak, for a night. 'Animal liberation' – I don't know why I said this, it suddenly just came into my head."

I didn't ask her to elaborate, nor did she volunteer what she had been doing during our read-athon. Her life obviously was full of entanglements I hadn't imagined. I only asked, "His dad lives in New York now?"

"Did Xander tell you that? Really, my boy has a very broad imagination. He was just with his father the other night."

"He seems quite gifted."

"Yes, but a pity, so far he shows absolutely no interest in painting . . . And you? Do you have children?"

I shook my head, wriggling out from under the boy. In the kitchen we had tea, or rather, I had tea while Bettina mixed herself a Bloody Mary. It was clear that we were not about to tear off our clothes and have frenzied sex on the kitchen floor. Not that I greatly minded. We passed the afternoon chatting and looking through art books. When Alex awoke, we took him to the corner playground, where we watched him swing and play on the slide. The sun, chasing away shredded clouds, moved in a low, fleeting arc through the January sky. When it came time for me to leave, Alex gave me a hug and pressed two hard kisses upon my cheek. Bettina and I exchanged a little wave. We never so much as touched.

Ten

It was a strange record for a former hypochondriac: in my seven years of teaching at Franklin I had never once called in sick.

Back from Berlin, however, I had to cancel not one day of classes, but an entire week. Worse, the second semester had just begun, always a frantic time. But I had no choice. During the return flight it became clear that the virus, far from vanquished, had merely regrouped to mount a more potent assault. I arrived at Logan stiff and uneven with fever. During the bus ride back to Pittsfield, it began to snow. Moisture invaded the cabin. Swirling eddies of snow buffeted the bus, which slowed to a crawl. Wracked with chills, I gathered myself into a ball, unable to control the chattering of my teeth.

"My sick animal!" R. exclaimed when she met me at the bus station. As soon as we got home, I collapsed, an inert mass, on our bed. R. retreated to the guest room.

On Monday morning I rose early to prepare for my ten o'clock class. No sooner had I stood up than our bedroom windows performed a neat trick, spinning a half-revolution. I sat on the edge of our bed, trying to figure out how they had done this. But the bed was playing along, too, pitching and rolling like a jet in turbulence. My mouth was parched, and when I tried to swallow, I had to shut my eyes to avoid crying out. Sometime later, when R. peeked in, I was still sitting on the edge of the unruly bed. "Have to teach," I whispered.

In my mid-twenties I had longed for a nineteenth-century-style voluptuous illness, a physical analogue to my depressed mental state. Nothing life-threatening, just one of those obscure maladies, like neurasthenia, that would require taking "the waters" in Baden-Baden. A nurse with gigantic Nordic eyes and pillowy breasts would wrap me in camel-hair blankets and push me along gravel paths in a wooden wheelchair, and later would serve me tea and recite Rilke as we sat together on a wrought-iron balcony overlooking a field of ice sculptures from Parsifal. To my disappointment, I remained tenaciously healthy. My body refused to serve as a trope for my mind. Now the opposite was the case: my body had succumbed to a rare and malign virus, as if punishing me for my happiness.

For a week I wallowed in isolation. I could hardly fault R. for keeping her distance, though Florence Nightingale she wasn't. She would enter the hot zone a few times a day to deliver honey-laced chamomile tea and cherry icicles, the only foodstuffs I could endure. Talking on the phone was impossible. Even reading was hard; after a few pages, my eyes would close on their own accord, and with all my joints aching exquisitely, I'd fall into a state just short of sleep, a semi-conscious haze.

Fortunately, Bettina kept me company. The experience bordered on hallucinatory – I would feel her presence not so much beside me, as *in* me, interwoven in the fabric of my self. This made me acknowledge what I hadn't entirely realized in Berlin: that I had fallen in love. My new love didn't exclude R. On the contrary, it was generous and accommodating. R. would also enter my mind, and there were times when I could not distinguish between the two women. One would become the other, or the two would merge in my fever into a single being, enveloping and oceanic.

Recovery came abruptly. The following Saturday night, I woke up, sodden. The next morning I made myself an egg. I was wobbly and had lost nearly ten pounds, but still dressed for the office.

R.'s expression was incredulous. "You've been half-dead, you look awful, and suddenly you have to go running out on a Sunday?"

"I've got to prepare – I missed a whole week of classes."

"So? You're tenured, remember? You run the show. And you've taught this stuff a thousand times. You could do it with your eyes closed. Now you need rest. Anyway, there's something I want to tell you. We've hardly talked since you got back."

"Later, I promise. I'll be gone just a couple of hours. And I'll be sitting at my desk – no exertion, honestly."

After depositing a peck on her cheek, I rushed off to my office, desperate to know how *CDB* had gone over. At an airport bookstore in Berlin, I had found a copy of William Steig's classic. What the Steig was doing there is anyone's guess. I had jotted a short inscription – *To make the thing work, you have to adopt American phonetics. CDB = See the Bee. German pronunciation (Say Day Bay) won't exactly work. Got it? xxoo Daniel* – and mailed it just as they called my flight.

Dozens of e-mail messages were waiting for me. Tamara Starr, the naked Miss Julie, e-mailed asking whether I'd advise her independent study. There was also a note from Rosalind Roth: *Morning, as in, "hello" (a salutation). I'm glad the muggers didn't slash your throat. That would have depressed me more than I already am (my dog has worms – ugh). Drop a line when you repatriate. You know where to find me.*

Sandwiched between an announcement for new Aladdin software and the daily bulletin from the *Chronicle of Higher Education*, I found what I was looking for:

Hello Dee, L-X-N-R N I N-Q 4 D . . . book. Steig is a genius. Tomorrow I fly to München – no intoxication of paint, just consulting. It is already vampirishly late and I go to bed with thoughts of your green eyes. Bee.

Then, several messages later:

Hello Professor Wellington (that sounds so official . . .), What heartache! Still no word! I am getting paranoid that maybe my message ended up in Siberia. Or maybe you are just extremely busy and Berlin is already a distant memory. But Xander will be very sad if you don't write immediately! His mom, too. So pleeaassse, let me hear from you. Still buzzing, Bee.

In my twenties, I was much taken by Schopenhauer's argument that pain is a more philosophically interesting experience than happiness. Pain, he observed, has roused the human spirit to its most fierce and stormy creations, whereas happiness invariably expends itself in a rainbow of bland cliché. And while pain can assume limitless forms and intensities, happiness restricts itself to a comparatively narrow palette. As an example, Schopenhauer turned to his nail-picking habit. All inveterate nail-pickers have on occasion picked with such reckless determination that the nail bleeds and becomes infected. One night, Schopenhauer's thumb was so inflamed that it visibly pulsed, and the pain was so astonishing that he could not sleep. That pain, from a partially torn thumbnail, was more intense, he claimed, than any corresponding feeling of happiness he had ever felt. For many years this made sense to me, but that afternoon I felt sorry for Schopenhauer. Obviously he had never felt what possessed me at my teak-finished desk: the transformative power of pure happiness. It ushered me to a state of heightened aliveness, my every sense acute and receptive. A superabundance of energy coursed through me. Had

I ever felt like this before? Perhaps once – when I had fallen in love with R.

At the computer I typed:

Dear Bee,

I wanted to write, but was sick the entire week with plague-like symptoms. Sustaining me were dreams of a very tall and "extremely fantastic" Berlinerin. I miss you and your freakishly precocious child and your B-U-T-F-L lips.

xxoo Dee.

By the time I got home, it was dusk. R. was napping on the living room couch, a knitted throw tucked around her legs. She looked handsome in the drained light, her dark hair framing the pale smooth skin of her face. I was so happy with my good fortune and the bounty of life that I wanted to cover her with kisses.

I prepared us a modest dinner – pasta and salad, all very continental. She smiled when I led her to the kitchen. "This is very sweet, but you shouldn't have. You're just getting over God knows what, and you need to rest."

"I feel great, one hundred percent. My skin feels deliciously cool."

"Okay, but just don't rush things."

"Not to worry."

"And here, I got you a present while you were sick." R. handed me a small jeweler's box. It contained a new wedding band, identical to the one that was stolen.

"Oh, it's beautiful . . . it's even real."

"What do you mean?"

"Just kidding . . . I thought, like with the car, you might give me a little toy."

"I assure you, this one's quite authentic."

"Really, it's gorgeous. Thanks." I slid it on. The fit was snug. "Come, let's compare." And I held my hand next to hers. "Look how shiny it is. I feel like a newlywed again."

"Give it a few weeks. Gold loses its luster quickly. But it's very nice isn't it?"

"I love it. It's beautiful. Thanks." We kissed moistly.

"You glad we're still together?"

"What kind of question is that?" I exclaimed. "Of course." And we kissed again.

"Did you get a lot of work done this afternoon?" she asked.

"Yeah, a fair share." I told her that I had gone over my class notes and had taken care of some departmental business. "You'd be amazed at how much junk accumulates in a week."

"I bet . . . Though you forgot to mention the real reason you went in."

"I did? And what was that?"

"To call that German woman, the new painter."

This was something of a surprise. "I hate to disappoint you, but I swear I didn't call her."

"You e-mailed her then."

"Well, yes, okay. I did e-mail her."

R. laughed, or maybe snickered. "Do you have any idea how simple you are?"

"I've never claimed to be complicated. Haven't I always said I'm simple?"

"So, what did you write her?"

"Nothing of great literary interest. Just a brief word of hello from the world's last superpower."

"Does she have a name?"

"Bettina. Bettina Schlachtenhaufen. The last name literally means 'slaughter heap.'"

"Oh, come on," R. exclaimed, "No human can have a name that disgusting."

"I'm afraid it's true. Can you imagine a doctor saying, 'What seems to be the problem, Ms. Slaughterheap?'"

R. laughed, flashing her perfect teeth. Her smile was a gem of genetics, a dental triumph absent the slightest orthodontic intervention. "You look very cute tonight," I said. "I missed you."

She touched my hand, but was undeterred. "And was there an e-mail from her waiting for you? At the office?"

"Hmm? Yeah, just a short thing checking to see whether she had, you know, the right address. Is that kosher?"

"Speaking of which, did you fuck her?"

"What?"

"I said did you fuck her. You know" – and R. made a poking motion with her forefinger.

"No, of course not, I told you that."

"Are you sure?"

"I think I'd know."

"Swear."

"Look, this is ridiculous. Yes, I swear."

"What do you swear?"

It was back to this adolescent game. "I swear I didn't have sex with her. For Christ's sake, I never even *touched* her."

"Look me in the eye."

I've mentioned that R. believes that my eyes betray me when I'm lying. When I'm telling the truth, my gaze is direct; when I'm not, it shifts, guiltily, to the side, or so she claims. Frankly, I'm confident of my ability to tell the most outlandish lie with the most penetrating stare. Still, I was well aware of R.'s lie detection system. So when I insisted on my innocence, I did so with averted eyes.

"So you did . . ."

This time I said nothing, simply looked down.

"You bastard. I knew you screwed her. I knew it that night when you called from the tub. I could tell just from your voice, that goofy, baby-talk thing you do."

"I'm just pulling your leg," I exclaimed. "I told you, I never touched her. I swear."

"Then why did you just do that thing with your eyes?"

"Because I know you think that when I'm lying . . . Look, I swear, I didn't touch her. Scout's honor."

"Now I don't know what to believe. She touched you, then. Sucked you off."

"Christ, no. Nothing, zilch. Goose eggs. May my tongue turn to black, may my intestines turn to sawdust." And I confirmed this with the most riveting, Rasputin-like stare.

*

Through the rest of the meal R. eyed me strangely. The silverware clattered loudly like in French movies about bourgeois unraveling. "What?" I said, but R. shook her head, then sighed. I could hear the fizz from the mineral water. All at once, without having uttered a word, she blushed deeply. "Is everything okay?" I asked. R. nodded, then shrugged as if having reconsidered. She reached for her water, then put it down without taking a sip, then reached for it again.

"Daniel?" Now she looked peculiarly serious, maybe accusatory.

"I *swear* I didn't touch her."

"I have something to tell you."

All at once my mouth felt peculiarly dry. "*You're* having an affair."

R. shook her head.

"Well, what is it?"

"I need to know you've changed. I mean, from the first time, from when I had the miscarriage."

"What on earth are you talking about?"

"I need to know that this time you won't freak, that things will be better."

"Could you please try to be a little – "

"Do you remember the tiny sweatshirt?"

"The sweatshirt – ?"

"We're going to need it."

"The tiny Yale thing – ?"

"Because we're going to have a baby."

A heavy silence fell abruptly over the table. Even the water stopped fizzing. "Come again."

"You heard me. I'm pregnant."

"That's . . . impossible."

"That's what I thought. But it's true."

I examined her expression. Her eyes were laughing but not her lips. Was she toying with me the way I had toyed with her? "I even had an ultrasound while you were sick to make sure it's not ectopic."

"What about having your tube tied? Did you have it untied? Can they do that kind of thing?"

"Of course not. But apparently fertilization can still happen. The doctor said it's not that unusual. I mean, it *is* very unusual, but not altogether freaky, not something that gets me into the medical books."

"You sure you're not lying, just pulling my leg, jerking my chain, throttling my whatever?"

"Positive."

I tried to express the full range of my raging emotions. "Panspermia . . ." I stammered.

"It is pretty ironic when you think about it," she said. "I mean, it took me a year to get pregnant with two functioning fallopian tubes, and here I get knocked up with none."

"Wow." I didn't know what else to say. Under the circumstances I doubted my ability to speak clearly, as well as reality's willingness to submit to speech. But it was clear I had to do something other than sit dumbfounded.

"This . . ." I said, embracing her, ". . . this is straight out of the Old Testament."

Her eyes looked like quivering ink. "I know you're in shock. To be honest, when I first got the news, I was, too. I had so steeled myself against the idea of having a child, I thought the whole thing was almost cruel. You were flying back the next day, and I didn't want to tell you over the phone. So at night I walked around the pasture wondering what to do. It was an incredibly clear night and cold, too. The horses were following me, exhaling these little clouds of steam. I could see the milky way and Venus clearly, and I waited for a sign. I really thought there would be a brilliant shooting star, or some other amazing event. But still, just standing there I realized how wonderful it would be to gaze at that night sky with a child, pointing out the constellations, what a gift that would be . . . Maybe I *was* rash when I made that decision. At times I've had pangs of regret and felt like a neutered creature. And I know I hurt you. But you have no idea how horrible that experience was. First, seeing you lose it, and then losing the baby. I simply wasn't prepared to bear anything like that again. But now . . . God willing, we'll have a child next fall. Think of that . . . Only I'm not prepared to be saddled with an infant *and* a basket case. Do you understand that?"

"Yes, of course."

Later, when we climbed into bed, I lifted R.'s nightgown above her belly. From the rise of her hips, her stomach formed a firm flat valley. I ran my cheek along the taper of raised skin, the scar from the procedure. With my pinky I poked her belly button, a standard "innie." I thought about the riddle concerning Adam – did he have a belly button? In the paintings of Michelangelo, Cranach, and Gossaert, his was always depicted as peculiarly cavernous, a darkly shaded hollow. Lips pressed to her skin, I addressed the tummy directly. "Hey, you in there – Can you hear me? This is your father speaking. You've been conceived under mystical circumstances. Not to put pressure on you, but we have Messianic expectations. And remember, five fingers on each hand, ten in total. Ditto for the toes."

With my arm curled around R., I lay awake, turning the news over in my mind. To my relief, I saw evidence of my maturation: I wasn't in the grip of malarial-like chills, breathing irregularly, or snacking on bark. In many respects it was an ideal time to have a child: tenure was settled, we were financially secure, and my career was on a promising track. Still, there was the sheer improbability of it all. Was a child conceived against such odds destined to be aberrant in multiple respects? Would it be graced with unusual luck, or would it be star-crossed, perissodactyl, prone to bizarre accidents? And I thought of Bettina. Such craziness, human emotions. In the space of a week, I had gone from wanting no family to now wanting two.

*

The following day, still aglow from the news, I received a letter from the director of the Imperial War Museum in London. The museum, which I had visited as a graduate student, explored both the technical and human sides of war. There were rooms of tanks, half-tracks, missiles, and other gadgets of mass destruction; meticulously reconstructed trenches and triage stations; and scenes of battle painted by the likes of Sargent and Owens. The director wrote that the museum was interested in creating a permanent exhibit on the Holocaust; would I be prepared to serve as a consultant? Elated, I promptly wrote a long letter of acceptance, ignoring the line of students outside my office. The rest of the week passed in a hectic blur. The college issued a press release that described my appointment to the Berlin memorial commission. My book, which had already gotten a short favorable notice in the *New York Times Book Review*, now received a long and enthusiastic write-up in the *New Republic* (which described it as a "superb example of criticism that melds the personal and the collective, the aesthetic and the political"). And classes went well – too well. My course, "The Art of Atrocity," had to be moved to one of the college's largest lecture halls. Like everyone else, students flock to celebrity – even of the marginal academic variety.

The class was so overenrolled I had to hire a teaching assistant. Tamara Starr applied for the position, but I didn't trust myself to work with her for a full term. In a brief e-mail, I also apologized that I was too busy to sponsor her independent study.

And so I hired Vercin Kahn. This was the improbable name of the young Jagger look-alike who had discovered me hugging the largest sycamore east of the Mississippi. The term before he had written a bewildering but brilliant seminar paper on Otto Dix, and on the artistic challenges facing those who struggle to transform profound trauma into meaningful art. *In posttraumatic terms, Dix's decadent figures assume poses of self-annihilation, masquerades that celebrate the ironic triumph of futility.* He arrived at my office with pistachio-colored hair and long narrow sideburns to discuss the terms of the work.

"This is a new look," I commented.

"Yes, I call it retro Eurotrash. It should help me establish meaningful communication with the undergraduates."

We talked briefly about his responsibilities. "Will this be your first time teaching at the college level?"

"Well, sort of, but not entirely . . . You see, my dad was a professor for a while, and sometimes when he was feeling a bit, uh, dissipated, he would have me teach his classes."

"I'm not sure I follow. When was this?"

"Uh, when I was in high school."

"You taught college students when you were still in high school?"

"Yeah, but only when I was on vacation from Hartfield – I'm an alum – "

"So I recall."

"Well, I filled in when Dad was, uh, temporarily out of commission."

"You grew up near here?"

"Actually out on the West Coast, in Seattle."

"And what's your father's field?"

"He used to teach film studies. He cut back on the teaching after he won, uh, his first Oscar."

"Your father won an Academy Award?"

"Uh, yeah, a couple."

"For what?"

"Pretty obscure stuff, actually. You know, documentaries, that kind of thing." He mentioned several films that I had never heard of.

"And what about that name of yours – were you named for a pioneer of documentary theory?"

"Vercin? It's the shortened version of Vercingetorix. He was the Gaulish general who, uh, refused to surrender to Caesar, and killed himself instead. That was, like, 45 BC."

"Is your family of Gaulish descent?"

"No, but my mother committed suicide."

"I'm very sorry to hear that."

"Yeah, thanks. I was twelve at the time. To be honest, she hadn't been all that there for some years. The night when you were doing those back exercises, you know, when I saw you, my first thoughts were of my mom. She used to climb up trees and bray at the moon, that kind of thing."

"Yes, you mentioned that."

"I did?"

"I even remember that you used that exact expression – 'bray at the moon.'"

"Really? . . . Hmm . . . Anyway, I hope your back is better."

"Yes, much, thank you."

I spent the remainder of the week responding to a flood of invitations to give talks at schools, conferences, and institutes. The Shoah Educational Travel Bureau asked me to serve as the scholar-in-residence for a summer trip to the leading Holocaust memorials in Poland. I was flattered, but declined, if only because I hoped to be shuttling between Berlin and London. The attention suddenly showered on my work drew little response from my colleagues at the college, though. Members of my own department sent a few notes and words of congratulations, but that was about it. Sebastian Winkie, having learned of the invitation from the Imperial War Museum, scoffed, "That dusty sanatorium down by Elephant and Castle? Can't say I've ever been all that keen on the history of armed projectiles." Another colleague said dismissively, "I guess all you have to do these days is mention the Holocaust and you get into the news. I should try that."

The only kind words came from Jonathan Stein and Rosalind Roth. "My sister reports that your name was in all the papers," Jonathan said. "She promised to send me a bunch of the articles. That must have been pretty exciting."

I acknowledged that I had had a good time. Poor Jonathan did not look good. His skin condition had worsened again and his forehead and chin were covered with greenish flakes.

"See, what did I tell you? You're on the gravy train. You should hit the dean up for a raise. I'm absolutely serious. You've got to play the game, strike while the iron's hot. Take it from this flame-out, the chances don't come that often, and when they do, you've got to make them pay."

I shrugged. "So what's new with you?" I asked. "Any more news about the cannibal? How's Mom and Mel?"

"Don't try to switch subjects, Mr. Humble. Your stock's on the rise – live by the market, die by the market. It's time for the dean to cough up big bucks."

In an e-mail, Rosalind Roth wrote:

> *You're a superstar, not that I had any doubts. Just don't let them build anything designed by Albert Speer.*
>
> *RR*
> *PS. You're a lousy correspondent, though. I'm pissed. Seriously.*

A couple of days later I caught sight of Rosalind on the quad, walking a dog. Hurrying to overtake her, I said, "Is this the canine that cost you an apartment?"

Rosalind appeared to have been lost in thought. "Oh, hello . . . Anubis, say hello to Professor Wellington." The dog was a piebald mutt, elements of retriever predominating. He wagged his tail furiously, setting his entire rear quarters in motion, then slobbered on my coat.

"He likes you."

Rosalind looked pale, ghostly rings around her eyes. It was the first time we had seen each other since the party.

"He's very bouncy," I observed.

"I'm afraid he's just immature for his age."

"And the worms?"

"Under control."

It was a clear blustery day. Micro-breezes materialized out of nowhere, sending dry leaves into orbit. Rosalind wore a miniskirt missing dozens of gold sequins, and a short coat that looked like it had been cut from a black shag carpet. Her hands were retracted into the sleeves.

"You haven't answered my e-mails," she said, teeth chattering.

"I'm sorry. I got the flu coming back from Berlin – I mean the real flu, not some little virus that everyone calls the flu. Since then things have been a bit crazy."

"All that fame to deal with."

"Yeah, that must be it."

Rosalind wiped away a bead of clear mucus from the tip of her nose. "I've never really understood wind chill," I said, to break what was threatening to turn into an awkward silence. "I mean, does it affect just our sensation of cold, or does it affect physical objects, too? For example, would wind chill make water freeze faster?"

Rosalind looked at me doubtfully. "You sound like a dumb-ass humanities type."

"Isn't that what we are?"

"I guess so, but I started at Brown as a physics major. I was pretty good at it, too." It was actually quite easy to picture Rosalind hunched over a lab desk, doing quantum mechanics in tattered black tights, compulsively chewing her lips – which, in the winter air, were beginning to bleed.

"I suppose it's none of my business, but why don't you invest in some Chapstick?"

She dabbed her lips with an ungloved hand and frowned. "It's actually a medical condition, thank you, with a very long name . . . Have you sought medical attention for your nail-picking?"

So she had noticed what for R. was a source of considerable disgust. And it wasn't a fresh observation either, seeing that I was wearing gloves. "No," I acknowledged, "but maybe I should – it's a pretty ingrained habit. Did you know that Schopenhauer was also a nail-picker? Darwin, too."

"Didn't Darwin also suffer from depression?"

"Also Churchill – his 'black dogs.'"

"And Dickens."

"We could probably go on like this for some time," I said. "Are you an only child?" The question came to me in the moment, like the sudden gust of wind that made us turn our backs.

"I guess it's pretty obvious. I take it you are, too."

I nodded. "My father wanted a second, but my mother was afraid of the cost. She had a thing about inflation."

"My parents wanted just one so we could travel, only we never went anywhere. My Dad developed Parkinson's as a young man."

"I'm sorry to hear that."

Anubis tugged at his leash, barked at a squirrel.

"I should go," she said. "As for my proposal . . . let's just say the ball's in your court."

"Understood. But recall, I *am* married." This didn't seem to impress her deeply. Was she picking up on signals that I was inadvertently sending? Had she somehow learned that the apartment search the year before had really been for me and not for the proverbial "friend"? In any case, I tried to set the record straight. "In fact, now we're even pregnant."

Her coppery eyes fluttered brightly. "I guess congratulations are in order." She planted a kiss on my cheek. "No blood," she added, reading my thoughts. "Was that why your wife got you that toy Volvo?"

It took me a second to catch the reference. "Yeah, exactly."

"I thought so at the time. I figured it had to mean something like that. How's that for prescience?"

"Very impressive."

"But I wouldn't use that 'we're pregnant' line too often. It might cost you friendships. Seriously."

"I agree, it's awful. I don't know why I said it. I've never used it before."

"Look, I'm sorry if I was too forward . . ."

"There's no need to apologize."

"But seriously, I'm sorry. It's just that people have all sorts of marriages."

"I know that. I just don't think I'm one of those people."

"That's probably just as well."

"Your dog looks cold." I said. With an exchange of waves, we parted company.

When I returned to my office, this was waiting for me:

Hello Dee DoubleU, I was soooo happy to get your newest e-mail. München was tiring – these days of endless negotiations about networks, digital lines, and fiber optics. So today I am taking the day off. And guess what I'm doing? Yes! I am addicted to canvas and the smell of oil pigments! I'm having a first go at a still life of my beloved siphons. Did I tell you that I am a fanatic siphon collector? Screaming out loud like a David Bowie groupie whenever I see one? (I bought two in München.)

Dee, I miss you sooooo. It's so crazy. I spend one day with a married, jet-lagged American and now all I do is think impossible thoughts.

Bee

Eleven

Every first-term philosophy student learns the law of the excluded middle. Originally articulated by Aristotle, this axiom claims that a statement is either true or not true, there being no middle ground. Take the sentence "George Washington is dead." If Washington is dead, then the statement is true; if, lo and behold, he's still alive, then it's false. But the claim can have no other valence: it must be one or the other. The institution of marriage is based on its own version of this law: to be married to A. excludes being married to B. This proposition states something more than a legal fact: it is an axiom of the logic of love.

However irrefutable, the law temporarily had released me from its hold. I was unsustainably happy.

During this period, I flooded Bettina with e-mails, clippings, postcards, packages, and gifts. She saw an Edward Hopper show in Berlin; the next day I FedExed her a copy of Gail Levin's Hopper biography. She wanted to read a novel about professors; I sent her Nabokov's *Pnin*. She loved it and wanted to read more by Nabokov, so I promptly sent her *Speak, Memory*, which she also adored. Having never fully understood what a consultant does, I studied Accenture's Web site. This didn't clear things up, but it did permit me to drop phrases like "harnassing potential," "delivering cost-effective solutions," and "outsourcing human capital," in ordinary e-mail. And I kept Alex happy with a constellation of books about the universe.

Our correspondence, though conducted by computer, was like a nineteenth-century epistolary romance. We never spoke. Her job outfitted her with the latest cell-phone technology, but she never called me, and I never called her. Nor did we exchange photographs. Not long after returning from Berlin, my visual memory of her faded. I could picture her outsized lips and doughy nose, but not her face as a whole. But instead of a photo, she e-mailed me a portrait she had painted of a young woman. I kept this on my computer's desktop, often examining it. It was not a self-portrait, but as the only picture available, the painting came to supplant my lingering mental image. Over time, I came to believe it captured her likeness.

We exchanged several messages a day, switching between languages. Bettina's English was far from perfect, but this made me treasure her writing all the more – its humor, its attention to quirky detail, even its malapropisms and Teutonic syntax. *In an antique store I stumbled on a sympathetic sculpture of a fish.* I lived for this mail, constantly checking my inbox and rereading her notes. I culled my days for stories to share with her, often repeating these same stories to R.; I wanted to keep both women in the same orbit of intimacy.

If that sounds strange, to me it felt entirely normal, even essential. I once read a memoir by a British poet about his father, the perfect Victorian gentleman. A former soldier who made an early fortune in the ammunitions business, the father retired early to raise horses, manufacture his own wine (this, in northern England), and collect sports cars. Handsome and mustached, he married a beautiful woman and had three children. Like other fathers of his generation, he was aloof and formal, but also humorous and kind. He died young of a heart attack; at his funeral, his family discovered that he had been a bigamist. Not only had he married another woman a mere two years after his first wedding, but he had had three children with this second wife, and had lived in a house that looked very much like his first. Neither family had known of the existence of the other even though only twenty miles separated the two households. The news had scandalized Britain, though the poet, writing years later and perhaps showing how much he was his father's son, was less interested in the moral question than in the logistics of the feat – how the father had managed to shuttle back and forth between his twin lives without arousing suspicion. Today, I suppose we would call him a genius of compartmentalization. I'm just the opposite. That's why I mentioned the story: to draw a contrast. I've never been one to seal things off, keep a secret, maintain a psychic quarantine. Bettina figured importantly in my life, and I wanted to share this with R. How can a marriage remain healthy without open communication? I felt obligated to create byways of connection, channels of intercourse, however subtle.

And so, sitting together in the living room, I asked my wife, "Did you finish *Pnin*?"

"Didn't I tell you? I read it through two nights ago when I couldn't sleep. It was absolutely delightful, one of your better recent recommendations. I loved the bit about the soccer ball. I didn't know Nabokov could be touching and sentimental."

"*Speak, Memory*, his autobiography, is also terrific. Why don't you try that next?"

"Okay. Do we have it lying around?"

It was a happy time. I was the good husband, nice, loving, solicitous, even to a fault. I shopped for organic food, loaded the dishwasher, folded the laundry, and cleaned the toilet. I overcame my own repulsion and cooked her liver with sautéed onions. I got her special oils, salts, and soaps for her bath, and even a natural exfoliating sponge from

Burma. I assembled and plowed through a shelf of books about pregnancy and parenting: *What to Expect When You're Expecting; What to Expect, the Toddler Years; What to Expect, The Teenage Years; Simple Ways to Raise Your Child in a Terrifying World; Non-Toxic Parenting.* I took pleasure in charting the changing topography of R.'s body: the new Doric flair to her hips, the Rubenesque roundness to her belly, the lovely inviting fullness of her breasts. I read to Zygote in utero, first Dr. Seuss, than anything to accustom him to the sound of my voice and the pleasures of reading: Evelyn Waugh, Flaubert, Kafka.

It was also a happy time for R. Although I encouraged her to rest, nap, and generally veg out, she had an abundance of energy that she devoted to an ambitious tree-planting project (a mulberry, hickory, and tupelo in the pasture, and a weeping cherry and Japanese maple in the front yard). When she wasn't planting, she was writing. Since abandoning the coelacanth project, R. had returned to freelance work, at first with reluctance, then with greater enthusiasm. In the diary I had bought her she experimented with different kinds of writing: dialogue, description, even Haiku. She adopted a new, more personal voice in her assignments, turning them into reflective essays on the natural world. One piece, a wry meditation on eating one's pets, was picked up by NPR. Together with friends we listened to her nasal voice describe how a longing for fresh eggs ended in rooster *au vin*.

Finally, I should mention that R. loved the Joop! perfume. (Having forgotten to dump the stolen merchandise, I had to present it as a gift after she discovered it in my bathroom drawer.) On R., the fragrance carried less of a charge than on Bettina, like a spice past its use-by date. But this was alluring, too. I had often complained that R.'s perfume smelled like men's deodorant, and we were happy finally to find one we both liked.

*

"You the couple with the little miracle?"

The technician, a heavy-set woman, less fat than block-like, with a rippled neck and immobile face, huffed as she moved. R. sat on the examining table in a Tommy gown. Goose bumps dotted her arm. It was her first ultrasound since the one that established the embryo wasn't ectopic. The technician was Southern and no-nonsense. "That must have been quite a special surprise for y'all. I'm all for surprises, just not the bad ones. That's why you're here this fine morning. We're going to make sure the critter is following its marching orders. Now, hon, I'm gonna squeeze some of this gel on your tum, it might feel a little cold, ready?"

The applicator, shaped like a cafeteria mustard squeezer, erupted in a flatulent squeal.

"Well, *excuse* me." We shared a mortified laugh.

The technician manipulated the scanner across R.'s slathered abdomen, her small pale eyes riveted on the monitor. "Hold on . . . It's in here somewhere, that's for sure . . ." On the screen, gray masses shifted about like satellite images of a gathering storm, an offshore hurricane, a tropical depression.

"Playing hard to get . . . ? C'mon . . . There we go – now we're cooking with gas."

R. craned her neck to see the screen. The uncertain meteorological formation had resolved itself into a fetal apparition. At its center quivered a furious amoebal pulse.

"I guess y'all can see that strong little heart clear enough."

R. reached out to me. We squeezed hands and gazed into each others befogged eyes.

"Okay kid, let's see if you measure up."

On the screen, the technician tightened a digital halo around pockets of gray. "Kidneys, one, two . . . Lungs, I count one, I count two . . . Liver – we'll settle for one . . . Okey-doke."

We exchanged another misty gaze.

"Now it's still early in the game and this one's a squirmer, but if y'all want, I can try to let you know whether to get the pink or blue wallpaper."

We looked at each other. We hadn't anticipated being asked to decide on the spot. The technician's bearing distracted me – she was overplaying the tough but tender Texan card. As we conferred, a doctor entered the room.

"How's everything looking here?"

"Peachy."

His eyes skimmed over the measurements and squinted at the screen. "That's a crisp shot of the little shortstop. He's looking good."

"Actually, doctor, they didn't – "

"Oh, gosh, I thought – "

"I'd just asked them if – "

"I hope I didn't spoil – "

And so we learned the sex of our child, the would-be heir to Derek Jeter. Though R. chided the sexism (she had played a reliable second base on her high school varsity softball team), the doctor's words powerfully affected me. All at once I glimpsed a skinny kid with long unkempt bangs booting a routine grounder and launching an errant throw, a real moon shot, in the direction of a disgusted first baseman: myself. In backyard practices with my father, I had always snagged the short hops and tossed ropes, only to commit pathetic errors under the pressures of the game. I saw another generation doomed to replay the same hapless scenario, and then another, until, by some genetic fluke, the family produced a stellar athlete – or, more likely still, the planet tumbled into the sun.

The exam over, R. hurried into the connecting bathroom. Moments later came the sounds of her throwing up. "Believe it or not, that's music to my ears," said the technician, her words punctuated by R.'s forlorn retching. "To me, it's the sign of a body fully accepting the glory of pregnancy. I always worry when women don't have any morning sickness. Now before I forget, let me give you the first picture for your baby album."

A paper issued from the ultrasound, like a fax from a distant galaxy. "He's actually much smaller," she said, "and a whole lot cuter."

Dumbfounded I examined the picture, this image of sheer potentiality, of life on the cusp of life. A host of feelings roiled inside: pride, fear, joy, worry. Suddenly, though, a horrible premonition seized hold of me. In a terrifying gestalt switch, the image of prospective life transmogrified into one of death. My hands held a picture of the skeletal remains of a child exhumed by archaeologists from an ancient burial pit. Before me was the Lindow man or some other star-crossed ancestor who had taken a false step in a dark bog scores of centuries ago. He was curled on his side, nothing but bones with a few bronze trinkets and decayed arrows throw in for good measure. When R. emerged from the bathroom, I half expected her to blanch at my expression. Instead, she shrugged embarrassedly. "I haven't done *that* in a while. It must have been nerves." Studying the macabre image, she smiled. "A boy, amazing . . . It's strange to think that a creature with a dick is growing inside me. Let's hope he has my arm."

*

Fortunately, there was little time to linger on my morbid thoughts. The next day a fax from the Berlin Holocaust Commission arrived, proposing meetings for mid-May, after the end of my term. I accepted – provided I be flown Business Class.

"That goes without saying," said the assistant.

That night I discussed the plans with R. I made her look through the *Rough Guide to Berlin* with me, showing her all the terrific sights:

the Reichstag, the Museum für Naturkunde, the Pergamon Museum, the Liebeskind museum, die Neue Gemälde Gallerie. "There's even a delicatessen where you can get chocolate-covered ants." I all but begged her to come.

She shook her head, her lips pressed together in her expression of unalterable resolve. "I don't think so, Daniel. Not when I'm pregnant. In a couple of years when the memorial is finished, then I'll go to Berlin. That would be exciting."

I shrugged. The important thing was that I had made a good-faith effort to convince her, hadn't I? But what would happen without R. around to keep me in check? What did I want? These were the kind of questions that reduced me to my most feeble. Because unanswerable they were best left unposed.

"You sure you don't mind me going? Who'll make you asparagus and goat-cheese omelets at midnight?"

"I'll be fine, Daniel. It's you I worry about. Can I trust you with that woman?" So it was on R.'s mind, too.

"What do you think?"

"I don't know. That's why I'm asking you."

"Of course, I'll be good." And again, I did that shifty thing with my eyes, looking away, and down, all very incriminating.

"You think this is some kind of joke?"

"No, but have I ever given you reason to doubt me? I told you, I never even laid a finger on her. Not a peck on the cheek, not a brush of the arm, not even a good-bye handshake. Nothing. You're the one always making eye contact with strangers, flirting in cafés, not me."

"I just worry that this would be a brilliant way for you to act out all your anxieties and ambivalence. I mean, it has the making of a truly classic male-flight fuck-up."

"Excuse me, love, but I wish you would stop judging me by what happened last time. If you hadn't noticed, I haven't had a single panic attack, not one. Credit where credit is due."

"I know. You've been remarkably normal."

"And that's the way it's going to stay. You can put that in the bank."

That afternoon Bettina wrote:

So you want to know more about me? EVERYTHING? That is maybe a little difficult to comply to, but okay, I'll tell you this: at night, after Xander is asleep, I like to sneak a little curry and ice cream. I take this into bed with me and read Patricia Highsmith or watch "Dynasty" reruns. You want to find abnormalities in me: How about this – I don't like supermarkets with long aisles. I fear I might disappear, vanish without a trace, the only marker of me left behind – a basket of muesli and quark and unripe bananas. And since you enjoy sharing your dreams, I will tell you mine (I fear it is very boring!): I am in an apartment, looking out the window. On the street outside my building, two cats are fighting, really very viciously, making a terrible noise. I try to open the window to call to them to make them stop, but I cannot open the window. (Why are windows always stuck in dreams?) Then I notice that my apartment is on fire. It is very visual: I actually see the flames reflected in the glass of the window. Now I pound on the windows, not to stop the cats but to save myself, but the pounding does make them stop and they look up at me startled, as if they know that I will not be able to escape. Of course, then I wake up. What does the famous professor make of this? Should I mention that my mother has a phobia for cats? And should I add that my father (who loves cats, and Ella Fitzgerald, too!) comes originally from Dresden, was six at the time of the attack, and remains until this day terrified of fire? And what about this: my grandfather lived with us during the last years of his life when he was very depressed. He had lost a leg (no, not in the war! Much later, in a tram accident!), he was becoming blind, and he liked to feel sorry for himself. All the days he threatened to kill himself. My father ignored these threats, but when Opa said he intended to gas himself in the kitchen, my father became very furious. "You will blow up the entire house!" he screamed. "Why don't you jump out the window like other old people?" I am happy to report that Opa never made it out the window. He died of natural causes, easily in his sleep. What else should I tell you, Professor Dee? That I am soooooo EX-CITED to see YOU. There will be two extremely fantastic shows here at the time, Max Beckmann, one of my very favorites, and Anselm Kiefer, with his gigantic conflagrated landscapes. But not until May! How will I possibly survive?! Bzzzz.

*

No sooner had I made the arrangements than an urgent fax from the Holocaust Memory and Memorial Commission arrived at my office. It reported that beneath the planned site in Berlin, municipal engineers had just discovered a mass grave dating from 1631, the height of the Thirty Years War. Experts had identified the unearthed bodies as those of Lutherans, massacred by a frenzied army of Imperial troops and German Catholics during the Siege of Brandenburg. Later that day, I got a call from Dieter Baer, the director of the commission.

"Ach, this discovery is a terrible setback for our work," Baer said. "You see, an interfaith group, the Deutsche Toleranzverband, has now resurrected the argument you so intelligently refuted in your lecture here. They insist the memorial be a collective monument for all victims of persecution, both the Jews in World War II and the Lutherans in the Thirty Years War."

"They want to memorialize victims of the Thirty Years War?"

"It sounds a bit unusual, but with the discovery of this grave . . . You see, it fuels the arguments of those who say, 'But we Germans have also suffered. We Germans have also been victims.'"

"Victims of . . . themselves?"

"That is one way to see it . . . But the Thirty Years War remains a sensitive topic to our collective memory, a little like your Civil War. For better or worse, we have a very long history. In the Palatinate, one can still find people flying the flag of Frederick V's militant Calvinist force. The Swedish King Gustav still enjoys a cult-like reverence as the savior of the Protestants. Admittedly, many Catholics consider him a savage war criminal. Perspective is all."

"Yes, of course." I tried to remember what I knew about the Thirty Years War. I recalled that it started with someone being tossed from a window in Prague and ended with a quarter of the population of Central Europe dead.

"As you can imagine, the Jewish community here is up in arms. You see, the Lutherans were historically terrible anti-Semites, worse than the Catholics, though perhaps not so bad as the Calvinists. Though this too is a matter of debate, as some groups claim the Catholics were the worst anti-Semites and the Calvinists the most mild. Of course, the Catholic community is also terribly upset because the Siege of Brandenburg was in retaliation for the Sack of Magdeburg in which thousands of Catholics were slaughtered, a truly horrible episode.

"In any case, the Jewish community says better not build the memorial at all, than turn it into a farce. I am certain that the whole thing will soon blow over, especially now that the Bundestag is considering a special memorial dedicated to the Thirty Years War in Münster. But until this is resolved, I think meeting will only make the controversy worse. The press will follow our every move, and that wouldn't be productive. So reluctantly, Professor Wellington, I have decided to postpone our planned meeting."

"I see."

"I hope the inconvenience isn't too great and that this doesn't upset your arrangements. Let me repeat that your participation on our commission, both as a noted expert and as a child of survivors, is greatly valued. I will call you as soon as I think it makes sense to reschedule."

After the conversation, I headed to the library and got out C. V. Wedgwood's classic tome, *The Thirty Years War*, then took a walk. The campus was littered with thinning clots of gray slush, the last vestiges of a lusterless winter. The trees were still bare, the grass yellow and tinsely. The only sign of spring was a mild odor of manure carrying from the nearby National Register dairy farm. With dusk came rain, first gentle, then with a driving monotony. The wind picked up; a single murderous breeze mutilated my umbrella and toppled a row of recycling bins. I hurried back to my office. I had a plan.

I would go to Berlin regardless. The flight was paid for, the hotel room reserved; I would only be gone a couple of days; R. would never even know that the meeting had been canceled. Or would she? I carefully reviewed the possible sources of information, eager not to compound deceit and recklessness with complete self-destructiveness. From every angle, though, the plan seemed safe. If somehow I died during the trip – plane crash, taxi accident, hotel fire, bombing, mugging – she would probably call the memorial commission and it would all come out. But if I returned safely, R. would never know.

My decision left me jittery. I'm not cut out for deceit. It's a moral matter, but not that alone – it's bodily. I cramp, sweat, palpitate, become balloon-headed. This was taking things to a whole new level, one that imperiled marriage, future family, all this newly found happiness. Then again, wasn't this happiness largely a product of my relationship with Bettina? If seeing Bettina was good for my mental

health, then it was good for my marriage. The logic was as unassail-
able as it was insane.

I continued to debate the matter. That I needed words to speak
to myself only contributed to discomfiting feelings of self-disassociation.
The whole idea of addressing oneself by name – *C'mon, Daniel, come to
your senses, old boy* – struck me as vaguely schizophrenic. I arrived home
feeling depersonalized.

R. greeted me with a kiss. "That's too bad about your meeting."

"What do you mean?"

"The director of your commission called. He said he urgently
needed to cancel. I told him to call you in your office. Didn't he reach
you?"

"No, no, he did."

"That's a shame. What happened?"

I told her how the Holocaust had become caught up in the
Thirty Years War.

"That's what I love about writing about natural history," she
said. "Animals don't know when they've been wiped out; the survivors just pick themselves up and get back to work digging their holes,
burying their nuts, building their nests until the next time that disaster strikes and the whole cycle starts over again . . . Maybe people
need to forget a little more. Maybe collective amnesia is the key to
moving on."

"That's possible . . ."

Honestly I was relieved. Or maybe crushed. Probably a combination of the two. After dinner, I skimmed the Wedgwood. *Whether
Germany lost three-quarters of her population, or a small percentage, it is
certain that never before, and possibly never since, in her history had there
been so universal a sense of irretrievable disaster, so widespread a consciousness of the horror of the period which lay behind.* I checked the copyright
date. 1938. That explained that.

Only I couldn't bring myself to tell Bettina about the cancellation. In part, I didn't want to disappoint her, but it was more than that alone. Our e-mail romance had been building toward a meeting, our intimacy had gathered a critical momentum; it couldn't withstand a rendezvous being put indefinitely on hold. Yet the longer I put off informing her, the more difficult it was to break the news. The deadline I had set for telling her passed, and the next one, too. It was a self-made mess that I was making worse and worse. I understood how a petty gambler must feel in the days before the loan shark comes to pulverize his knuckles and flatten his nose.

Then came the miracle, the *deus ex machina*. It took the form of a letter from the Imperial War Museum, inviting me to London for two days of preliminary discussions about the proposed Holocaust exhibition.

Ecstatic, giddy, spooked by this run of luck, I wrote to Bee, explaining the change of plans: *I know you had your heart set on Berlin, but I'll bring a very large umbrella, and we'll eat Indian food and ride in romantic black cabs. Also my sources tell me that London is the world center of antique siphons, and I hear that there are some pretty decent paintings in the National Gallery and the Tate. And I swear there'll be no more sudden changes. So please, please, PLEASE meet me there. Whadya say?*

Later that afternoon, I received the shortest message Bettina ever sent me:

Agreed.

*

Vercin Kahn had never learned to drive, so I chauffeured him to our house for dinner. When I arrived at his apartment to pick him up, he was sitting on a Turkish rug, applying silver nail polish to his toes.

"I hope you'll excuse my, uh, uncharacteristic tardiness," he said. "I got off to a late start. It took longer than I envisioned to download the material you asked for."

"Were you able to find it?"

"Maybe eighty percent is, uh, total drivel, but there's definitely some serviceable recent work on visual display and curatorial praxis."

"We'll see what we have after dinner."

With the trip to London looming, I was hard at work on my presentation. The director of the Imperial War Museum wanted the exhibition space both to facilitate the visitors' encounter with the displays and to resonate architecturally with the subject itself. The U.S. Holocaust Memorial Museum had deeply impressed him, and he hoped for something comparable on a smaller scale for the Imperial. This made perfect sense to me until I realized that I knew nothing about the subject and had fewer ideas. Determined for once to head off a disaster-in-the-making, I called the director to confess my absence of experience in museum design. "I appreciate your candor," he answered, "but I was just reading something on this very point. Let me find it . . . Yes, here it is: 'In dealing with a subject as fraught as the Holocaust, it is not enough to have an aesthetics of display; what is needed is a *theory* of space.'" It was a line from my book. We agreed that I would supply that theory.

Preparing for London, I worked closely with Vercin. Over the course of the term, he had proven to be an impressive leader of discussions. ("The dude is awesome," reported one student. "He's just like us, only really, really smart.") As his hair color evolved from pistachio to tangerine before settling into black with a platinum corona, he began assisting my research as well. At every turn he impressed me with his intelligence, diligence, and resourcefulness. Talking to him could prove a harrowing experience – dreadful pauses punctuated his baroque syntax – but he was more interesting than the vast majority of my colleagues. I came to like him.

Waiting for his toenail polish to dry, we sipped Pellegrino and listened to music that sounded like water dripping from a pipe. His lips were full and unusually red. Did he use lipstick? His apartment was tastefully decorated, remarkably so for a grad student's. On the walls hung original prints by David Hockney and Eric Fischl. ("Gifts to my dad – they're kind of friends.") On an elegant coffee table sat a mini-CD player and earphones, a folded pair of sleek sunglasses, a minimalist clock, and a teddy bear. Issues of a magazine called *kaPutt* were stacked on the floor. I flipped through the contents: *Mode/Style/ Beauty/Art/Music/Design/Food/Ideas*. He also had a private greenhouse, filled with lush succulents and priapic cacti. I had speculated that women must find his androgynous beauty irresistible, but now it dawned on me that Vercin had to be gay.

R. had set the table in the dining room with brass candlesticks and pewter napkin rings. A hand-painted Italian tureen contained carrot soup, and for the main course she had prepared cauliflower-potato curry, accommodating our guest's vegetarianism. Vercin sampled this studiously, then said in his halting monotone, "Correct me if I'm wrong, but doesn't this recipe come from the *Sutra Raan Cookbook?*"

"You saw the book when you came in," R. said.

"Really I didn't. I just happen to be very familiar with it. It's one of my essential texts."

"Essential for what?" I asked.

"For, uh, cooking. You see, cooking is my favorite contact sport."

"That's great," R. exclaimed.

The topic could not have bored me more, but I was glad to see Vercin at ease. "Do you also know wines?" I asked. But as I made to pour, his hand gently but firmly covered his glass.

"I'm afraid I'm not much of a drinker. I suppose it's a form of rebellion against my upbringing . . . Dad's been on the wagon for, uh, several years now."

So I found myself drinking alone.

"My husband tells me that your father has won two Oscars."

"Two? I guess that's right. Though maybe he shared a third – I don't really keep track . . . I mean, I don't want to take anything away from Dad, because he is, uh, awfully smart and technically something of a wizard, but his films are not what I'd call wildly innovative or brilliant."

"Would we know his work?"

"I doubt it – well, maybe . . . Documentaries get like next to no market in this country. His stuff is mainly screened at these tiny film festivals in loser cities, and also in Europe. Apparently he has a pretty devoted following in Germany. But maybe you know this one he did in '86 – it was about the Army's program in the Sixties of testing the possible military uses of LSD on a group of totally unwitting recruits."

"That rings a bell." Both R. and I nodded, though frankly I drew a complete blank.

"That won him his first Oscar. It was considered a pretty evocative portrait of the period and also this brave indictment of a cynical government policy, though I think he just wanted an excuse to experiment with hallucinogens." He took a bite of curry and munched with excruciating delicacy. "Then he did this pretty notorious one about polygamy among contemporary Mormons. I still think that was his most accomplished. It earned him a lot of death threats, but formally it was, uh, very tight. Philip Glass did the sound, and for once Dad didn't over-edit – he let the material breathe. Now he's doing a film about lap dancing that's, uh, nominally from this progressive feminist perspective – you know, empowering the dancers – but I think Dad's just really into the porn."

R. laughed. "And what does your mom think about that?"

"Uh, my mom's dead."

"I'm very sorry . . ."

"She committed suicide when I was twelve."

"Oh my God, that's terrible – "

"I thought I mentioned – " I felt awful about my oversight, but Vercin did not seem to mind. I had never seen him so voluble.

"It was definitely the nadir of my existence, but by the end she was so far gone that in a way it was a relief."

"She had cancer?"

"No, she was insane." Vercin consumed a tidy bite, then took a sip of water, holding the glass with long, tapered fingers and exquisitely manicured nails. "It's hard to say how much of it was innate or the result of all her substance abuse. Over the years Dad consumed truly Olympian quantities of controlled substances, yet it never really affected his work. At times he was, uh, pretty ragged, but he always stayed focused. He always got me to my drum lessons on time and could spend like thirty straight hours in the editing room. But Mom was a different story. It's like she was looking to bid adieu to reality."

The line made me laugh, but R.'s forehead was furrowed in the tick-tack-toe pattern of extreme concern. "And even with the new generation of psychiatric drugs, nothing worked?"

"Her main problem was she lacked the will to be sane. Seriously. Dad's default lament was, 'You're not crazy, you're undisciplined.' At the time I thought this was maximally insensitive, but in retrospect I think he was essentially right. Because first she'd go on a psychotropic binge, mixing her meds in truly novel combinations, and then she'd stop taking them altogether, burying them in our garden next to the zucchini. It was all fairly adolescent." Emotion registered in Vercin less in his voice, which remained largely absent of affect, and more in his cheeks. They were pinking up.

"If you don't mind me asking," I said, "how did she kill herself?"

"Pretty unimaginatively. She washed down a pile of pills with a bottle of tequila Dad bought in Oaxaca. We wouldn't even have been sure that it was, you know, purposeful, but next to her bed she had left this video cassette – she had been a pretty skilled editor until she became so unreliable that Dad had to sack her. So instead of a note, she had, uh, prepared this suicide video, nothing all that elaborate, just her talking into the camera." The ruddiness of his cheeks had clarified into two precisely contoured crimson circles. "The whole thing was addressed to me, not even a mention of poor Dad. What was amazing was how coherent and even humorous she was. I mean, this was a woman who believed that all the sprinkler systems in the neighborhood obeyed her commands, and here she was speaking in this totally sane and tender manner." When Vercin next lifted his water glass to his lips, a slight tremor rippled his grip. "She'd obviously prepared the video months earlier, because you can see the bare limbs of the trees out the window. So ending her life must have, uh, been on her mind for a while. I guess I'll never know why she waited until she did, though it didn't particularly help that it was the day before my birthday."

Thankfully R. broke the ensuing silence. "How often do you watch the video?"

"It's funny you should ask, because I'm always surprised that *more* people don't want to know exactly that . . . Anyway, I've only watched it three times – once when it happened, and twice since. At the time I nearly threw it out, or to be, uh, more precise I *did* throw it out. I was feeling pretty sub-par, and, as you can maybe guess, I'm not exactly the smash-objects type. So I removed the tape from the VCR and dropped it in the trash, very gently, you know. But Mercedes, our maid, secretly rescued it and kept it for a few weeks while I behaved, uh, very reclusively. Then she gave it back to me.

Now I'd have to say the tape is my most cherished possession. I've made two backups, and keep the original in a safe deposit box. I've only watched it three times in eleven years, but I remember exactly what Mom says, what she's wearing, how she moves. Her last words are, 'I'm so sorry I have to go now, honey. But I promise I'll see you again.'" Vercin's voice had turned into a whisper and I feared he would be unable to continue. Then the moment of raw emotion passed. "At first I thought that line was just a sorry bit of New Age horse. But then I realized that by making the tape, she had in a sense honored her promise, because I *can* see her whenever I want."

We fell silent. I sipped my wine and they, their water. Then R. said, "Daniel's grandmother also committed suicide." I glanced at R. sternly. This story was properly my mother's, and the fact that Vercin chose to share his familial afflictions didn't obligate us to reciprocate.

"I'm sorry to hear that."

"Well, that was all before I was born," I said, "None of us really know all the details."

"Except that as a result Daniel's mother has been basically dysfunctional all her life."

I shifted in my chair. "I would hardly call my mother dysfunctional. Also, I don't think Vercin really wants to hear that children of suicides are destined to lifelong impairment."

"You're right, I'm sorry. Your mother could be far worse, given what she's gone through."

Vercin tactfully changed the subject. "I noticed that you also avoid drink. Does uh, intemperance also run in your family?"

"My family?" R. laughed. "I'm afraid the closest thing to an addict in my family is my father, who compulsively watches CNBC. My grandmother did have a second cousin with a harelip who was a heroin fiend back in the Twenties. Anyway, the reason I'm not drinking is because I'm pregnant."

"Honestly? That's truly robust. Did you just find out?"

"We've known since January."

"I would never have guessed."

"It's the clothes. When I'm in my undies, it's pretty obvious."

The conversation had started to rankle me. The meal was over, there was work to be done, but my assistant was growing more loquacious by the minute. "I can't wait to have children. I'm drawn to large even numbers, four or even six, also evenly spaced, like one every two years. I also like the idea of twins, preferably identical." Frankly I had a hard time imagining this androgynous Martian-haired creature with silver toenails and various braided bands looping his wrists as a paterfamilias. There was no shutting him up. "In high school I had a Catholic friend who had so many siblings that he didn't even know all their birthdays. I was incredibly envious of that breathing room, that centrifugal force. I suppose that's the legacy of being a single child in a subatomic family that imploded big time."

"I think everyone reacts to conditions differently," R. said. "Daniel's also an only child from a dysfunctional family, and yet he's terrified about having even one child – "

"That's ridiculous. I'm incredibly excited."

"But you were – "

"That was completely different – "

And so the story of the Sycamore tree came out.

"To be honest, I never believed the thing about the back spasms," Vercin said, shyly.

"On that note," I said, "perhaps it's time for us to do a little work on the visual display of atrocity." After retrieving some papers upstairs, I reentered the kitchen to find Vercin and R. standing by the counter, examining a cookbook. Or rather, the cookbook lay open on the countertop, and they stood face to face, talking. There was nothing remarkable about this – they were discussing northern Indian cuisine

– but there was something odd about how they were positioned. It was as if they were standing on a crowded subway car, pushed by forces outside themselves to share the space intended for a single person. They seemed to be resisting some invisible force that would propel them closer still, her head colliding into his prominent Adam's apple.

"Are you ready?" I asked.

"Eager," said Vercin, and then to R., "That was truly delicious. If you ever want help preparing an Indian meal, please let me know. I'll bring some Garam Masala that my dad brought back from Bangladesh. It's supposed to be an aphrodisiac or a soporific, uh, something like that."

Twelve

"I suppose you know this building once housed the original Bedlam, the great nineteenth-century mental institution." The director of the Imperial War Museum leaned back in a sumptuous worn leather chair and smiled, revealing fine, slightly yellowed teeth. Charles Worthington was the first Knight I had ever met. (To use the English parlance, he "had gotten his 'K'" a decade before, in 1991.) In his early sixties, Sir Charles had the height, trimness, watery blue eyes, and thinning platinum pate born of generations of sensible breeding. Eton, Oxford, Savile Row: privilege hung about him with unapologetic ease, as if inherited wealth were a natural right conferred upon an elite judiciously chosen for its good taste, civic mindedness, and inborn sense of etiquette. "And I fear some of the old spirit still persists," the director added, turning to the museum's secretary. "Wouldn't you agree, Jeffrey?"

"One could say we've merely exchanged one form of insanity for another," said the secretary, a thin, slightly stooped man who faded into the office's mahogany wainscoting.

"Yes, but by displaying the madness of war," I said, "the museum performs a vital pedagogic function."

"I believe our secretary was commenting on the Imperial's internal administration, not on its function as a gallery of modern warfare." The correction came from Edward Pugh, the third member of the museum's administration present in the director's vast, handsome, yet gloomy office. If Sir Charles looked like a triumph of the species, Pugh was a visible reminder of the losers in the Darwinian scheme. Somewhat older than the director, he was rumpled and fat. His cheeks sagged in loose baggy jowls. Dense fur clogged his nostrils. Truculent hazel eyes scrutinized me from beneath an outrageous growth of bristly eyebrow. "War has admittedly been associated with some of man's darkest moments," he continued, "but it has also provided man's spirit with untold opportunities for glory. Wouldn't you agree?"

I had never heard anyone propound such views, except maybe in a Monty Python skit. At a loss, I exclaimed, "War – man's finest hour!"

Pugh reddened. The director of the museum coughed into a balled fist, and I realized that this affectation was not a contrivance from Noel Coward movies – British men really did deploy phlegm to defuse social tension.

Sir Charles removed a silver cigarette case. "Would you mind terribly?" he asked. "My American friends find my habit all very old world."

"Not at all."

"And to think," Pugh observed, "even with your public bans, cigarettes still kill as many Americans every year as did the entire Vietnam campaign." Yet he, too, joined the director in lighting up.

"Now then, Professor," said Sir Charles, exhaling in a manner that would have been the envy of my students, "I take it that you survived your flight and find your hotel agreeable."

In fact I had arrived straight from Heathrow, stopping by the hotel only to drop off my luggage and write a quick note for Bettina who was to arrive in the afternoon. But thanks to Business Class, I had actually managed some sleep en route.

"It's a shame," he continued, "that you shan't be in the hotel my assistant originally booked for you. It's a splendid place."

"Maybe next time . . . An old friend happens to be in London on business, so I decided to stay in his hotel."

"How serendipitous."

Pugh blew his nose explosively. As he excavated his nostrils with a monogrammed hanky, he asked, "I don't suppose there's any family connection to Arthur Wellesley?"

"Arthur . . . ?"

"The first Duke of Wellington," said the secretary, mournfully.

"Waterloo," added the director.

"Oh, of course," I said, "It's just that Americans usually call him . . . anyway, no, there isn't a family connection – at least, not one that I'm aware of."

"But such a proud English name," said Pugh. "Whereabouts do your family originate?"

Feeling no need to explain that my grandfather had changed the shtetl Weinstein to the manorial Wellington in a fit of Anglophilia, I merely answered, "The East."

"The East? East London?"

My stomach rumbled gaseously. "No, not London – to be honest, I'm not sure where exactly."

"I see . . . I must apologize, Professor Wellington," continued Pugh, "but during the introductions, I somehow missed your Christian name."

"I don't have a Christian name," I said, staring coldly at the tangled eyebrows. "But I do have a first name: Daniel."

The director and secretary coughed simultaneously. "As an art historian," said Sir Charles, "you simply must see Goya's marvelous portrait of Wellington that hangs in our National Gallery."

"It was painted during the Spanish campaign," explained the

secretary, "directly on the heels of the victory at Salamanca. If memory serves, Wellington took the painting with him on to the north, but then sent it back to Goya to have his new medals added. As it is, the medals are completely wrong and the uniform inaccurate."

"Still, it's far superior to Goya's equestrian portrait of Lord Wellington that hangs in Apsley House," said Sir Charles. "There I'm afraid the Lord looks a tad stiff in his mount."

I nodded. Resting on the corner of the director's inlaid Edwardian desk was a squat tome, *German Sidearms and Bayonets, 1740–1945, Vol. II*, next to a copy of *Military Motorcycles of the Second World War*. What on earth am I doing here? I wondered.

Sir Charles stabbed out his cigarette, while Pugh puffed away, oblivious to the crooked finger of ash that threatened to collapse on his lapel. "Professor Wellington has come a considerable distance to speak to us about the Holocaust, so why don't we let him begin?" The director turned to me.

My talk started with an overview of the different strategies of display used by existing Holocaust museums. Focusing on the Museum of Tolerance in Los Angeles and the Holocaust Memorial Museum in D.C., I weighed the strengths and weaknesses of various approaches, and offered my own recommendation: that whatever its shape, the Imperial's wing had to challenge the orthodox theory of exhibition. Museums generally strive to organize their space in a manner that is friendly, accessible, and logical. In the case of the Holocaust, it was imperative for the museum to disorient, challenge, even confuse. "This is the great achievement of the D.C. building," I said. "It manages to be both attractive and sinister, attacking the assumption that a museum should be an innocuous, neutral environment. All the same, it's visually striking and it uses architectural tropes to stunning effect – like the tapering wall of photographs designed to suggest the chimney of a crematorium." Less successful, I argued, was the newly opened Dokumenta Zentrum in Nuremberg, built in the shell of the Nazi's gargantuan and never-completed Kongreßhalle. The Dokumenta Zentrum, a museum of Nuremberg's involvement with Nazism, followed many of the strategies of the D.C. museum – exposed brick, unpolished darkened steel, jarring angles – but it made one colossal mistake. The entrance was designed to look like a spear thrust into the side of the building, a visual pun on Albert Speer, Hitler's architect and the original designer of the builder.

"Avoid visual puns," muttered Sir Charles, as the secretary took copious notes with a fountain pen the size of a cigar.

"At the same time," I continued, "it's important to remember that there's more to a successful exhibit than successful architecture." Here I said that a museum had to create its own memorial space, otherwise the exhibit risked turning into a display of the techniques and logistics of genocide, a museum of the perpetrators. To avoid this, the museum had to establish and make clear the human element of suffering; it had to penetrate the numbing arithmetic of genocide by telling personal stories. In short, it had to create a narrative that would pull its viewers through the exhibition.

"Create narrative," Sir Charles repeated. Only now it seemed that his eyes had glazed over, not with inattention but with something more profound, a meditative reflection. The secretary continued to scribble furious notes, seemingly far in excess to my spoken words. As for Pugh, he was fast asleep, his rattling half-snore providing a metronome for my presentation. Sir Charles and the secretary registered their mortification with tense smiles, but refrained from rousing him.

No sooner had I ended, though, did Pugh's dry yellow eyes open. He blinked once, then launched into me, confident that sleeping through my talk posed no obstacle to vociferous disagreement.

"Frankly, Professor," he began, "I absolutely cannot fathom what you mean by – now what was the phrase? – yes, 'the unrepresentable qualities of the Holocaust.' It seems to me that historians and others have been representing the Holocaust just fine for some time now."

"My talk tried to spell out how such an extreme event in human history resists being captured, or represented, in conventional historical, literary, or visual idioms," I answered.

"I'm not asking you to repeat your presentation," he said. "I'm just telling you that when I hear words like 'unrepresentable,' I think 'rubbish.' I don't mean to be rude, but I feel I must be frank."

"I also dislike academic jargon and theoretical claptrap," I said, folding my hands in an effort to match his expression of pugnacious calm. "But I guess I've never considered the verb 'to represent' particularly difficult."

"It's not the verb that troubles me, Professor, it's your use of it. Let's return to Goya. Wouldn't you regard the *Disasters of War* series as one of the great depictions of human suffering? And Goya was hardly the first – think of Callot's *Miseries of War* etchings from the Thirty Years War. So what makes the Holocaust any less "representable" than, say, the battle of Austerlitz or, for that matter, Tilly's siege of Magdeburg?"

"Perhaps," Sir Charles interjected, "we should attend to those points raised by our guest that are more germane to our project."

"Come now, Charlie," Pugh grumbled, "this isn't just some argument before the Oxford Union. It goes to the heart of the professor's proposals for our museum. Wouldn't you agree, Professor Wellington?"

I had no choice but to nod.

"So, then, what makes it so unrepresentable?"

I repeated my argument: the depth and magnitude of the horror, the unique qualities of its implementation, etc. Pugh was unmoved. I noticed that a single wiry hair sprouted defiantly from the end of his nose. Certainly he could have had it plucked. He clearly took pleasure in repelling people.

"Perhaps, Professor, we can pursue this from a different angle," he continued. "In anticipation of this meeting, I was looking over your writings, and came across something that truly baffled me. In one of your essays, you praise the work of a young German artist who constructed a wonderfully precise model of Birkenau. This little model, I recall, was built from Playmobil pieces. Perhaps you can explain to me why you find this work so worthy of praise. I should have thought 'offensive' and 'insulting' would have better characterized the work, particularly issuing from a German artist."

The reference was to an introduction I had written for a museum catalogue of an exhibition of contemporary German art. At the time I had been unfamiliar with the work of the artist in question, but had been flattered by the invitation to write. My payment had been an original Richter offset print from the museum's archives. I recalled the excitement of the opening – the crush of well-known artists, the press coverage, the fabulous finger food. "I wouldn't for a second consider such a work right for this museum."

"Most reassuring, but I would still benefit from learning why you find this piece so remarkable."

I glanced at the director, hoping he might again intervene. But his expression of impatience had turned to one of growing interest. The secretary, for his part, followed the colloquy with expressionless, filmy eyes.

"I never claimed *Playmobil, Birkenau* was a great work of art – "

"'Path-breaking' and 'important' are, I believe, the terms you used. Yes, let me quote, 'The monumental and carnivalesque coalesce in this daring interrogation of the received pieties of "safe" art.' 'Safe' is in scare quotes."

Hearing my work read aloud made me shudder. "All I was trying to claim," I said, "was that the power of the piece came from the fact that Playmobil was, well, so obviously, an inappropriate medium for representing the Holocaust."

Pugh's expression of skepticism was now mirrored in the handsome face of the director. "I must admit, Professor Wellington," Sir Charles said, "that I, too, found your remarks about this Ischinger fellow rather puzzling. Perhaps this kind of formal experiment flies in Germany, which remains, even today, such a deeply metaphysical land. But what can I say? We English are a more figurative people . . ."

"Even pastoral," added Pugh.

"Would it be fair," Sir Charles continued, "to describe your viewpoint on these matters as highly conceptual? My question isn't meant to hide criticism. I merely want to make sure I fully understand your orientation."

"Maybe I misunderstood my assignment," I said, "I thought I was asked to supply you with a *theory* of Holocaust exhibition."

"Yes, of course," the director said. "But a *practical* theory."

Even the dour secretary joined his colleagues' cataract of laughter.

After the mirth, Pugh's face remained flushed, a dreadful infarction hue. "What I should most like to hear is an explanation of why we should have a Holocaust exhibition at the Imperial in the first place – and a permanent one at that. It's absurd."

"We've been over this terrain often enough," said Sir Charles, impatiently.

"Yes," said Pugh, "but perhaps the professor has views that can move our thinking forward."

The director turned to me, waiting.

"I'm sorry," I said, "but, again, I thought the question of building the exhibition had been settled, and my responsibility was to consider the issue of design."

"Nothing's been settled," Pugh grumbled.

"The board has voted preliminary approval," the director corrected.

"Which, as you know, Charles, means very little. The board also voted approval of the Falkland wing and what became of that?"

I turned to Pugh. "I'm sorry, but just as you missed my first name in the rush of introductions, I'm afraid I missed your role in all of this . . ."

Sir Charles's placid brow furrowed as he explained that Edward Pugh was the chairman of the museum's board and its principal donor.

"Oh. I see."

"And still no one has explained what the Holocaust has to do with us Britons," said the obstreperous benefactor. "It's perfectly appropriate to have a small display about the liberation of Belsen – there we were at least involved. But an exhibition on the whole Final Solution? What sense would that make? This is London, not Berlin. Let the Germans build a monument or memorial or whatever they've decided to erect fifty plus years after the fact – the more the merrier. And let's be honest, the only reason the Americans built that monstrosity on the Mall was because the Jews are a powerful, wealthy, and well-organized tribe, and Jimmy Carter wanted to win their support. And they still voted for Reagan and his tax breaks."

"If you have no interest in putting your money into a Holocaust exhibition, that's one thing," I said, trying to master the emotion in my voice. "But that's no reason to make statements that sound dangerously like anti-Semitic clichés."

My heart thudded for battle. Instead, Sir Charles smiled sympathetically, as he might at a foolish child. "Edward an anti-Semite? In addition to chairing our board, Edward Pugh runs the largest Jewish philanthropy in Britain."

Helplessly I nodded.

"Perhaps I should add that Edward first came to our country via a *Kindertransport*," continued Sir Charles. "These were the trains that . . ."

"Yes, of course. I know – "

"Unfortunately," Pugh said, "My parents were not able to join me. They traveled in the other direction, to the little Playmobil building."

"I'm awfully sorry . . ." I felt myself turn a crisp sun burnt red. Duped by that Anglo name and Dickensian face.

"No need for apologies," said Pugh. "It was coy of me not to mention any of this earlier. But much as I'd love to see the Queen Mum convert, I can't see why we, and now I'm speaking for my adopted country, should devote any more attention to the Holocaust than to the Armenian genocide."

"Not to quibble," the director cut in, "but I wouldn't call the Armenian experience genocide proper – it lacked a central administration. It would be more accurate to say mass murder."

"Oh, for God's sake, Charles!"

Initially charmed by the director and repulsed by Pugh, I marveled at the sudden change in my impressions. Obviously Sir Charles was nothing more than a hair-splitting patrician; Pugh was the beetle-browed conscience of the community.

Unbidden, the secretary entered the fray. "We have seen a fifty percent decline in our admissions in the past five years." His remark struck me as a non sequitur, an answer supplied to a question that he alone had heard. But then its relevance became clear.

"Ah," said Pugh, as if waiting for this. "So that's the bottom line, so to speak. What's the phrase, Professor – 'There's no business like Shoah business'? I suppose there are worse things than pandering to voyeurism."

"It's not pandering," objected Sir Charles. "We're educating the public, teaching the dangers of intolerance and racism."

As the squabble continued, my gaze traveled through the office's leaded picture window. The forecast had predicted rain, but the sun was shining brightly. On the grounds of the museum was a park; boys and girls in cheerful navy and red school uniforms were playing on swings, kicking a ball, playing tag. The sky, a voluminous blue, was etched with contrails. Bettina had already landed. She probably was already waiting at the hotel. Overcome by a fit of impatience, a feeling of life wasted, I suddenly yawned. Not a discreet, head-tilted-to-the-side, hand-over-the-mouth, stifled yawn. No, it was a vast, sluggish yawn, a Sunday morning, still-in-underwear yawn, the kind that accompanies a lazy stomach slap and a pinky poke at a knot of belly-button lint. It was a yawn of the unshaven and slothful, of the loutish, overweight, and under-exercised. The three officials stared at me with astonishment. Immediately I apologized, but the point had registered. "Perhaps this is enough for one day," Sir Charles said. "Tomorrow we shall doubtless have the opportunity to discuss the substance of Professor Wellington's provocative ideas more closely."

"I look forward to it," I said, sheepishly.

*

Bettina and I had booked separate rooms in a small hotel off Ladbroke Grove. The concierge confirmed that she had already checked in. I showered, then shaved for the second time that day. (I had shaved twice in a day only once before – for my wedding.) For the forty-eight-hour trip to London I had completely overpacked, sparing myself the need to decide what to wear in advance. Towel around my waist, I laid out all the clothes across the queen-sized bed and arranged various combinations. It was then that I noticed the absence of fresh underwear. Absentmindedness is not one of my principal problems, and I cursed the mistake, obvious fodder for the Good Doctor. After a quick check, I reluctantly slipped on the pair I had worn all day. Dressed, I rebrushed my teeth, then noticed a patch of toothpasty froth clinging to the breast pocket of my shirt. I tried dabbing it away, but only succeeded in leaving a huge damp spot on my chest. In disgust, I peeled off the shirt, threw it in the corner, and pulled on another, my fingers fumbling helplessly with the buttons on the cuffs.

Before Bettina's door, I paused to master my breathing, then gently knocked.

The door opened a splinter. "It's you!" Bettina cried. "Come in." We greeted each other as we had parted in Berlin, without a kiss or hug, but both smiling madly. What I noticed first was that she was barefoot, that her blouse revealed a thrilling shadow of cleavage, and that the air about her trailed the scent that had turned me into a thief. What I noticed next was on the bed, leaning against a bank of pillows, and watching cartoons: Alex.

"How are you, my little friend?" I said, trying to conceal the avalanche of disappointment. "Whoa, look how you've grown."

The boy didn't react to my proffered high-five. In plotting our rendezvous, we hadn't discussed the Alex issue. I simply had assumed, or hoped, that Bettina would leave him with his father. Perhaps Bettina thought I realized that he'd be coming along. In any case, there he was, sullenly absorbed in the animated adventures of a British postman.

"Oh, Daniel, I'm sooo happy to see you," Bettina said. "And don't mind Xander – he's often shy in a new environment. He says his stomach hurts. It's his typical complaint."

The boy did look a little pale. When we first met, I had been unable to detect a trace of Bettina's genetic contribution. In the intervening months, though, certain features had emerged from the chrysalis of young life – his mouth now stenciled the outline of his mother's sensuous lips. For her part, Bettina looked the same, though I was shocked once again by the daring assemblage of exaggerations that formed her face. She was far less attractive in a conventional sense than R., but who cares about convention? I was fatigued with desire. My spirits lifted when Bettina said, "Darling, your sitter will be here in minutes. Would you like a bath?"

"Dude – a bath! Now that sounds like fun! Whadya say?" I'm not sure where the rodeo voice came from, but it wasn't convincing anyone. The boy grunted, an indication that I was blocking the screen.

"So what are you watching there? How about working up a hello for your old pal?"

Silence.

"Hmmm, not exactly in a conversational mood, are you?"

Just then he moaned, "Mama, my stomach feels funny."

"Oh, Xander, your stomach always feels funny. Would you like a glass of bubbly water?"

"No!" He crossed his arms, as if he couldn't understand how his mother could possibly make such a moronic suggestion. "My stomach feels *very* funny."

She sat on the bed, rubbing his cheek. "Xander, my sweetheart, what am I going to do with you?" Then, turning to me, she said, "This is our normal ritual. Don't worry, he becomes a happy little animal once the sitter arrives."

His moaning, which had briefly subsided, took on a fresh intensity at the word "sitter."

"Mama, I don't want you to go out tonight," he cried, tears beginning to drizzle.

"Xander, *Schätzchen*, it will only be a few hours. And you like this sitter. It's Emi who used to come to us in Berlin, now she lives in London. It's like seeing an old friend."

"I *hate* her. She speaks English even worse than you. And she smells."

I was taken aback by the boy's cruelty.

"Now don't behave like a beast. She's very sweet, and together you can watch television and read your new books and order dinner from room service – you always love this."

"But my tummy! – it's *killing* me."

Bettina frowned, her lips curling down like a clown's. "Oh, Xander, this isn't the start of another one of your bugs, is it?" She pressed her hand to his forehead, and, in apparent obedience to some Teutonic folk tradition, examined his tongue for grayness. A complex expression settled upon the boy's face, at once shy and sly, vulnerable and manipulative – the quivering smile of a neophyte poker player on the verge of an improbable win.

"I declare you absolutely fit, you brave little warrior," Bettina concluded, tousling his hair. "I predict an extremely big portion of French fries and chicken fingers for you tonight – "

The boy moaned miserably. Then he shrieked at me, "GET OUT!"

"*Tierchen*, you must behave, do you understand me?" Clearly this kind of tantrum was familiar. "Now get control of yourself and give me a hug." The boy, sobbing fiercely, consented to a brief hug then broke free and dashed into the middle of the room. There he froze, as if zapped in a children's game.

"Xander, what is it?"

All at once a torrent of vomit erupted from his mouth. He righted himself, his eyes wide and startled. Then he doubled over and a second wave of watery puke splashed across the carpet, television, bedspread. The boy wept quietly.

"Oh, my sick little *Würmchen*, I should always listen to you. Come to Mama, and let me clean you up. I'm so, so sorry . . ."

I retrieved some towels, dabbed at the mess.

"Please, Daniel, do not bother. We can get the maid service." She called down, then helped her son into fresh pajamas. On the television a voice said, "I fear the letter was eaten by a donkey."

"Daniel, I feel so awful . . ." Bettina said.

"Don't be ridiculous, these things happen. I just hope Xander's okay. Do you want me to call a doctor?"

The maid arrived and set to work on the disaster area. I felt terribly awkward in the presence of a woman employed to clean up a stranger's vomit. Looking away, I handed her a fresh wad of paper towels every time she deposited a soiled one into the garbage. Experiencing no such discomfort, Bettina pointed and said, "Excuse me, miss, you missed an area by the television."

Alex had returned to the bed.

"Feeling a little better, Xander?"

"Don't call me that! Only my mom calls me that."

"My sincerest apologies. Hey, I like those jammies. They're pretty cool."

"They have all the characters from Thomas the Tank on them," the boy answered. "Here's Henry, and James, and Gordon, and Thomas."

"They look more like trains than tanks to me."

"Thomas is not a tank, he's a tank *engine*! That's a steam engine that doesn't need a tender." Still surly, but very talkative now.

The maid was just finishing up when the sitter arrived. She and Bettina conferred by the door, speaking quietly in German. By the look on her face, the sitter didn't appear all that surprised by the situation. Alex glanced at her both shyly and suspiciously; she waved, flashing him a weak short-lived smile. He simply looked away. Bettina handed the woman several bills, which at first she refused, but then folded into a purse. It was agreed that they would talk again the next morning.

After the sitter left, I rose. "Should I get a doctor?"

"I think he just needs rest."

"Well, then . . . I guess it's time for me to pack it in."

"Oh, Daniel, you're welcome to stay," Bettina said. "We could order in food. Of course, I don't want you to catch Xander's bug . . ."

"I think I'll head back to my room, get some sleep."

Bettina and I briefly discussed the plans for the next day. I had meetings at the museum scheduled through the afternoon. Assuming the boy had improved, we would arrange something for the evening and night.

"Tomorrow," she said, as I left.

"Yes," I said, "tomorrow. Hey, feel better little friend."

By now he was too absorbed in Wallace and Gromit to answer.

*

The next morning as I was shaving, the phone rang.

"Professor Wellington? This is Fiona Andrews, assistant to Sir Charles Worthington, director of the Imperial War Museum. I'm afraid Sir Charles has taken ill. With regrets he must call off today's meetings. He assures me that he will ring you in America within the week to reschedule. In the meantime, please accept his sincerest apologies."

After the debacle of the day before, I greeted this news with something close to euphoria. I promptly called Bettina, leaving a short message when there was no answer. "You guys are probably still snoozing, but I wanted to let you know the director of the museum has come down with Alex's bug. Hope the little guy's better, and give me a call when you're up. I'm free the whole day." After breakfast, there was still no message from Bettina, so I knocked softly on their door. No answer. The receptionist smiled brightly. "The German lady and the little boy? They were certainly up bright and early – went out at half past seven or so."

Either Alex had recovered in record time, or they had gone to the doctor. A vague worry took hold of me. I returned to my room and waited. Shortly after ten, I gave up. I'd call every hour or so to check for messages.

The weather was again lovely. Low fleecy clouds roamed the sky, and Kensington Garden was in spring blossom. I probably should have returned to the Imperial to familiarize myself with its collection, but the prospect of spending my one free day in London with prototypes of the V-2 and the first tank didn't thrill me, so instead I rode the tube to Covent Garden, where I bought two pairs of designer underwear. Without a specific goal I wandered down Whitehall and paused by the Cenotaph, once the destination of a million private pilgrimages, now covered in a sooty film of exhaust from the double-deckers and cabs that roared indifferently past. I people-watched in Trafalgar Square – it was crowded with the typical variety of tourists, pigeons, beggars, addicts, and students. A man with a loudspeaker shouted about the dangers of cloning to a stone lion. In the National Portrait Gallery, I examined lush paintings of proud English monarchs who had had their heads chopped off or had otherwise met a similarly violent end, invariably at the hands of a trusted advisor, or a family member. Every so often, I'd find a phone and call the hotel. Finally I sought distraction at the National Gallery, but by then was too overwrought to attend to the sublime. I rushed past Titians and Rembrandts like a person on a power walk.

Back in the hotel, I calmed myself with a bath, then knocked on their door around five.

Bettina answered. "Oh, Daniel, excellent timing – we just came in." Alex came running and grabbed my hand.

"Is everything okay? It looks like someone is feeling better."

"Yes," said Bettina, "It was one of those typical twelve-hour stomach flus."

"I see." Twenty-four hour bugs I had heard of, but twelve hours? Perhaps German viruses operated on an abbreviated schedule.

The boy tugged at me. "Come see what I got." In the middle of the room, covering whatever stains might have been left from the night before, were two gigantic bags from Hamley's, filled with Lego sets.

"Whoa, looks like you bought the entire company."

"Isn't this cool? It's a Lunar Rover. Did you know that the real Lunar Rover had wheels made from piano strings? It's true."

"Very impressive. So you spent the whole day in Hamley's?"

"No, silly! We saw Big Ben and the Thames and went to the Science Museum. I saw the Rocket, which actually isn't a rocket – it was the first real train!"

"It sounds like you two had a lot of fun."

"Me and Emi even took the Underground!"

"You and Emi? Where was Mom?"

"Where do you think?" said Bettina. "I shopped and threw myself into art. I saw a fantastic show at the Royal Academy of young British sculptors, and went to the National Gallery, of course. Today I declare Titian to be the greatest painter of all, the supreme master."

"Are you kidding? I was there."

"No! What about your meetings?"

I explained the cancellations.

"You silly animal, why didn't you call my mobile? Didn't you have the number?"

I looked at her helplessly. In fact, I did have her cell number, but it had never occurred to me to use it.

"*Na ja,*" she sighed. "What can we do? Now you must go away and let me change. Emi will be back at six, right Xander?"

The boy nodded, this time all reconciled to his fate. We agreed that after the sitter arrived, Bettina would come to my room.

The next hour I was wracked with nerves. Should I dress to go out, or prepare for immediate lovemaking? I thought about the first time that R. and I had slept together, in a sleazy motel on the outskirts of New Haven on a hot summer afternoon. The room had fake paneling, a mirrored ceiling, and paper-thin walls, but it was the first place we ever had all to ourselves. When our order-in Chinese food arrived, R. tossed away the paper plates. "Eat off me," she said. We left a twenty dollar tip for the chambermaid who had to deal with the puzzling mess.

I answered Bettina's gentle knock. "Oh, Daniel, look at you! You haven't changed! What have you been doing?"

"I thought maybe you'd like to spend some time in my room."

"Oh, but I'm totally ravenous."

"We could raid the mini-bar and order room service."

"No, let's go out. I know this fantastic little restaurant in Westbourne Park. It's very close. I know you'll love it."

Bettina waited for me in the lobby. She was sitting in a chair, legs crossed, checking her cell phone messages when I silently approached.

"Expecting a call?"

"No, I'm sorry. It's my useless job. It occupies me so."

The evening was crisp and clear, though as we passed Stanley Crescent, a single gray cloud appeared over the rooftops, like a giant dirigible in the Great War. It left a trail of thick raindrops, then bundled away as quickly as it materialized. A bit later Bettina announced, "Ah, here we are."

A narrow metallic staircase led down to the restaurant. The ceiling was vaulted, the floor a mosaic of weathered stone. Clusters of candles burned like votives on each table, and oil-lamp sconces hung from the walls. It was like dining in a crypt. "Isn't it wonderful?"

It was so early that we had the restaurant to ourselves. The only people eating were the waiters. We took an intimate corner table.

"How do you know this place?"

"I came here a few times with my husband. He does have very good taste, at least when it comes to restaurants."

Bettina smiled. Her lips were glossed a mute lavender, and there were traces of color upon her exuberant teeth.

"I don't think I'll be able to eat a bite," I said, "unless I kiss you immediately."

"Really? How sweet. First tell me something about your wife."

This pulled me up short. In our e-mail exchanges, Bettina never asked about R. and I never volunteered an abundance of information. She appeared in our correspondence obliquely, through ellipses, fleeting mention, and casual passing references. *Yesterday while my wife was with a friend, I decided to* . . . Like much of our relationship it was an arrangement based less on active deception than on convenient omission.

"What would you like to know? Want to see her picture again?" I meant this to be humorous, but it came out rather sharply.

"She is aware that I exist?"

"Of course. I told her about you right after we first met. I called her from the bathtub as soon as I got back from your apartment in Berlin."

"Does she know that I am here in London?"

I hesitated, then nodded.

"She does? Isn't that odd?"

"Over the years we've reached an understanding."

"Really? What kind of understanding?"

"We both respect each other's freedom."

"What does that mean? Has she her own affairs?"

"I suppose. I've never really asked. We're a bit like the U.S Army – you know, 'Don't ask, don't tell.'"

My words sounded dreadfully hollow, and I wasn't surprised to hear Bettina say, "I could never live such a way."

"Well, it is pretty much a travesty as a matter of government policy. But it works well for us, I suppose."

"So *you* have had affairs?"

"Well, no, never. In fact, I've never so much as kissed another woman since I got married."

"So why all this talk about freedom and open marriage?"

"To be honest, I have no idea what I'm saying. My brain has turned to mush. After we kiss I'll be more coherent."

"Something you've never done with another woman since you are married?"

"Exactly. I swear."

"I believe you, of course." But instead of taking my hand or pulling me across the table, Bettina flagged down the waiter to order a bottle of sparkling water. I nursed my white wine, nibbled at a roll. An unwelcome silence descended upon us. The restaurant was still empty.

"Oh, Daniel," said Bettina. "This cannot possibly work."

"What are you talking about? Of course, it can. In fact, it is – it's working absolutely brilliantly."

"But you're married and thousands of miles away, and I have my career and my extremely neurotic child."

"So? That's hardly new information. I'll be coming to London and Berlin regularly now, and we'll meet and look at paintings and be inseparable companions and have all sorts of unspeakable fun. I mean, you can't call this off before we've even kissed, can you?"

Bettina smiled. "It's crazy, isn't it? What a harmless little affair! But yes, I think that is what I'm doing. Please try to understand, Daniel. I too was looking forward to this 'unspeakable fun.' Only it's not possible now . . . You see, Robert and I are getting back together."

"Robert? Who's Robert?"

"My husband, of course."

"I thought he was screwing around with your friend at work."

"That situation has changed. Robert broke things off. And Ute – the other woman – she's been transferred to our Bochum office, which is extremely ugly. It's devilish of me to say, but she has also gotten very fat! Of course, that's not the reason Robert ended the affair. He and I started talking again at work, which at first was very uncomfortable. But we agreed to go on a few dates, just as an experiment. This felt very odd, you can imagine, especially at the beginning. But I was surprised by how much fun I had, how happy I felt. Robert seems older now, less like a spoiled boy. And Xander, of course, wants us to be a family again. He adores his father. You see what a struggling child he is, how needy and hysterical."

I nodded, a clump of half-eaten roll wedged against the inside of my cheek.

"Now Robert and I are both assigned to a gigantic project to privatize the Russian telephone system. Can you imagine? What a nightmare! Soon we will be traveling every week together to Moscow. Of course, we'll bring Xander with us and keep the apartment in Berlin."

Because nothing else came to mind, I said, "My wife and I took a trip to Moscow once."

"You've been there! It's funny, Daniel, but that makes me so happy."

"It was in the early nineties. We stayed in a hotel that doubled as a clinic for amputees. There was a ramp in front of the hotel, and these guys without legs would race down in their wheelchairs, making hairpin turns, like kids on skateboards. You should have seen them. They were incredible."

"This is one of your stories, isn't it?"

"The guys were all veterans of the war in Afghanistan. I have no idea what the clinic was doing in the hotel. Maybe it was because the building had one of the few functioning elevators in the entire city. Next to the hotel was a huge open-air market where we got an antique Leica that turned out to be a fake, a pair of decommissioned Soviet night vision goggles, and nesting Matryoshka dolls in the shape of Lenin, Stalin, Khrushchev, and Gorbachev. I wonder if that market is still there . . . So this means no affair?"

"I don't think that would be the most healthy way to reconcile."

"How about just tonight? We could compress a lifetime of happiness into one mad, joyous, tragic love fest."

Bettina smiled but shook her head. "No, Daniel. But you know what? I am certain that you and Robert will like each other. I may have been bitter when I first described him, but he really is very wonderful, and you two have lots in common. He's very funny, speaks five languages, loves Nabokov, and has seen *Robocop* maybe five times."

"I don't love Nabokov," I said. "Just that one novel."

"Daniel . . ."

"And why didn't you e-mail me about the grand reconciliation with Fred?"

"Robert . . . I don't know; it was like secret consulting negotiations – and I wasn't at all sure it was going to work out."

"I think we call that hedging our bets."

"Hmm? Yes, maybe . . . I'm sorry, Daniel. Maybe I haven't behaved well, but you live far away and you still love your wife. Don't pull faces, you know it is true. And I was so confused . . . I went to a therapist, did I tell you? It was the strangest experience. He interviewed me for, I don't know, maybe two hours. He asked about childhood, marriage, work, food, pets, movies. Everything. Then he asked me to take off my clothes, down to the underwear. Of course, I found this very strange – one hears such odd things about therapists. So I was very wary. When I was in my underwear, he asked me to hold my arms out straight in front of me. He took each hand and examined it very carefully, first the top, then the palm, and then he ordered me to push down while he pushed up. After this very peculiar exam, he declared, 'Frau Schlachtenhaufen, I believe you are in excellent mental health. I see no benefits for therapy.' Can you imagine? He rejected me as a patient!"

I smiled, wanly. "We should all be so lucky."

"What? Yes, of course . . . Oh, Daniel, now you're sad."

"Just a bit emotionally devastated."

"Please, Daniel, don't be. Now we'll always be best friends, okay? We'll e-mail, and you will visit in Berlin, and you can even stay in our apartment. But it never could have worked, especially now. You see, I have a secret . . ."

"You're pregnant."

"How did you know?!"

"Clairvoyance."

"That's remarkable! . . . Obviously it came as an incredible surprise to us. We hadn't been intimate for so long, and after just one time – well, now this! Xander does not know yet. At first he will misbehave, but I think a sibling will make him a more happy child."

I congratulated her, then watched a couple seat themselves at an adjacent table. The woman appeared to be considerably older than the man, though perhaps it was the lighting. "Guess what," I said. Without waiting for a response, I told her that R. was also pregnant.

"What? Is that true?! When did you learn this?"

"Shortly after I got back from Berlin."

"So long ago? Why didn't you tell me?"

I waved at certain explanations, though nothing sounded particularly compelling, except maybe the idea that I didn't exactly want to admit to myself that I was planning on betraying a pregnant wife.

"I can understand that."

"To be honest, there was also the fear that if you knew, you would have been less inclined to have an affair with me."

"That's not pretty but certainly true."

"And I don't know, maybe there were other reasons, too."

"But you're happy about becoming a father?"

"Sure, of course . . . Basically. I mean, I've always wanted to have a child, or, to be more precise, I've always wanted to want one."

"You're losing me . . ."

Having never told Bettina about R.'s first pregnancy, I didn't feel like telling the whole sorry story. I picked at my food, overplaying my wretchedness. Between energetic bites of her roasted capon, Bettina looked at me, her eyes tremulous with emotion. "Oh, Daniel, just think, we'll both have babies the same age. Maybe one day they will be friends . . . You will be such a wonderful father. Xander adores you."

"Yeah, I can tell."

"He was just sad because he is needy and loves illness. He really thinks of you as a great friend."

"Umm. Like mother, like son, huh?"

After dinner, on the way back to the hotel, Bettina took my arm. It was the very first time we had touched. In the lobby she held my hands and faced me, her eyes gazing down on mine. "Would you like to kiss me now?"

"No, it's okay . . . I wouldn't want to interfere with your reconciliation."

"It's kind of you to think about Robert. Do you also think about your wife?"

I didn't answer. Bettina pulled me close. We didn't exactly kiss; her lips simply lingered upon mine. It was obvious: I would never see her again.

The next morning I flew home. When I reached our house, R. was out. The kitchen was tidy, but smelled powerfully of curry. On the countertop I saw a bag of spices. The label, identifying the contents as Garam Masala, was written in a hand I recognized – Vercin's.

Thirteen

Sir Charles never did call. A week or so after returning from London, I received the following letter:

Dear Professor Wellington:

Please accept my apologies for canceling our second meeting. A nasty bug laid me up for the better part of a week. Since returning to the office, I have had the chance to review matters with Mr. Pugh, the chairman of our board, and with Mr. Baker, our secretary. We all agreed that yours was a splendid presentation, one that provoked us to reexamine our basic goals. You will be pleased to know that as a consequence, we have renewed our commitment to create a permanent exhibition devoted to the Holocaust. We have agreed, however, that the exhibit shall be organized according to more traditional and less conceptual notions of display.

Please do not construe this decision as a repudiation of your excellent work. We asked you to help us clarify our purposes; you have done admirably.

I have asked Mr. Baker to work out the details of your remuneration. Best of luck with your Berlin project, and we do hope you shall include a visit to the Imperial in your future trips to London.

Yours sincerely,
Charles Worthington, KBE

P.S. Apropos our discussion of Goya, the British Museum has the chalk sketch of Lord Wellington that Goya executed as a preliminary to the formal portrait that hangs in the National Gallery. Rarely has conté been used to such haunting effect. I urge you to spend time with it.

I read the letter over several times, folded it, and neatly tore it to shreds. Obviously my conduct had appalled them. I inventoried my gaffes – displaying ignorance about England's greatest military hero; insulting the museum's benefactor; defending the aesthetic merits of a toy death camp; yawning like a bored student. The bite of rejection was sharp. I had started to picture myself as an international artistic consultant, jetting to the great capitals of Europe, dispensing aesthetic advice. Now I was again nothing more than a dweeby professor, flying steerage to dull conferences on "Historicist Conceptions of Weimar Art." An envelope arrived the next day by express mail containing a check for five thousand pounds. When I did the math, this worked out to roughly $200/hour, modest by the standards of high-powered professions, but hardly farcical. This only aggravated my regret. But worse than the lost income was the prospect of fading back into the anonymity of college life, the futile committee work, the tedium of teaching bewildered heirs.

The Berlin project meanwhile remained mired in memory's sinkhole. I inquired about the possibility of a summer meeting, but learned less from the evasive chairman than from Jonathan Stein. Together we lunched at the faculty commons.

"How's life on the gravy train?"

"So, so." I gave him a brief rundown of the debacle at the Imperial.

"A temporary setback, a mere blip in the steady inexorable rise of Franklin's young, bright star. It's just a matter of time before Harvard and Yale come courting. Then we'll say, 'Yes, we knew him when . . .'"

"That's enough, Jonathan."

"And I hear the Germans have decided to include the victims of the Thirty Years War in the Holocaust memorial. Maybe they could also add a monument to the Huns killed during the sack of Rome." Jonathan cackled at his own joke. He finally had replaced his faded, frayed, and encrusted Michigan sweatshirt with a new Michigan sweatshirt. He stabbed at his salad Cro-Magnon-like. "They could call it the pillar of pillage. And what do you make of the city's proposal to move the Holocaust memorial out of the center and place it in the 'burbs near Adolf's Olympic stadium?"

I smiled. Or maybe frowned.

He studied me and chewed more excitedly. "Well, what do you think?"

I sipped my iced tea.

"You mean, you haven't heard?"

"Jonathan, I'm on the design commission. I think I'm in the loop."

"Commission or no commission, this isn't *ain bubbe meiseh*."

"I'm afraid my German doesn't always help with Yiddish," I said, losing patience.

"You don't know that expression – 'a grandmother's tale'? Didn't you learn any Yiddish from your parents?"

"My parents? My parents know about as much Yiddish as Saddam Hussein."

"So what was their native tongue? German? Polish?"

"What are you talking about? Try English."

"But I thought your parents came from Europe . . ."

"Brooklyn and Pittsburgh is more like it."

"They're not survivors?"

"Survivors? Of what, each other? No, of course not. Where'd you get that idea – ?"

I swallowed the end of my sentence. I knew exactly where he had gotten the idea. From the same source that had supplied him with information about the Holocaust memorial.

"Is your sister still at the *Frankfurter Allgemeine?*"

"She left that job four months ago. Now she's a news editor at the *Berliner Morgenpost* . . ."

I nodded, taking this in. Of course, Jonathan had read the articles in the Berlin papers describing me as the child of survivors. Presumably also the interview that discussed my past. I should have felt mortified, embarrassed, maybe even panic-stricken; instead, I found myself thinking about the time Jonathan had invited me to dine with his mother. The four-foot-something matriarch had ignored my questions about her childhood in Hamburg and escape to Shanghai, and instead had spent the meal telling me what her son had been like as a child: how he was born with a tooth, was potty-trained at nine months, and was so cute as a little boy that strangers would stop on the street to pat him on the head.

"I don't get it, Daniel. Have you turned into one of those nutty Holocaust wannabes that makes up a past to join the victim parade?" Jonathan chewed his peas with great brio, excavating a trapped green mass from between his teeth with a long-nailed finger.

Finally I said, "A decent amount of that was true."

"Really?" He continued his aggressive chewing. "What part is that?" When I didn't promptly answer, he shook his head. "Christ, Daniel. Don't you remember that guy over at whatever college who won all those awards for his books on Begin and Carter and Camp David? Then it came out that he had made up all this shit about his time in the CIA doing undercover work in Guatemala, really gratuitous stuff that had nothing to do with his books. He was ruined, finished. I mean, c'mon, Daniel. How long have you worked here? Your colleagues already resent you to death – you're a success, you go places, you get attention. If any of this leaks out, they'll eat you fucking alive, and I don't mean like our cannibal friend. No, that poor schmuck will get off easy compared to the shit you'll be dragged through."

"How could it leak out?"

He stared at me, baffled, appalled, even angry. "I don't think that's the point, my friend. I think someone's moral compass needs a correction. Look, I'm hardly one to lecture anyone about anything, but this kind of thing only ends in disaster, sooner or later."

I agreed completely. It was important to set the record straight.

Back in my office, I promised myself no fresh lying. This seemed like a reasonable compromise. Then I e-mailed the chair of the Berlin design commission to learn if the rumors of the site change were true. Finally I read a message from Bettina:

Dee, guess what? Robert and I are going for a week to Capri! To learn to scuba dive! (The doctor says it's okay.) I'll send you a postcard.

The note left me sad, but not because of its brevity. I was saddened by my own indifference. A correspondence that had been the center of my life now seemed pointless, dispensable. The relationship had run its peculiar, amputated course. It was easy to foretell: we'd keep e-mailing, shorter, more sporadic notes, then one of us would simply neglect to respond and that would be that. I wrote her a short reply. That alone was an effort.

More ominous was the change in my behavior toward R.

Meteorology was partly to blame. Early June typically smiles on New England: days of smooth skies and nights dusty with stars. The campus is lovely, largely student-free, and only slowly preparing for the invasion of summer programs – Nike tennis, D.A.R.E., SAT review. In the past, strolling beneath the ancient oaks and sugar maples on Central Quad, I often felt like a guest at an exclusive psychiatric retreat for movie stars and the insane offspring of billionaires. This year was different. First, the college opened its summer facilities early so local SWAT teams could practice counter-terrorist maneuvers. For ten days the school was in a state of siege: snipers positioned on the transept of Merrill Chapel, shock troops belaying down Johnstone Science Center, EMTs performing triage on scores of groaning victims from the theater department scattered on North Lawn. One afternoon at lunch I was startled out of my chair by a tremendous thud. A battering ram with an explosive charge had shattered a mock door installed by the entrance to the faculty dining commons. A dozen helmeted commandos stormed through the cafeteria in fatigues and bullet-proof vests, wielding automatic weapons. I watched them exit through the kitchen. By the time I had finished my cheese sandwich, they were resolving a hostage situation in the Admissions Office.

Then the heat wave struck. Barely out of May, the dog days of summer were upon us: stifling heat, soymilk skies, storms that lashed the steaming earth with angry, belligerent rain. The weather left me incapacitated, limp. R. doubted the health benefits of a refrigerated environment, so we made do without air-conditioning. In the morning we'd shut the windows and draw the curtains, sealing the house like a sepulcher, and at night we'd open them to the clotted air. Sticky and sleepless in bed, I'd pick tiny flies off my arm and dream of relief. But things only got worse. Doppler radar detected funnel clouds in our county. A microburst tore off the roof of a nearby picnic lodge. I was startled out of my stupor one night by a concussion of thunder that set off the motion sensors over our front door. Insects proliferated and died in biblical numbers, covering bulbs, books, and sheets with a buggy mash. The dehumidifier failed from overuse. Winds from the south carried ash from a distant wildfire, turning the sun into a dull red stub. The rare breeze bore the stink of silage from the nearby dairy farm. Yet R. didn't mind. She loved to sweat.

The expression "sinking into depression" suggests a slow process, a quiet descent down a staircase so long that each individual step conceals the gradually encroaching darkness. In my case, it was a plunge, a nosedive, a fall so sudden that you lose your wind and temporarily your bearings. What particularly depressed me was my depression. It was all terribly familiar: I was back in the same lousy place that I had been stuck in at the time of R.'s first pregnancy. All my progress – gone. The happiness had unmasked itself as chimerical and aberrant. Welcome back to Dread Head. It was my natural state. I took it everywhere, carried it in tow, for a straightforward and wretched reason: it was me.

My office had central air, but work was out of the question. Instead, I read books about artists and madness. Utrillo, Van Gogh, de Chirico, Gorky, Rothko: such a thrilling variety of schools and styles to choose from (not to mention critics, like Ruskin). Everyone knows that Van Gogh sliced off his ear and presented it to Gauguin, but few are aware that Munch once sent a woman a mole carved off his back. And while the list of artists who took their lives is long and impressive, few showed the industry of the British painter Paul Livingston, who slashed his wrists, drank poison and shot himself – all at the same time.

I thought about my grandmother. I had but a single photograph of her, which I placed on my desk, determined to rescue her from the blind spot she occupied in my imagination. It was a classical oval head shot, originally black and white but later blushed with the exaggerated pinks and greens of an indifferent Marshall coloring. In the picture she couldn't have been much older than thirty-five, though already her hair is gray, and her face, which must have once been beautiful, appears padded and loose. Her smile is kind, the teeth straight, and she might pass as normal were it not for a quality of her eyes. If the Mona Lisa's are said to track its viewer, my grandmother's do just the opposite. Her eyes shun contact. Her gaze travels elsewhere, to a point unseen or unseeable. I thought about that point: by the time of the photo, presumably it no longer belonged to the external world, but had moved to a place deep within herself, dark and unreachable by words and touch. Maybe that was where she kept memories of her daughter, the young girl with the fused spine who died on the operating table of Roosevelt Hospital's charity ward. I wondered if it was proper to speak of the residue of a child's life as mere memory.

One evening I returned home to find R. pregnant. Perhaps this is the way geometric progression works. In the span of a single day, she had gone from barely showing to looking bloated and defenseless, a sea creature stranded halfway in the evolutionary migration to land. The reality of the situation was forced upon me. In a couple of months R. would give birth. Watching her waddle to the refrigerator I tried to summon all the feelings of fierce protectiveness and animal pride that a husband should feel under the circumstances. Instead, I felt estranged. I couldn't help but note that in addition to the obvious bodily transformations, R. had changed in other, more obscure ways. Studies suggest that women speak on average a third more words per day than men, but this wasn't my experience. R. said ever less, maybe to everyone, certainly to me. She stopped reading the *Times*, and was oblivious to the disasters and calamities making the headlines; instead, she wasted hours thumbing through cutlery and garden supply catalogues. She bought clover-scented candles and sticks of Bangladeshi incense. In her car I found a small amphora tied by its throat to an air vent that contained a vial of mandarin orange oil. She made loud and demonstrative staccato hooting sounds as she practiced her breathing, an act she had previously performed without instruction.

Then I discovered the serpent on her back. Coiled at the point where arm met shoulder blade, the serpent made a perfect circle, consuming its own tail.

"When did you get that?"

"Last week."

"Is it henna?"

"No, the real thing."

"And you didn't tell me . . ."

"I did it for myself. I figured you'd notice sooner or later, and I knew how you'd react."

I struggled to absorb this. "You refuse to take a sip of wine or step into an air-conditioned room, but you get a tattoo? How'd you know the needle wasn't contaminated with HIV? That you wouldn't get blood poisoning?"

"The place is licensed by the state. The tattoo artist was an obese dyke with a beard. She was all very professional."

"And why the New Age snake? It's like something one of my students would have."

"It's a uroborous. It's an ancient Greek symbol of wholeness, the continuity of life."

Who is this woman? I wondered. Had she always been so opaque?

"Look," R. said. "You're the one who suddenly has started lighting Yahrzeit candles for total strangers. What's *that* about?"

True, I had lit a candle for Moses Wechsler, the little boy in Berlin. It seemed the right thing to do both as a gesture of tribute and prevention. If I honored the memory of this boy, then perhaps God would be less likely to visit disaster upon our offspring. This latter thought had begun to vex my nights. Lying sleepless I was prey to a wide range of morbid thoughts. They would spin through my mind like a newsreel while I passively observed. Some involved minor everyday tragedy – a bicycle clipped by an eighteen-wheeler, a neighbor's pool left unattended, a hardball delivered to the sternum, a piece of lamb chop lodged in the trachea. Others were more global in nature, involving galloping pandemics, economic collapse, chaotic weather, and spasms of unspeakable violence. These often had a strong visual dimension: I saw Bosch-like tableaus of mutant frogs emerging from toxic oceans, raging fires consuming elegant subdivisions, and skeletons in Nikes and spandex cluttering city streets. I remembered the question R. had asked before she got pregnant the first time: Why usher accidental life onto a doomed planet? It was meant rhetorically, but now I couldn't offer a sound answer.

Then there were the omens. The first involved the horses we boarded. It was the morning of our first substantial shopping expedition for Unborn, hours spent choosing the right developmental mobiles, nursing rocker, ultra-range nursery monitor and heavy-duty all-terrain buggy stroller. We arrived home to find the gelding behaving oddly: whinnying and dashing about the pasture, as if chased by a dagger of bees. Only later did we notice the mare on her side, legs stabbing the air, a cluster of flies trespassing upon her open eye. The sun had shredded the cooling haze of morning, and the body was beginning to bloat in the murderous heat. The gelding retreated to a far corner of the field to watch a tractor-crane lift the carcass onto a dump truck. "Good thing we got her loaded when we did," said the driver. "She was liable to burst. If you ever smelled a horse when the stomach goes, you'll know why we worked this one fast." I gave him an extra ten for his efforts. An autopsy revealed the mare had died of an allergy-related asthma attack. Imagine: a horse allergic to hay.

A week later, I grabbed a carrot from the fridge. Rinsing it, I stood by the sink, transfixed. The vegetable was grotesquely misshapen, its base bifurcated into two "legs" wound together like those of a Gumby doll. Its skin was warty. In the crevice between the twisted stalks tunneled an army of minuscule worms.

Even the little black Volvo: stare at it long enough and it turned into a hearse.

I'm not the superstitious type – the number 13, cracks in the sidewalk, broken mirrors have never spooked me. Yet I couldn't shake the suspicion that these events, far from random, carried symbolic weight. The ultrasound, the horse, the carrot, the Volvo – the signs were not good. The least I could do was light Yahrzeit candles. I recalled that once in a casino in the Black Forest, I had seen the identical number come up four times in a row on a roulette wheel. The odds of such an occurrence were one in a million. I had no money down on the number, but still had thrilled to the freak happening. Now I wished I hadn't been there. It confirmed that anomalies are part of reality, and suggested I might be a magnet for them. The pregnancy provided additional proof. And for every good freak, there must be a bad freak. Math teaches us this. One could write a thick medical textbook about all the devastating birth defects that occur with far greater frequency than one in a million. In fact, given the complexity of the structure – the opportunities for a chemical to miscode, an enzyme to malfunction, an encryption to go haywire – it seems nothing short of a miracle that any child is born normal.

No fool, R. said, "I feel I'm losing you again, just like last time. It's that prepartum dread. I can see it in your eyes."

"It's the weather, honestly. Everything will be fine once this heat wave breaks. Christ, I feel like I'm going to die . . . I'm going to take another shower, okay?"

There was a final fear. It involved me, and it wasn't new – that I would lose my mind. The thought didn't upset me directly, though it did greatly contribute to my worries on behalf of Unborn. What could be worse than having a father who celebrates the birth of his son in a psychiatric hospital? I imagined us sharing the same facility – R. in the maternity ward, me in the behavioral wing. Two orderlies would bring me to see the baby and resting mother; I'd stand in the corner catatonically and then be ushered back to my floor for ping-pong and crafts. The whole thing was again viciously circular: my fear that I would become insane was making me insane. But that's the perverse logic of dementophobia – it's the purest, most highly distilled form of hypochondria.

For help, I turned to Klara. We hadn't spoken since I first told her that R. was pregnant again. That wasn't altogether strange. We could go without talking for months, then chat several times in a single week.

"Ah, at last," she exclaimed, when she heard my voice. "We wondered what deep dark cave you've been hiding in. It's been so long – you haven't heard our big plan."

"Plan? What plan?"

"We're moving to Albuquerque!"

"What? Albuquerque? Why didn't you tell me?"

"You should try to respond to voicemail every now and again." I recalled that she had left a couple messages after I sent money to help cover some emergency dental work she had needed. I hadn't called back. "Yes, its all planned. I tell you, this shit weather in the Northeast is turning me into porridge. And another year with these conservative Pawtucket morons will drive me to the brink."

"But I still don't get it. Why Albuquerque?"

"It's time to move. I read some books, and Albuquerque is dry and affordable. Also I considered Sacramento. Which do you think is nicer?"

"I don't really know. What does Oliver think?"

"Oliver is like you – he likes to stay in one place and complain. In the meantime, life gallops along. It's time for a change, something exotic."

"I'm not sure that's the right word for Albuquerque. Have you ever even been there?"

"Don't you remember? We went there together, on a holiday."

"Klara, that was the Grand Canyon. We were nowhere near Albuquerque."

"Still so averse to experiment? You should see the packet from the Chamber of Commerce. The city is very rapidly growing and the heat is dry, very low humidity . . ."

I listened to Klara go on. Never content merely to follow her feelings, she had long subscribed to the belief that the more impulsive and ill-formed a decision, the more it was to be trusted. She disappointed quickly, but never lost her faith in the restorative power of sudden gratuitous change. Maybe that was preferable to my dreams of a risk-free existence.

Gradually the conversation moved on to my morbid feelings about the pregnancy. Klara listened closely, then said, "I don't think dementophobia is your real problem. I think you're a futurophobe. You're afraid of tomorrow."

"As opposed to what, being afraid of yesterday?"

"Sure. Why not? I mean this seriously. I'm much more fearful of my past than my future."

"What sense does that make? Everything that can possibly go wrong in the past already has. The future, though – the possibilities are endless."

"What an odd way for someone with such a good life to think. At times I understand why your wife believes you simply must stop feeling so sorry for yourself."

"What do you mean 'my wife'? How do you know what she thinks?"

"She called."

"What?"

"Yes, she called, maybe just a week ago. She's worried about you, you know. We had a very nice conversation. We both think you need to try a little harder to be an adult."

In my astonishment, I didn't know what to say. "I'm amazed she called you. And what do you mean about trying harder – you think I enjoy being this way? Do you have any idea how hard I struggle to master these fears?"

"I know you do, but maybe that's part of the problem. Instead of trying to think through all your dread, try ignoring it. Just pretend it isn't there."

"Pretend I'm normal?"

"Exactly. I mean this seriously. If you think, 'a normal person would act happy in this situation,' then act happy, even if you are feeling misery. If you can do this successfully, then I think you really are okay."

I thought about this for some time. Was Klara's ability to pull herself out of her purple funks a result of her fluid understanding of personal identity? Maybe my problem was too strong a belief in the continuity of self over time. Maybe I needed to take the whole idea of the coherent human subject more casually, even if that flew in the face of my narcissism and liberalism. Depressed about my prospects, I placed another call. Rosalind Roth answered on the first ring, as if expecting me. After a brief chat I asked if she would like to get together.

"Right now?" she said.

"Now? Actually, I thought . . . well, okay, sure. That works."

I met her on North Quad. The smell of orange-flavored beef wafted across the campus – a new pan-Asian restaurant with a large deck had opened in town. Rosalind was standing in the stagnant shade of a sugar maple, smoking. She wore orange-tinted sunglasses that matched her rust-colored hair, and, perversely dressing against season, dark paisley slacks. Anubis lay at her feet, threads of saliva dangling from his panting mouth.

"You don't look well," she said.

"I feel like your pooch. The weather is killing me."

"Come. I know a spot that's relatively cool."

We traversed the athletic fields, a broad plain of manicured baseball diamonds and soccer fields carved out of the rolling hills of the Hitchcock Range. The fields were quiet, save for the faint laughter of a couple tossing a Frisbee and the ticking of the in-ground sprinklers. By the tennis courts – the most per student of any university in America, claimed the Admissions Office – we picked up a trailhead for Frost Wood. The narrow dirt path followed a railroad bend, then plunged into the forest. Walking slowly to conserve energy, we passed a mucky pond choked with frogs. Many had tails. Mature tadpoles, or the mutants from my nightmares? I remember R. telling me about a global frog die-off, the result of the sensitivity of their skin to environmental degradation. The woods were strangely silent and birdless. An occasional squirrel or chipmunk darted across our path, but Anubis was too tired to give chase. The trail opened into a meadow that ended in a copse of ancient gnarled maples.

"I love this place," she said.

The conversation was overdetermined from the outset: Rosalind had taken us to a cemetery. The trees formed such a thick canopy that little sunlight penetrated, and a brook cooled the shaded air.

"You've never been here before, have you?" said Rosalind. "It's one of my very favorite spots. It's called Graves' Cemetery – if only everything were named so lucidly."

We examined the stones, slabs of dark crooked slate engraved with images of death's heads, Edward Gorey-like urns, and macabre angels with hollow eyes and wings fluttering in the place of ears. The cemetery, named after the family that had most generously contributed its members, contained perhaps thirty Graveses. Here lay Ishmael Graves and his wife Resigna, Elijah Graves and his wife Immaculate, couples stiffly paired, resting from abstemious lives of gritty work and gloomy New England piety. The clan had seemingly died off in the mid-nineteenth century, when the Skibiskis and Perkowskis took over.

"There goes the neighborhood," said Rosalind.

Rows of headstones sketched uneven lines. Some were cracked or toppled; others completely effaced. The smallest, fuzzy with moss, marked the children: infants, their age recorded in days or months, and toddlers – whole families of little ones carried off by trivial diseases and minor accidents, such grief designated by these mute slabs. I thought of the urban necropolis in Queens where my mother's sister was buried. It was odd to think that in the earth lay the skeleton of a twelve-year-old girl, and now my mother was nearing seventy.

"Wouldn't this be a nice place to lie down?" Rosalind said.

"You mean, forever?"

"Actually, I was thinking in less metaphysical terms."

"Me with you?"

"Not necessarily . . . I thought you nixed that idea some months ago."

"I did?"

"That's my recollection. Cold day outside, lots of wind, disappointing conversation. Unless you've had a change of heart . . ."

"Have I?"

"Okay, one of *those* moods."

We sat. Rosalind's leg was touching mine very lightly, not quite purposive contact. She removed her sunglasses. A shaft of light fell across her face, turning her irises a dazzling golden brown. She wore a T-shirt, *Texas, Hard to Be Humble*, and no bra. Her breasts looked to be exquisitely formed.

"Stop staring at my rack."

"Fine. How about the lips? They appear to be much better."

"Thanks. It's a seasonal thing, anyway. Any progress on the fingernail front?" She took my hand for an examination. "I guess not." But she kept hold of my hand, massaging my palm. She asked me how I became interested in the study of war memorials.

"I'm not exactly sure. When I was a kid, cemeteries used to terrify me. I'd hold my breath every time I saw one. I thought that as long as I didn't breathe, death couldn't take hold of me. It wasn't until pretty recently that I found out that holding one's breath at graves is a pretty common superstitious practice. But I came to that all on my own."

"Didn't Freud have a name for that kind of thing?"

"Probably. I remember once taking a car trip with my parents, when we drove by this huge cemetery. I tried holding my breath, but the cemetery was vast—it just wouldn't end. My parents noticed I was turning purple, so they pulled over, right by the main entrance. I made furious gesticulations for them to keep driving, but by now they were frantic, wondering what the hell was wrong. Finally, I couldn't hold out any longer and started breathing again. 'Just drive,' I cried, but my parents kept screaming at me, trying to find out what was the matter. It was awful."

Rosalind laughed. Her teeth, stained with coffee and nicotine, were not her strongest asset. "I've never been afraid of death," she said, matter-of-factly, as if talking about an unfairly maligned insect. "To be honest, at times I've positively longed for it. I went through a period, not my happiest chapter of my life, when I could hardly look at people. Everyone looked so gross, not just particular persons – everybody, myself included. They say that when blind people have their sight restored, they can't believe how strangely repulsive human beings are. It was kind of like that. And everything seemed so dull and chaotic. Life felt like a dreary high school re-union – lots of Abba and a broken disco light. Death seemed like an attractive alternative, a state of order and tranquility. No Abba, and no me."

"I take it you never acted on this feeling?"

She smiled. When not chapped, her lips were attractive and full, even a little plump. In fact, it was possible that the whole package was quite beautiful. "Now I feel very different. Now I like human beings. I think the world would be a much sadder and more barren place without a creature capable of self-consciousness. I think that's why I love cemeteries – there's something so profoundly decent about expending all this care and loving on the dead. Cremation seems so callous, so empty by contrast."

It turns out we both preferred burial. "Did you know," I said, "that in Germany there are all sorts of laws against cremation? You'd think this would have to do with their history – the bad connotations – but in fact it's religious. Germans who want to get cremated have to go to the Netherlands." I told her about an article I had written about an artist who had poured the ashes of his grandfather, a former officer in the Waffen SS, onto the Berlin neighborhood of Charlottenburg from a rented helicopter. The artist had been promptly arrested, and his case had turned into a cause célèbre for the Berlin art world.

For a time we sat in silence, listening to the trickle of the brook, as if sound itself could cool our bodies. Then Rosalind said: "In graduate school, I was involved with this guy Tim – we were engaged, actually – until his younger brother got murdered. We were living in Berkeley, and the brother was in San Francisco. We'd see him once or twice a week. The two of them were very, very tight, and played together in this pretty decent band. I mean, Tim totally loved his little brother and Stephen adored Tim. One night, we got a phone call that Stephen had been stabbed to death in his apartment. At first the cops thought drugs were involved, even though Stephen was this total straight-arrow. Then they thought it might have been gay-related. Finally they just gave up. Stephen's murder was never solved. The whole thing destroyed Tim. He completely unraveled. He stopped work on his dissertation, and just sat around all day watching Mexican soap operas and eating junk food. Then he started hanging out at the airport, watching planes take off and land, until finally security got suspicious. That's when he started writing angry letters to the police, accusing them of purposefully failing to solve Stephen's case."

"Why'd he believe that?"

"Fuck knows. He always was pretty paranoid. Though I wouldn't put anything past the Frisco cops – they were a rancid lot. After they threw in the towel on the investigation, Tim became totally obsessed with the city's crime log, memorizing all the violent crime statistics. Every time there was a murder – and we're talking, like, almost a daily occurrence – he would suffer a relapse. It would bring the whole thing back, he just couldn't get on with his life."

"What's he doing now?"

Grazed again by the light, Rosalind's eyes were now an improbable rich soil color, almost terra cotta.

"After he dropped out of grad school, he worked for a couple of years in a bookstore. Now – get this – he's a high-priced lobbyist *against* gun control. He truly believes Stephen would be alive today if he'd had a gun. I once visited him in D.C. – that's where he lives now – and he insisted on taking me gun shopping. We went to this store the size of a Wal-Mart that was filled with some *very* dubious looking types – very pale and unshaven white men outfitting themselves with some serious-looking hardware. Tim tried to get me to buy this little Chinese handgun with a nice brushed metal finish. We even had lunch with Charlton Heston – they've gotten very close."

"C'mon, is all this true?"

"You're a very distrustful person. But if you'd ever bother to get to know me properly, you'd know I never lie. Really, never. And if you want, I'll put you on the NRA mailing list. The stuff Tim writes is pretty interesting, in a fascist kind of way."

"He sounds a tad screwed-up." It felt unexpectedly good to be able to say this about someone other than myself.

Absentmindedly Rosalind drew figure-eights on my palm. "To be honest, even before Stephen was killed, Tim wasn't exactly Mr. Normal. He was always something of a downer, pretty kinky, too. Into the gross stuff – you know, sexually."

The pressure of her nail on my palm was pleasurable. Her fingers were long and thin. "Do you mind if I ask what?"

"Nothing particularly interesting. Stuff you'd associate with arrested development."

"Like . . . ?"

"You're really curious, aren't you?"

"I don't want to pry, but yes, I suppose I am."

"Well, let's see . . . once he beat off into a salami sandwich and asked me to eat it." Anubis, who had been napping, awakened with a start and looked at Rosalind.

"He did not."

"He most certainly did."

"Christ, that's so . . . Philip Roth. What did you do?"

"I think you're giving Tim more credit than he deserves. His literary tastes ran more in the direction of *Snatch*. But it seemed a shame to let all that perfectly good salami go to waste."

"You didn't really, did you?"

"See, you're being distrustful again. But like I said, I never lie. And to be honest, it wasn't all that bad. Not that I'd put it on the menu of a restaurant or anything."

Just then, Rrosalind took my hand and pressed it between her legs. I held it there, cupping the great heat. The sun had dropped a notch in the sky. I wondered how late it was. With my hand between her legs I couldn't see my watch. Rosalind moved against me, flinging her arms around my neck, moaning in my ear. All at once I stood up.

"We should head back," I said.

"What are you talking about? Things were just getting interesting."

"I really think we should go."

"Christ, you're such a faggot."

"You think?"

"I was speaking figuratively. But you really are a confused pup."

We walked back to campus in silence. Dusty light seeped through the foliage. Anubis trotted ahead. We parted where we had met.

"You sure you don't want to come back to my place?" Rosalind said.

"Is it air-conditioned?"

"Arcticly."

"When was the last time you cleaned?"

"That bourgeois side . . . Maybe Hanukkah."

"Perhaps another time."

I headed back to my office, unable to get the salami story out of my head. What intrigued me wasn't the boyfriend's prurience but his temerity. Where do people find the courage to act on their debauchery? How did he know that Rosalind wouldn't react with disgust and fury? I once read an article by an anthropologist who divided people into two basic camps – the "nothing ventured, nothing gained" group, and the "nothing ventured, nothing lost" group. It wasn't hard to figure out which one I belonged in.

Or maybe it was sick to envy a pathetic pervert. Maybe the poor toad couldn't help himself.

Lost in these thoughts, it wasn't until the Essex Street inter-
section that I noticed across the street stood Vercin's apartment house.
The building was one of the more attractive college houses for grad
students, built of elegant brick in the 1930s with patina gutters and a
slate roof. I debated dropping in on my assistant, but as I waited for
the traffic light, I saw something familiar yet out of place: my Honda,
parked in the building's lot. I hadn't driven anywhere since arriving
at my office that morning, but the car, proudly sporting its NPR and
Amnesty International bumper stickers, was definitely mine. Then I
remembered that I hadn't taken the Honda: R. had brought it in for
servicing, leaving me to use her car. No sooner had I figured this out
than R. and Vercin emerged from the building, climbed into the car,
and drove off.

Startled, transfixed, I looked for an innocent explanation to
make sense of what I'd seen. Of course – R. must have invited Vercin
over for dinner, probably another vegetarian Indian dish, Sag Something. But when I got home, the house was empty. In the swelter-
ing kitchen, next to a stick of molten butter that one of us had
forgotten to put in the fridge, was a terse note: *GNO xx*. "GNO"
stood for "girl's night out." In a long-standing practice, we each
went out one night a week alone, time to ourselves. My BNO's were
typically devoted to Hollywood spectacles of computer-enhanced
gore. R. preferred concerts, and more recently had joined a writ-
ers' group. More mystified than disturbed, I couldn't imagine how
Vercin figured in her plans. I remained convinced that there had to
be an innocent explanation, only I drew a blank trying to come up
with one.

R. returned at quarter to one (12:47 a.m. to be exact). Reasonable by urban standards, unusual by ours. She was obviously surprised
to find the light on in our room.

"You still up?"

"Yeah. I've been calling all the local police stations, missing persons bureaus, emergency rooms, and morgues."

"I'm sorry. I had no idea that you'd wait up."

"It's too hot to sleep. And you know I worry."

"And you know I wish you wouldn't. I can take care of myself." She yawned widely, making clear her exhaustion. Then she undressed quickly, her ovoid shape silhouetted as she flossed. Clicking off the light, she heaved herself into bed. "Night." She deposited a dry kiss on my lips, then turned away, her arms and legs flung around the giant snake of her "pregnancy pillow."

A tiny noxious insect landed on my cheek. I swiped it away.

"So where'd you go tonight?"

"Hmm? A movie."

"Really, what did you see?"

"That French comedy at the Phoenix."

"Was it any good?"

"Decent. You'd probably hate it – it was *very French*" – and her voice became heavily accented – "but I thought it was pretty cute. I'll tell you all about it in the morning."

"What about your writing group."

"It was canceled. Julie and Abby are sick."

"So who'd you go with?"

"Alone."

I lay on my back, hands clasped behind my head, staring hard at the dark ceiling. A moth bumbled about, colliding again and again with the overhead fixture. The bulbs must still have been hot; the odor of singed wing filtered down.

"And what did you do after the movie?"

"Tomorrow. I'm exhausted."

"I haven't seen you all day. Aren't I entitled to ask my wife a couple of questions before we go to sleep?"

"Fine." She remained on her side, back to me, fortress-like. "I went to the Haymarket Café, had tea and dessert, and did some writing."

"Who'd you go with?"

"I told you. Alone. Now go to sleep."

A sodden fold of sheet fell across my foot. I kicked it away.

"What *is* your problem?" she said. "Stop that."

"So you think I'm a futurophobe?"

"What?"

"A futurophobe – you know, someone scared of tomorrow."

"Daniel, what on earth – "

"You called Klara."

She sighed. "Oh. Is that what's bothering you? You'll be pleased to know that she and I had a very nice chat. She's much more level-headed than you make her out to be."

"What did you talk about?"

"About why you like to harangue people who are trying to sleep."

"No, seriously."

"Tomorrow, love." R. adjusted her leg across the snake pillow and sighed again, this one more like a well-practiced technique for achieving relaxation and wellness.

"And what were you doing with Vercin? I saw the two of you leaving his apartment."

"Oh." Her nonchalance sounded forced, artificial. "The two of us cooked together."

"Who arranged this?"

"A few weeks ago – I think you were in London – he left some spices for us. When I called to thank him, we made plans to try a new recipe, okay? Now good night."

"So what did you cook? Earth to wife, come in wife – "

"A dish from South India, Madras."

"Was it good?"

"Very. Enough, okay?"

"Then what did you do?"

"I told you. I went to a movie. Alone."

"And why didn't you tell me about these plans to cook with Vercin?" She didn't answer. My heartbeat muffled the crickets. The moth had vanished or fried itself. "Well?"

"I don't know, I forgot. We can continue this in the morning, if you like. I'm exhausted and need my sleep."

"I saw you guys drive off in *my* car. What was that all about?"

"Jesus, we had to go shopping for some ingredients, okay? Now enough third degree."

Two nights later Vercin called. Since London I had hardly seen him. He came by my office once to hear about the debacle at the Imperial War Museum, and again, some time later, to discuss the final grades he had submitted for my course. Otherwise, we had no contact. Because the Berlin project remained mired in the Thirty Years War, I had little work to give him; he was spending the summer on his own research. I was surprised to hear his voice, but also glad. I had already apologized to R. for my suspicions, but still welcomed the opportunity for corroboration.

"So how'd you like the movie?" I asked.

"Movie? What movie?"

"Oh, I thought you and my wife saw some French flick together."

"No, she, uh, invited me, but I had to complete some reading. Anyway French cinema isn't exactly my thing, though as I told her, my Dad dragged me to Truffaut's funeral when I was a kid."

"So how was the meal? Delicious, I heard."

"It was pretty successful, under the circumstances."

There was a pause. What circumstances could he have meant? "And how's the research going?"

"Okay, I guess. Though I think our library would benefit from the presence of books. The empty shelving must, uh, be on the order of acres."

There followed another pause, this one more dreadful than the last. Finally Vercin said, "Uh, Professor, would you mind putting your wife on the line?"

"My wife? Sure, just a sec."

It was only after R. picked up that I realized the obvious – that Vercin had called to speak to her, not me. And speak they did, for almost an hour. For me, talking to Vercin was excruciating, tortuous even, so what was I to make of R.'s effortless gabbing and constant laughing? Once she hung up, I waited for her to volunteer an explanation.

Finally, I could stand it no longer. "Have a nice talk?"

"Umm. He's totally delightful. He reminds me a bit of you, though not really."

I wasn't sure how to take this. "Did you make any plans for more meals?"

"No, I'm going to take him to the Bird Sanctuary."

"You're what?"

"When we were cooking he said he'd never been. And he doesn't drive – "

"Yes, I know – "

"So I said I'd take him. What's there to get so pissy about?"

"I'd hardly call my behavior pissy. But it does occur to me that I've never been, either."

"That's because you hate birds. And you can't spend a minute outdoors without moaning and griping. But if you want to come along, fine, be my guest."

"Nah. I wouldn't want to intrude on your fun."

I hoped R. would say something like "don't be absurd" or "stop being petulant," but she reverted to her perfidious strategy of silence. I had no choice, then, but to continue. "You have to admit, this is getting a little weird."

"What's weird, Daniel, is your paranoia. Instead of getting all worked up, I suggest you concentrate your energies on preparing to be a father."

Fourteen

To use Jonathan Stein's favorite word, maybe the jealousy was an epiphenomenon, another of the unbecoming masks my dread wore. Objectively speaking it was odd. I recognized this. R. was more than slightly pregnant and I was the one who had flirted with an affair. But jealousy corrodes reason. That is its genius. It exploits conjecture, turning absurd suspicions into dreadful certainties. R. once showed me photos of the Angler Fish, a truly malign-looking denizen of the blackest depths of the ocean. The creature comes with its own built-in fishing pole that sticks out of its head and ends in a brightly colored lure to attract prey. Only sometimes the fish is so vicious and stupid that it confuses its own lure for its prey and takes a greedy bite out of itself. I was like this fish.

When R. returned from the bird sanctuary hours late, I resolved to remain calm. "You might have called to say you weren't coming for dinner," I said.

"I left a note that I might not be back."

"Yes, love, but your message could have been clearer. It made it sound like I was I supposed to wait for you, and if you didn't show up, conclude that you weren't showing up. Anyway, it doesn't really matter, though I *was* starting to worry."

"You're right, I should have planned better. Sorry." R. poured herself a glass of water and leafed through the day's mail.

"So did you have a nice time looking at the 'birds'?" I used my fingers to make scare quotes, though I meant this humorously, not belligerently.

"Yes, very nice, though I didn't see as many species as last year with the Audubon Society. But we did spot a scarlet tanager. It was absolutely stunning."

"I suppose Vercin is an accomplished lay ornithologist."

"He does know quite a lot, actually. He spotted the tanager."

"That's no surprise. Didn't his father win an Academy Award for his documentary about the mating patterns of the polka-dotted king bloater and the rainbow-crested baby bustard?"

I expected her to laugh, but instead she said, "Daniel, is this really necessary?"

"What's happened to your sense of humor?" I exclaimed. "For Christ's sake, that was a joke. I mean, maybe it's not as funny as the one about my wife dating my research assistant, but still, I thought it was pretty good."

"I'm not *dating* Vercin."

"I know, I know. I was just kidding. I'm just curious what you two do all those hours together."

"You mean, when we're not screwing?"

"Screwing, not screwing – whatever. I'm all ears."

"Vercin and I like each other, period. For God's sake, Daniel, he's a child. He's almost *ten* years younger than me. Just chill out."

"That reminds me. Did I ever tell you the story about Klara's grandmother? She left her first husband, pretty gutsy behavior for a German woman in the early 1930s. She didn't remarry until she was forty. Guess how old her second husband was? Twenty-five. Let's do the math – a fifteen-year difference, and they went on to have *two* kids."

"She sounds like a fascinating woman, way ahead of her time. I'll be sure to ask Klara about her next time we chat. But I don't think you have any cause for worry. I'm *already* pregnant, if you haven't noticed."

"Did you know the Internet is filled with porn sites of guys having sex with pregnant women?"

"I'm glad to hear you're using your days so constructively."

"Just reporting a fact. After all, you still look perfectly attractive. Your butt's all round and your tits look great. Vercin – his mom kills herself when he's a kid, so obviously he has some very deep-seated maternal complex, and maybe he fantasizes about you carrying him around in your womb."

"You're truly deranged, do you know that?"

Admittedly I hadn't controlled myself as hoped. But if it was crazy to believe that a thirty-four-year-old woman entering her third trimester would have an affair with a twenty-five-year-old graduate student, why did she behave the way she did? In the past I had at times caught her brazenly returning the stare of a stranger in a restaurant, or writing a postcard to a man she met on a train. Now when I strayed into the study while she was e-mailing, her laptop would quickly clap shut. An interruption of her diary writing triggered the same response: book closed, clasp locked, pen capped.

I dryly observed that her behavior might be considered suspicious.

"I like my privacy," she answered, "I've always liked my privacy, and I always will. This is not new information, Daniel."

"And you can't write when I'm standing ten feet away?"

"It's disruptive."

"Even if I'm just looking for a book?"

"What book? You just like to hover, monitor."

I left her in peace and went into the living room. There, in the stereo cabinet, I discovered the alien CDs. Stereolab, Tricky, the Verve,

Wilco, Beck, P. J. Harvey. It was pointless to ask where they had come from. The liner notes were handwritten, cut to size and carefully fitted into the plastic disc cases. *Note the sublime guitar work that introduces track 4. . . . Having seen the wisdom of my choice, my father decided to use the opening licks of track 11 as a prelude to his film on lap-dancing. . . . No doubt you will recognize this edgy industrial cover of a Neil Young classic (track 14).* It wasn't so much the juvenile infatuation betrayed by the notes that upset me, but the idea that R. liked the music. Not that it wasn't tolerable. Reclining on the couch with headphones, I concluded that, as with art and fashion, Vercin's taste in music was fundamentally sound. Indeed, it was *my* kind of music, not R.'s. If she had to flee every time I cranked up *Achtung Baby*, there was absolutely no reason for her to like Radiohead. At least, no good reason.

Still, things might have turned out differently if I hadn't received, out of the blue, a letter from Tamara Starr. I had barely seen Tamara since *Miss Julie*, and it wasn't until I read her letter that I even realized that she had graduated the past spring:

I've moved to Brooklyn, and found a job, doing promotion for stAge, an online theater magazine. It seems pretty cool – it pays my bills and gives me time for auditions. And it's strange – it's only been a couple of months, but already Franklin seems so distant. Anyway, I still have some furniture in storage, so I'm going to rent a U-Haul and drive up one of these weekends. And when I do, I was hoping to see you, Professor Daniel Ben Wellington. I'm sorry we kind of lost touch during my last semester. I never got a chance to tell you how much I loved your course; I still think about the phrase, "A space that creates the mood for memory." And can I now confess – once I almost raised my hand and asked, "Professor, do you think I'm fat?" My last semester was pretty rough, though. I broke up with my boyfriend of four years after he completely freaked on my birthday. It's not bad being a single woman again, but all the guys at stAge *seem so young – that or gay. Anyway, will you be around in the next few weeks? We could grab a coffee . . . or better yet, a stiff one. (I'm something of a lush.) Game?*

Also in the envelope was a copy of a poem she had published in a literary quarterly. I hadn't heard of the journal, but the poem was strong and mature. In the corner she had written, "For DBW, who taught me to find beauty in the grotesque."

Carefully I studied the letter: ". . . a single woman again, but all the guys at *stAge* seem so young. We could grab . . . a stiff one." It was all so unexpected, transparent, and welcome. If R. could have Vercin, wasn't I entitled to a little romantic attention from Tamara? After the reversals of late, I was gripped by a child's sense of entitlement, a petulant belief in just deserts. In any case, it provided me with the opportunity to test the thesis of Jacob Burckhardt, the great Swiss historian, who believed that the great disasters in history were the consequence of self-pity.

I immediately fired off an e-mail:

It was great to hear from you, and I loved the poem. Who knew that inside all that theatricality was a young Elizabeth Bishop? As for your letter, I'm glad to hear you've largely gotten over the breakup with your boyfriend. That kind of pain is something we all struggle with, at all stages in life. Believe me. As far as "grabbing" goes, what is your preference? Be honest now . . .

Promptly she answered: *Is there really any doubt?*

I wrote back: *I figured as much. I thought, though, you might be interested in a meal as well as a drink.*

Her answer followed fast: *Why not? I have quite an appetite.*

Me: *Any preferences?*

TS: *Way too many. I'm willing to try just about anything.*
Me: *Really?*
TS: *Really.*
Me: *Even something . . . out of the ordinary?*
TS: *Try me.*
Me: *Okay, how about a salami-and-cum sandwich?*

Hitting the "send" key filled me with instantaneous horror and excitement. What had I done? Miss Julie's voluptuous, mature body beckoned. I recalled the small tattoo on her thigh, a packing-crate arrow pointing upward, gesturing to what? And how would I answer Tamara? She challenged me as Miss Julie, the powerful erotic force standing akimbo: *Do you think I'll stay under this roof as your easy lay?* What would I say? As usual, I found it impossible to think clearly, my capacity to divine my own desires short-circuited by the prospect of cyber-titillation. In my head, I composed a dozen responses, each more randy than the one before.

The next day, the heat wave broke as abruptly as it had started. No cataclysmic storm, no explosive light show staged by histrionic thunderheads, just a daybreak so clear and cool as to make the weeks of misery seem like a passing fever. Only Tamara did not write back. At first disappointing, by the following day I found her silence a source of mild alarm, then as more days passed, of embarrassment and finally relief. I considered writing her an apology, but opted instead for palliating silence. Instead, I resolved to spend more time at home. I hoped this would give R. and me a chance to smooth things out before the baby arrived. But having rarely quit the house during the stretch of beastliness, R. all at once had a busy schedule. She donated her L. L. Bean "schmatas," loose-fitting cottony dresses designed for matrons pottering around their dahlias, to Goodwill, and, thanks to a mail-order maternity boutique, began wearing short skirts (the pregnancy had smoothed away the boniness of her knees) and low-cut blouses to show off her new cleavage. Joop! once again scented the air around her, and Evening Blue mascara, last seen on our honeymoon, enlarged her eyes. One afternoon as she prepared to leave, I was struck by how good she looked. Tell her, I thought. Tell her she looks beautiful. What came out was, "Why the hell are you dressed to kill?"

She had already slipped on her sunglasses – a new pair? What happened to her sensible Serengetis? Her expression was as opaque as she claimed my behavior to be. "It just so happens that getting dressed up makes me feel better about myself. If you had to go around all day looking like you just swallowed a bathtub, you might know what I'm talking about."

"And the Joop! Is that just for yourself?"

She fumbled for her keys.

"Does Vercin like the perfume?"

"Why not ask him the next time you see him?"

"I think I will. Yes, that's an excellent idea."

As luck would have it, I saw Vercin the very next day. I was in the library, flipping through journals, and he was at a catalogue terminal. But no sooner had I taken a step in his direction than he bolted from his terminal and hurried into the stacks.

"Don't you find that extraordinary?" The weather, refusing to submit to the pathetic fallacy, remained brilliant. For the first time that summer, R. and I were able to dine in our yard.

"He probably didn't see you."

"No, I'm *positive* he did. We virtually made eye contact."

R. shrugged. She wore a black maternity tank top. Most women gain weight in their shoulders during their pregnancy, but R.'s remained slim and toned. Tanned, too.

"So you don't find his behavior a bit odd?"

Again she shrugged. "I'm sure he just feels uncomfortable."

"What does he have to feel uncomfortable about?"

"I don't know. You and your wild jealousy."

"How on earth would he know that?"

R. didn't answer. Her teeth excavated neat divots from her corn.

"You told Vercin that I'm jealous of him? What the hell did you do that for?"

"Well, you are, aren't you?"

"That's completely and utterly irrelevant. Have you told him about my marriage to Klara? Did you tell him about my experiences in therapy?"

"No."

"Then why mention the jealousy except to create a special intimacy between you two? Well?"

R. smiled her rubber-band smile, the tight grimace on the verge of snapping. "I'm not the one who flew off and fucked Frau Slaughterslut," she said.

I shook my head, unable to believe what I had heard. "What on earth are you talking about? I never touched that woman. I told you that months ago."

"How do I know what to believe? You're always making weird faces, playing odd games."

"I was pulling your leg, acting like a goof basket. That lasted exactly one minute. And what are you suggesting, that there's a *quid pro quo*? Because of what I allegedly did – or rather, what you imagined I did – you're entitled to have an affair with my research assistant? – change that, I mean my *former* assistant. Next time you take him on a safari, make sure you tell him that I don't feel comfortable working with him anymore."

"You're truly an asshole."

"How would you prefer me to act? Like a loyal cuckold? Want me to roll over like a circus dog?"

R. squinted into the sun as it dipped below the hills behind the pasture.

"I think that *is* what you want, for me to be your pathetic little lapdog. 'Sure do whatever you like, I love being kicked, bow-wow, woof-woof. Kick me some more, please.'"

All at once, R.'s plate rose in the night air. Spinning like a little UFO, it discharged its contents in a midflight spiral – burrito, chips, and salsa, unwinding as they fell back to earth. Then came the cutlery, somersaulting in the sky, and tumbling to a rest near the recently bereaved horse. Drenched with water flung from the pitcher, I watched the vessel trace a trajectory over my car and spray a dispersion pattern of pulverized glass around the epicenter of the driveway. It was R.'s most impressive display since the conflagration of Klara's landscape.

"Trouble with your temper, dear?" I said.

The back door slammed with a concussion that shook the bulkhead.

*

The next morning I finally received my eagerly anticipated response from Tamara. It arrived, though, in an unlikely form: a voicemail from the dean of faculty. That afternoon I was in his office.

"Daniel, thanks for coming in. Any trips to Berlin recently? Here, have a seat." The dean motioned to a captain's chair bearing Franklin's seal. "Can I get you coffee? Juice? Soda? Water? You sure?" He sipped a Pellegrino with a hand in a cast. "Stupidest thing – I tripped over our front step and broke my wrist."

"Ouch. I'm sorry."

"It's not at all painful, just inconvenient. I'm not much of a summer sports guy, so it's no great loss. You're something of a tennis player, aren't you?" The dean was in his early fifties, with a loose, jowly face and moist, bulging eyes that made him look comically frog-like. But his appearance was misleading. The man was a quick study, equipped with a dangerously precise memory.

"I can hit the ball. I played on a high school tennis team."

"Well, I couldn't have made the kindergarten squad. Not that you could pay me to get on a court, the way the weather's been. Screwy, isn't it? That storm last week, did you hear it knocked out all the computers over in Poynter? Ted Seidner lost half his book on his hard drive. How anyone can forget to keep a backup is beyond me. And just when you'd normally expect things to get brutal, we get days like this. Christ, it almost feels like fall out there."

"Yes, it's very strange."

"Well, we live in screwy times, there's no doubt about it. You know, when I started grad school in the late sixties I lived in a coed dorm for a couple of years. Every morning when I'd go to the bathroom down the hall, I'd bump into this famous professor – you'd recognize his name, he was quite a moose head in his day, but let's leave names out. He'd be at the next sink in this communal bathroom, merrily brushing his teeth, buck-assed naked. No towel around his waist, the goods all on display. He was sleeping with one of his students, or I should say, with at *least* one, I'm sure there were others. And no one gave it a second thought. To be honest, it was considered pretty cool, a sign of progressive, liberated sixties thinking. I remember saying to myself, yeah, I can't *wait* to become a professor. Well, all that has changed."

I nodded fatalistically.

The dean thrust a note in my direction. It was a printout of an e-mail. "Looky here, Daniel. This former student of yours, Tamara

Starr, wasn't amused by your recent communication. She's been kind enough to send me a copy. She also sent one to the dean of students. The only good news is, that's as far as she's gone, we think."

My cheeks burned. Hidden beneath his desktop, my hands set to work. Using the head of a screw on the chair as a lever, I tore into a crescent of thumbnail.

"Now Daniel, you're tenured, thank God, and a big boy, so I don't need to tell you how this kind of thing can truly fuck up a promising career. You think you're in for some extracurricular activity, and then one fine morning you wake up with a big fat lawsuit hanging over your head. And believe me, Daniel, you don't want that. Now I don't know what kind of history you have with this girl, and I don't want to know. Frankly, it doesn't matter a hoot. Because if this mess ever turned ugly – read, legal – it's not just her word against yours. You've brilliantly left a paper trail, this priceless literary masterpiece here. So let's play out our little hypothetical for a moment. The attorneys for the college urge us to settle, because the college doesn't want the publicity of a sexual harassment trial, and the lawyers know that once a jury's involved anything can happen. So what then? We're stuck paying some whopping settlement, and for the rest of your career you're a leper, a pariah. Got the picture?"

"I didn't harass Tamara Starr." The broken nail resisted the first tugs, but then the fleshy anchor stretched and tore loose. The pain made me blink. "In fact, she was the one who – "

"Daniel, my friend, it doesn't matter what you say or think. She took exception to your snack suggestion. That's what counts. And it doesn't matter that she's got her degree, because she still might want a letter of recommendation. You might think it's relevant, but believe me, it ain't."

"I don't know what to say – I'm incredibly ashamed. I've never done anything like this before . . ." I glanced down: a bubble of blood covered the spot where the nail had been. Casually I wiped it on my dark sock.

"Daniel, I'm not here to demand fifty Hail Marys. How you get your kicks is none of my business, though I'll be honest – I think you better cut back on the early Philip Roth."

I nodded abjectly. The very thing I had said to Rosalind.

"And remember: your business becomes ours when your games get us in deep doo-doo. So for your sake and the college's, it's important that you write an apology. Take a look at this . . ."

He handed me a second paper. It was a form letter. *Dear [student's name]: I write to apologize for my unwelcome amorous advances . . .*

"A boilerplate?"

"A recommendation. Remember, Daniel, you're not the first person to have a midlife crisis, though you are on the young side by at least five to ten years. And you can call this anything you want, but you should see the messes that your colleagues get themselves into when they try to pen one of these on their own. All that learning and sophistication and they just step in it deeper. So take this with you. You might want to fiddle with it here and there, but I'd follow it pretty closely if I were you. Now isn't your wife expecting pretty soon? And how about letting me get you a Band-Aid for that thumb?"

Back in my office, I pulled at my hair like a madman. Because that's what I was. Only a crackpot would have sent that note. Maybe it would be best to check myself into a psychiatric hospital. Strictly as a prophylactic measure, before I could muck things up any worse. Online I ordered a brochure from McLean.

I wrote Tamara an apology, carefully following the college's form. (I added one sentence, blaming my obscenity on severe depression triggered by an undiagnosed developmental problem.) The following days were consumed in dread of receiving a call from the college's attorneys. Instead, calamity came from a different source.

The German accent on the line momentarily sounded like Bettina's. Then the woman said, "Professor Wellington? I am calling for Dieter Baer of the Holocaust Memorial Commission, Berlin. The next voice you hear will be Dr. Baer's."

"Daniel? Dieter here. Sorry it has been so long since we last spoke. I hope you have been well."

We exchanged pleasantries.

"As you can imagine, this job keeps me occupied," he said, annunciating with excruciating precision. "There are endless politics to take care of. But at least I have some good news to report. The crazy plan to move the memorial to the vicinity of the Olympische Stadion has been conclusively defeated. At last we can return to the difficult but happy job of considering the submitted designs. As you will see, many remain quite unrealistic, but there are a few interesting, perhaps even promising ones. Tentatively I would like to schedule a meeting of our committee for the last week of August. Does that fit your schedule?"

"I'll need to run the exact dates by my wife, but that should work fine."

"Excellent. Unfortunately, there is one more small complication that needs to be taken care of. You're familiar with the *Berliner Morgenpost*?"

"Yes, of course." My intestines twisted unpleasantly.

"In general German newspapers show greater respect for privacy than their American counterparts. But it saddens me to say that everyday the difference becomes less and less. In the last week I have received several annoying inquiries from a journalist at the *Morgenpost* regarding you, specifically your ancestors. Why he contacts me and not you, I cannot say. But it is a very intruding matter. You see, he insists that he has information that contradicts that you are the child of survivors. Really it saddens me just to repeat such ugliness, but I think it is important that you stop these insulting inquiries."

"Has anything already appeared in print?"

"No, of course not. Our libel laws would not permit that. And in my mind, they should be even stronger, precisely to stop these kinds of intolerable insults."

There wasn't enough nail on my right thumb to suffer fresh damage, but a jagged sickle remained on the left. My mail opener ripped it easily.

"Professor, are you there?"

"Yes, I'm just thinking."

"I know how very insulting this must be, but really I think it would be best for you to call this journalist directly. Let him know you are familiar with the German legal code. He is sure to stop this impossible behavior."

"And what if I simply resign from the commission?"

"What? Don't be ridiculous. It is simply a matter of putting an end to these rumors."

A bird – was it a tree swallow? did it matter? – flitted by the window and flew off.

"I think I'll just resign."

"But, why?"

I closed my eyes, reopened them, closed them again. I heard myself tell the director that I might have made some misleading statements when I spoke to the press in January.

Baer blew his nose loudly when I finished my account. "Please excuse my allergies. But I'm not sure I understand what you are telling me. Are you or are you not the child of survivors?"

"Well, it is true that most of my grandfather's family was wiped out. They lived in a small town near Grodno that's now part of Belarus. Fortunately, my grandfather had been sent to America when he was just a child. He came over with two brothers on the Lusitania. Later they started a poultry business."

"Professor, I don't believe this question is a complicated one. Maybe I am wrong. Are you, or are you not – "

"Technically speaking, I suppose not."

"What does this mean, 'technically speaking'?"

"No, I'm sorry – I'm not. Not at all."

"Not at all."

"Correct."

Baer fell silent. Coronas of orange appeared before my closed eyes from the pressure of my palms. I could hear his breathing, a faint wheeze.

"Ach, what a *Schweinerei*. Sadly I must agree that there's now no question that you must resign. The last thing we need is another Wilkomirski mess. We already have enough problems and controversies. This would be too much." Baer said he would tell the other members of the commission that I resigned because of personal matters. If the reporter continued to pry, I was to refuse to comment and Baer would do the same. I thanked the director meekly.

"It's for the benefit of all involved to keep this out of the news," he said with a fatigued sigh. "I just hope we are able to do so. I tell you Professor Wellington, sometimes I truly believe that the Holocaust is like a black hole that distorts everything that comes in contact with it. Did you know that in Germany today there is a broad sociological pathology of persons who falsely claim to be Jewish? These people are called *möchtegern Juden*, maybe you know the term. Yet in my view, more interesting are the Germans who falsely claim to be the children of perpetrators. Mind you, these are not crazy neo-Nazis or rightwing bullies. They are ordinary Germans, who need the connection, who want to feel part of history. Even I have felt this. When I was maybe a boy of thirteen, my grandmother showed me a photo taken of her in Posen during the war. She was very young in a spring dress standing on the porch of a house, smiling very prettily at the camera. 'What were you doing in Posen?' I asked. 'That was where your grandfather was serving,' she answered. 'Yes, but what were you doing there?' 'I was with your grandfather.' 'Visiting?' 'No, living. That was our house. Your grandfather was a guard, though it wasn't one of those awful camps people go on about these days.' As a thirteen-year-old I was astonished to learn this, but it also made me feel a certain satisfaction . . . I cannot explain it. We have a saying, 'Better Abel than Cain, but better Cain than Zero,' maybe you understand . . . In any case, I'm very sorry it has come to this. Your expertise will be missed."

I let the receiver drop into its cradle. The thumb was bleeding, but not badly. The nail itself lay on the floor. From my desk I mechanically removed the file that contained clips about my work, and read over my interview with the *Morgenpost*. What I remembered as a couple of misleading statements was, in fact, a whole web of lies, an entirely bogus family history. Not that my powers of imagination had been strong: I simply had stolen the story of the parents of Daniel F., my grade-school friend, even down to those details dubious in the original. *My father served as a leader of the doomed Treblinka uprising. He escaped by climbing over blankets that had been thrown over the barbed wire. Ukrainian guards opened fire, and he was shot twice in the leg while swimming across the Bug River. Having made it to the forest, he was taken in by a local farmer, one of the brave few who didn't betray the escaping inmates.* On a lark I Googled Daniel F. It took 0.25 seconds to locate him. He directed the department of radiology at a hospital in Greenwich, Connecticut. At least, he had come out unscathed.

The tube of antibiotic nail cream that I kept in my desk was flat out. I got in my car but drove straight past the CVS. The gas gauge was below empty; the fuel light burned a bright orange. I wondered if I had enough to get home, a twelve-mile drive. I came to the cluster of stations at Pelham Road, but kept going. There was a thrill in this, a minor but palpable thrill. Not exactly life on the edge, but a small step closer. About halfway home, the engine quit and I rolled to a halt on the shoulder of Route 118. For a time, I sat in the car, holding the steering wheel. My breathing wasn't quite right, so I followed the exercise from R.'s birthing class. In through the nose, out through the mouth: hoot, hoot, hee. And again. The outward scaffolding of my existence remained intact: I was still tenured, married to an attractive woman, living in a comfortable house. The world is a hostile place to most life forms. Millions, billions, would risk treks across the open desert, journeys across perilous seas, to be in my shoes. Why wasn't I one of them? Why was I the one stranded on the shoulder, hyperventilating? Just then, I noticed an opossum family crossing the road, a mother, trailed by five babies. Frozen I watched the mother lead the babies toward the meridian and the car bearing down on them. The car didn't slow down or alter its course. The mother crossed the meridian; the car didn't swerve. I looked away but not before I saw the mother disappear in a horrific pinkish spray. Now the baby opossum were in disarray. Two nuzzled by the plump quivering mess while the others scampered into the coming traffic. Cars slowed, weaving a crazy course of avoidance. Then a giant black SUV, a monster Lincoln Navigator with tinted glass, came hurtling down the road and hit two babies square. Before I even knew what I was doing, I leapt from my car and hurled a rock at the speeding vehicle. "Slaughterer!" I shrieked. "Murderer! Criminal!" The rock skittered harmlessly down the road. The remaining babies wandered like broken toys. Grabbing at the bald tail of the mother, I lugged the guts off the road, as motorists eyed me with disgust and suspicion. The babies followed, making a sound like speeded-up chatter. I left them at the opening to a rusty culvert, clueless as to what else to do. Then I trudged off for some gas.

When I got home, the trail of Joop! led me into the study. R. was on the phone. As I crossed the threshold, she hung up. I found words, though not the right ones. "Was that Vercin?"

"No. It was my doctor."

"Why? What about?"

"I've been spotting for the last day. She wants to see me. She thinks I should have another ultrasound."

Only then did R. notice my eyes and the tears. "Hey, she said it's probably nothing. What's gotten into you? And Christ, what happened to your thumb?"

Fifteen

The spotting was harmless and the ultrasound measurements were normal – so claimed the doctor. But under closer questioning, she admitted that the fetus had not kept up with the growth rate projected from earlier exams. I nodded gravely. All my suspicions were confirmed. When it came to explaining this laggard growth, the doctor was useless. Maybe it had something to do with R.'s diet, she said. It was hard to say.

During the drive home, I tried to offer comfort. "I'm sure everything will be okay."

"What do you mean?"

"I mean I wouldn't lose sleep over what the doctor said."

"She didn't say there was anything wrong."

"She said she didn't think there was *necessarily* anything wrong. There's still a chance . . ." I decided not to push this any further. "You want to go for lunch?" I suggested. "You want a smoothie? We could get smoothies at the Blue Bean."

"No, I'm okay, really."

"A smoothie would do you good. Or we could try that new Indian place on Steed Street. I heard it's pretty decent. You really should be eating more, you know." A vague terror roiled within me; it came out of the blue.

"I've been eating plenty, thank you."

"*Plenty* is something of an exaggeration. I've probably put on more weight during your pregnancy than you. This isn't exactly the time for dieting."

"Who the hell said I was dieting?"

"I didn't mean that seriously, it came out wrong. It's just that at times it seems you're trying to watch your calories."

"Daniel, just concentrate on your driving."

R. watched with silent curiosity as I made a detour, then pulled off the road and climbed out of the car. At the bottom of the culvert there was no trace of the little possums, just some crushed beer cans and broken glass. Crows had probably feasted on the mother, a fox or an owl finishing off the babies. I emptied a baggie of peeled carrots, celery sticks, and peanut butter and jelly crackers, and spread out the modest buffet. Someone might have survived. It only takes one.

A black fatiguing nap consumed my afternoon. When I woke up, R. was in the kitchen, fiercely scouring the stove with frothy Brillo pads. This must have been the fabled nesting instinct at work, the need to clean and order before the Big Arrival. Watching her reminded me of my effort to scrub the bathroom floor free of its terrible stains. And I remembered Klara's advice. What would a normal person do under these circumstances? The answer was clear. I went to work on the refrigerator, tossing out jars of crystallized jam and murky pickles, then attacked the pantry with its budding potatoes, bags of stale pretzels, and boxes of mouse-raided cereal. Next came the lawn. I mowed with military precision, in great trim swaths, but in high gear, moving along at a clip. With our lawn completed, I rode straight on to our neighbors' without slowing down. Al was a retired highway surveyor with an arthritic wife, and by exacting New England standards their lawn was looking a tad overgrown . As I raced along on my neighborly mow, Al raised a bony hand either in greeting, gratitude, or protest, I couldn't really tell.

Clarity came to me on our John Deere. It was like fog lifting to reveal a bleak landscape. It wasn't a pretty sight, but at least it was in sharp focus and could be measured for what it was. I had to leave. Leave R., the house, maybe even my job. I would check into McLean, and if it was all booked, Austin Riggs also came highly recommended. Maybe some facilities offered special summer rates, August discounts for when the shrinks were on the Vineyard. Or maybe I would take a small apartment. There were always the "barracks" down by the railroad tracks where I had sought refuge during my first crisis. But I had to get out. And soon. I had known it back then, and I knew it now. As Spinoza observed, people persist in being themselves. I had tried hard to suppress its truth. But if I didn't get out, I'd go insane and drive R. mad along the way. Maybe I was already a bit touched – the jealousy, the episode with Tamara, the dread. Everything was over-the-top and barely under wraps. So I had to go. It was the last thing I wanted – I craved normalcy, dull, taken-for-granted normalcy – but sometimes the easiest things are the hardest. Leaving would be best for all concerned. Convincing R. would be the tough part. I came back to the old arguments. That she would be fine, maybe even better off. Her father couldn't remain indifferent to his daughter's need, not with a grandchild in the picture. And I'd sign over most of my income and pension. Child support would be no problem. I'd sell everything I owned if need be. The Richter print had to be worth something. I would tell her all this, level with her, come clean. I wouldn't just flee, head north on my riding mower, however poetically that might confirm the reality of my problems. No, I would do it the responsible way: in person. A mature conversation between two persons who still loved one another. Because of that love I would leave. I would tell her this. That very afternoon.

I found her in the living room, kneeling, doing her labor exercises. She regained her feet with a sigh. "Daniel," she said, "I want to talk to you."

I nodded.

"I've been thinking . . . about us separating. Maybe you should move out."

All at once I burst into tears. "No," I sobbed. "No, no."

*

"But why?" I cried.

"I thought it might be good for both of us. Just for a time. Look, I thought you might actually think it was a good idea. It would give you a chance to deal with whatever it is you need to deal with."

"Does it have to do with Vercin?"

"Oh, God, not that again. Please, don't start. Please."

"Then what is it?"

"It really was meant for you. You're obviously struggling. Look, we can talk about it more later."

"Why later?"

"It's GNO. Don't cry."

"You drop a bombshell like that and then take off?"

"I'm sorry. I just wanted to start a conversation, give you something to think about. I really thought you'd react differently."

"How did you think I'd react?"

"More receptively. It seemed that you, well . . . I didn't mean to upset you. We can talk more when I get home. I'm sorry I mentioned it."

"Can't you take Girl's Night Out later in the week?"

"I'm sorry, Daniel. But I already have plans. Maybe you and I can go out tomorrow."

"Plans with who?"

"Not your nemesis, I promise. I'm sorry, Daniel, I really am. I won't be back late, okay?"

She kissed my cheek and left.

Odd how quickly human emotions can change, words triggering chemicals. R.'s announcement rocked me out of my stupor, blasted through my numbness. Far from leaving R., it was imperative that I stay. How could I have ever thought otherwise? Illness had made me think of flight, and health commanded otherwise. I knew what had to be done – it was clear the moment her car pulled out of the driveway. From the bottom drawer of R.'s desk, I removed her diary bound in pebbled Italian leather with a small brass locking clasp. I wasn't proud of what I was about to do, but necessity trumped probity. Otherwise I would never rest again. Not that I was looking for incriminating evidence. On the contrary. I wanted proof of R.'s innocence. The diary would provide that. The lock was more symbolic than practical; it wasn't designed to resist a serious marauder. It was willing to share its secrets, to show how benign they were. Once I knew she was guiltless, I would never browbeat again. That struck me as fair. The clasp quietly succumbed to my unsystematic attack with a screwdriver.

Seconds after opening the book, I locked it in terror. I was being watched. The feeling was uncanny, like a phantom breeze on the nape of one's neck. Wildly I spun around to a surreal sight. The surviving horse, the grieving gelding, was glaring at me through the living room window. He must have pushed open the pasture gate and wandered over to the house. His glassy eyes refused to blink. He was staring me down. His nostrils flared massively, steaming the window. He bared his teeth. Then, in a moment of pure madness, I noticed that his penis was descending like a refueling hose in a midair tanker. It reached monstrous proportions, dangling like an elephant's trunk. How could a gelding have an erection? More pressing than the how was the why. The horse pinned back his ears. I sat immobile – the slightest movement might further provoke the crazed animal. Gradually the hose retracted. Imagining what a character in a television drama would do, I grabbed a carrot from the fridge and coaxed the nightmarish beast to the pasture, slamming the gate behind him.

Back on the couch, I returned to the diary. I could still feel the animal's eyes on me. I tried reopening the book, only now the lock was jammed. Increasingly frantic jiggling with the screwdriver led nowhere. My grip slipped, the screwdriver stabbing my bandaged thumb. Pain blotted my vision. Clearly this was a sign that I should give up and put the diary back. Nothing good could come of this. Still, it was important to test the sign's strength. From the basement I retrieved a pair of needle-nosed pliers, but it fared no better. Obviously the warning had bite. I swore to desist, but first the claw end of a hammer deserved a try. The strap yielded to the pressure, loosening encouragingly. In the next moment it busted open, shearing off from the lock, which remained anchored in the clasp.

"Fuck," I whispered.

Another potentially catastrophic mess in the making. But damage control would come later. First there was work to do. Almost all the recent entries were about Vercin:

> *Found him alone in D.'s office, editing footnotes. He had moussed his bangs into a vertical point. It was the kind of thing that would look ridiculous on anyone else. He looked, well, beautiful. He said he was glad it was me, not D. who had come to the office, because*

he was being a slug. I figured that was my cue to take him on a little adventure. He finds New England so pitiful, compared to the West.

His mother. Whenever he mentions her, I get this terrible twinge. I find myself wanting to take care of him, cook for him, darn his socks. It must be the maternal hormones.

Listened to another of his tapes for me. Liz Phair. Turns out she went to my high school. He's got my taste down exactly – she's blunt, wordy, witty. One line stuck in my head: "I want to be cool, tall, vulnerable, and luscious." And even though I appreciated the glaring absurdity of the situation, part of me longs to be that way when I'm with V.

Went to a poetry reading at Voices – Yehuda Amichai. Vercin was there. I spotted him in the back row, wearing his black zip-neck tee. He came up to me afterward. He said he half-liked it; he loved the war poems but hated the love poems. Funnily enough, I was going to say the same thing. I half-liked it too, only the half he didn't. Lines like: "You had a laughter of grapes: many round green laughs." "I found that line particularly painful," he said. It's always like this with us. We're drawn to the same things, but for completely different reasons.

Met for tea at the Haymarket. He mentioned an idea for a screenplay, a thriller set in the Horsehead Nebula. Somehow it got us talking about children. He said again that he couldn't wait to have a child. He even had a name picked out: Livingston. He said everything is far better with kids. I wonder.

Tonight we cooked together again. The first course: wild mushroom fricassee with hazelnuts. I'd managed to find chanterelles, ceps, hens

*of the woods, morels, and cloud ears. I'd even bought a little brush
just for cleaning the mushrooms. Vercin brushed them meticulously.
For the main course – I had a very particular craving – we made
steamed sea bass with ginger and scallions. Crepes for dessert, filled
with sliced bananas and melted chocolate (dark, Belgian, of course).
At first Vercin was intimidated by my crepe pan, but halfway
through he took over and started flipping them into the air. One
time, in mid-flip, he even did a little spin. When we were done he
gave me the sweetest hug.*

To think – Daniel hates mushrooms and is allergic to bananas.

*

And so on.

Phrases, sentences disturbed and puzzled me. What was the "little
adventure" that she had taken him on? Why mention my (extremely
mild) allergy to bananas, except to highlight her greater kinship with
Vercin? And what was the meaning of her laconic "I wonder" punctu-
ating Vercin's statement about kids and happiness? All along I had
assumed that she was looking forward to motherhood with unalloyed
pleasure; was that a fiction of my narcissism?

All the same, R.'s tenderness for Vercin, however deep, betrayed
no romantic love or steamy erotic passion. I felt strangely becalmed.
All the jealousy – gone. Just like that. A storm that hits land and breaks
up harmlessly. If only she had let me read the diary weeks ago, so much
grief could have been avoided. Reassured, I happily kept reading. I liked
the look of R.'s script: jagged and angled, not in the least feminine.
She always surmised she was a natural lefty forced to accommodate a
right-handed world. And I liked the diarist's voice. I was eager to get
to know this woman better. To think, she was my wife.

Flipping to an earlier point in the book, I found this entry:

We drove to Gray's, the oldest and most poetic of the syrup farms. Massive century-old sugar maples lined the driveway, each wearing a ring of metal buckets. "Inhale," I told him. Clouds of steam billowed out from the gaps in the sugar-shack roof. He said the smell reminded him of something his mother took him to see when he was little, The Amazing Automatic Donut Machine. The machine, he explained, stirred the dough, punched out the little hole, tipped the donuts into hot oil, flipped them over, and ejected them at the exact instant of doneness.

We approached a gigantic maple. The February sun, warm on my hair, was making the sap flow. I held my finger under the tap, caught a drip, and had him lick it. I wanted him to try something new. I told him how raw sap is mostly water, and how it leaves just a trace of sugar on your tongue. I told him it takes 40 gallons of sap to make a single gallon of maple syrup. He tried a drop from my finger. "Is that supposed to count as new?" he asked. "Generally speaking, I prefer the outrageously new, the grotesquely new, or the painfully new." And yet I know he loved it, too.

Corrosive acids briefly bubbled up in my stomach. Though undated, the sugar-shack placed the diary entry in the late winter, before she had met Vercin. Who, then, was the shithead licking R.'s finger? And why was he telling her *my* story about the Amazing Automatic Donut Machine? Then came the shock of recognition: it was me. I was the shithead. We must have gone to Gray's shortly after my return from Berlin, yet the memory remained as hazy as the clouds of sweet steam. As for licking her finger, I drew a complete blank. Maybe I had been daydreaming about Bettina. I chuckled at my own stupidity.

Notwithstanding the tender sugar-shack story, it became clear that I played a minor role in the diary. My appearances were much like R.'s had been in my e-mails to Bettina – oblique, peripheral, relegated to the margins. This didn't upset me; instead, I was moved to ponder the logic behind R.'s writing. A lovely description of a Jack-in-the-Pulpit blooming in our yard was separated from the next entry by several months. Why had the blooming of a single flower deserved such loving attention when an entire winter warranted no mention? In a later entry, R. described sitting on a bench, listening to the watery call of barn swallows. What was it about that moment that raised it above the stretches of featureless life that she had consigned to oblivion? Never before had R. seemed so enigmatic.

Emerging from this exquisite melancholy, I wondered how to replace the diary so that it wouldn't appear violated. Repair was impossible. At best, I hoped to arrange it so that when R. next opened the drawer, the clasp would seem to snap on its own. I gently inserted the torn strap into the lock, but the book wouldn't stay closed. I tried wedging the strap, but it didn't hold. With mounting frustration, I jammed it with all my might, but this time the book popped completely open. It did so to a page I hadn't read. As I scanned the first lines, my heart stutter-stepped. A dizziness overcame me, as if cold gas had been pumped straight into my brain.

> *I bumped into M.D. at the Mad Hatter Café. He invited me to join him. He sipped his black coffee; I blew the steam off my Morning Thunder tea. I felt my cheeks grow hot under that incredible gaze of his: dark, spicy, mischievous, sleepy, inviting. Strange to think those eyes had seen me naked. "I raise miniature donkeys," he said, maybe the best come-on line I've heard.*
>
> *He invited me back to his house, and I agreed. Just this once, I told myself. Just once to indulge my eggless, desirous body. With the hairline scar patiently (lovingly?) stitched on my tum.*
>
> *From the barn's loft – we both knew we'd end up there – I could hear the rhythmic breathing of his strange, stunted creatures. Be-*

fore we even started he let drop that it had been six years, four months, and 14 days since his wife (he called her a "noble creature") gave him a certain pleasure. But who's counting?

What the hell, I thought. I slipped my hands into the back pockets of his jeans, and knelt down in the hay. I gave him my best, and my best is pretty good. By the end I was lying on my back, with my head braced against a wooden post. He came so forcefully that my head flew backward, banging into the sharp edge of the post. Instead of apologizing, he simply said, "Your turn."

After that we had a nice little rest, my head on his chest. I kissed his neck. "Mmm, salty. If I were a deer, I'd come to lick the salt off you all winter. Tell me one corny thing." "Impossible," he said. Then he whispered in my ear: "My gazelle." I climbed down the wooden ladder, wobbly and smiling crookedly, and drove straight home. Jumped in the shower. Threw out my undies. The whole thing had been remarkably easy. I suspect the hard part will follow.

My heart rocked violently. Dry, murderous heat coiled through my head, leaving my thoughts bloated and cracked. Somewhere a feeling of grim satisfaction took shape. The rancid, philandering bitch. All along I knew my suspicions were justified; now I had the proof. But who the fuck was MD? The only candidate was Michael Dumont, R.'s flamboyantly gay piano tuner. From the tumult in my brain one thought, clear and sinister, took shape. *Whoever he is, I will seek him out. And I will kill him.*

I prepared for R.'s return. In the bathroom I dumped the Joop! down the drain and refilled the empty bottle with water. This seemed an obvious first step. Then I carefully positioned the diary on our dresser, and took my place in our bed, opened some crap novel, then got up and reread the entry. Lodged in my mind was an image of R. from our honeymoon in Poland: fully dressed and propped up in bed, her hands folded behind her head, beckoning me with her eyes alone. The idea of her looking at another man in the same way made my head hiss.

Back in bed I sat, immobile, like a sniper in wait. Only my chest was rocking. A careful reconstruction of the timeline confirmed that her slutfest happened before I left for Berlin. And to think she had had the nerve to interrogate me about Bettina. Now I understood why: secretly she had hoped that I had also strayed, to relieve her own guilt. But I hadn't. I had bent, but not broken. There was only one cheater in this marriage.

To pass the time, I tore pages from the novel, crushed them into concentrated pellets, and hurled them across the room in the direction of the trash basket.

Finally she arrived. I was positively glad it was so late. It made my case all the more airtight.

She entered our bedroom noiselessly. I saw her take in a perplexing bit of visual evidence: the pellets of paper scattered on the floor. A moment later she exclaimed, "What happened to my diary!"

"I cut it open," I said nonchalantly, without looking up from my mutilated novel.

"What the hell did you do that for?"

"To read what you've written, of course."

"You read my diary . . ." she stammered.

"Because I knew you were unfaithful, and now I have the confirmation I needed."

"You cut open my diary and read it . . ."

"Because you lied. And deep down I knew you were a liar. Now instead of the obligatory mea culpa, perhaps you could start by telling me who this guy is. I plan to kill him."

"How dare you . . ."

"How dare I *what*? Ask about the identity of the human slime that *you* sucked off? I think I'm well within my rights to know, thank you. Now if you'll just kindly tell me . . ."

Dark wild eyes fixed upon me. From our dresser, R. grabbed a ceramic bowl, my gift to her to celebrate her first article in *Smithsonian*. She held it over her head, but I was not to be intimidated. I returned her stare with my own fury. An instant later the bowl exploded against the wall beside me. "What the hell are you doing?" I yelled. "You could have blinded me!"

She grabbed a second pot, this time a wedding present from friends. "You are never, *ever* to read my diary, understand?"

"For Christ's sake, put that bowl down. Have you gone crazy?"

"So help me, NEVER, do you understand?"

"Alright. Now put the goddamn bowl down."

She faked hurtling it across the room and instinctively I ducked. "*NEVER!*" she shrieked.

"Right, never. Okay. Sure."

Plunking down the bowl, she advanced toward the bed. I prepared myself for fresh violence, but she simply grabbed her nightgown and pillow.

So I admit: what follows couldn't have been self-defense. She was on her way out when she turned to kick a shard of the smashed bowl. It skittered to a rest before me. I picked it up: it was cobalt blue, obloid in shape. In college, I had played Ultimate Frisbee. What I lacked in speed, I made up in arm strength. The shard was much smaller than your standard disc, but still had the same basic shape. The grip is called "the classic" – fingers curled on the under-lip, forefinger on the under-belly pointing out. I wasn't out of control, I want to emphasize that. True, I screamed, "Bitch," but I was playing a role, just like Klara had suggested. The role demanded emotion. I was sick of R.'s temper. Or maybe I was afraid she was about to leave. Or enraged that I was being attacked for *her* infidelity. Or just fatigued by all the upheaval, all the everything. It goes without saying that the shard was meant to whizz harmlessly past her.

How it managed to strike her square in the forehead I cannot to this day explain. I've replayed the scene in my mind a thousand times, and still it remains a mystery. R. must have turned back toward me in the instant of the shard's release. At the same time, my release point must have been slightly off, sending the ceramic shrapnel on an errant trajectory. The whole thing unfolded with terrible slowness. But unlike a cartoon character, I couldn't arrest the projectile in mid-flight and pluck it harmlessly from the air. Instead I watched, frozen in horror, as it charted its malign course, and struck R. with an awful crack, like a walnut hitting pavement. She staggered back and sank to her knees. The skin on the center of her forehead parted, like a new eye opening for the first time. Then: the blood.

There are no accidents without trust. Without trust every harm is born of malice, every injury of intent. And we had long exhausted our reserves of good faith. From the fridge I grabbed Mr. Happy, the cold compress with the smiley face purchased for future infant mishaps. R. held Mr. Happy to her split forehead as I drove to the familiar emergency room, murmuring bewildered apologies. I hadn't forgotten the way.

The wound took nine stitches to close. With the white bandage across her forehead, R. looked like a woman's tennis star from the 1970s, though she refused to acknowledge the comparison. We told the physician, a bearded homunculus, that she had walked into an open door. He accepted this without suspicion. "It is true that pregnancy can affect balance and spatial relations. We're lucky that you haven't gone into shock. That could have been perilous for the fetus."

He wanted to keep her overnight for observation, but R. refused. At our car, she demanded the keys.

"Shouldn't I drive? You're probably still dazed."

"I'm fine."

She climbed into the car without unlocking the passenger door.

"Uh, hello. How exactly am I supposed to get home?"

"Home? No way," she said. "You're out."

PART 3

Sixteen

This morning the Amtrak was on time. The days remain warm, though leaves have begun to yellow and fall, the foliage thinning. When the diesel roared into the clearing, I could see the driver in the lighted window of the cab, a classic engineer's cap atop a thimble of head. I waved.

I couldn't fall back asleep, so I paced the apartment, Rosalind Roth's old place, the very one I put a deposit on before R.'s miscarriage. The little girl next door was crying: it's the same every night; she's terrified of the train, and earplugs don't help. While she cries, I pace. It's really not a bad little apartment, except for the smell, this odor of vanilla mixed with cat urine. The center hall leads into a living room; off the living room is a small dining space; this empties into a modest kitchen; the kitchen connects back to the entrance hall: a nice tidy loop, perfect for pacing, two hundred and fifty laps to a mile. I hope my steps lull the girl back to sleep.

Her father is an academic nomad, drifting from college to college in search of a permanent position. For the past three years he has found sanctuary in our sociology department. His wife, a doctorate in linguistics, works as a receptionist at a local HMO. Twice they've brought me something freshly baked – once, a plum pie, and a week later, a loaf of beer bread. They steer our conversations toward benign generalities. Peering out my kitchen window, I watch the girl, long-limbed and pig-tailed, swing from the swing set in the yard. She offers her father detailed pushing instructions. "Not too high, not too low; not too fast, not too slow." Happily he obliges.

Today I saw something odd: Jonathan Stein, sitting in a spanking new stop-sign red BMW, eating a sandwich, watching my apartment. When he saw me looking out the kitchen window, he nodded then drove off.

*

Out of the blue Ted Margolis invited me over to watch preseason football. When he first joined the English department in the mid-1970s, Margolis was considered a rising intellectual force on the national scene and a powerful presence on campus, his reputation secured by an acclaimed study of the literature of the Vietnam War that he had published fresh out of grad school, and also by the fact that he played a sturdy bass in a jazz band. Then everything went south. The story goes that his wife, a stunning clothing designer from Stockholm, ran off with her yoga instructor, catapulting Margolis into a funk from which he never recovered. He stopped publishing and, according to my students, teaching as well, ending each class with a weary sigh, "Enough wisdom for eighty minutes."

We were introduced years ago, but never got close. He remained a reclusive, cautionary figure, an example of life derailed. I was surprised, then, by his invitation – so surprised I accepted. "It's open," he bellowed, when I rang the door. "Come on in." I followed his voice to a rickety screened porch, where Margolis, dressed in a stained work shirt and greasy chinos, lounged in a battered recliner. "Grab a seat," he said, gesturing to a stiff metal garden chair. We watched the game on an old Zenith with floppy aerials and a fuzzy screen. "You watch a lot of preseason ball?" he asked.

"Actually, never . . ."

"Oh, you're in for a treat." But he didn't elaborate, as he slowly sipped a birch beer, oblivious to the march of carpenter ants across the flagstones.

The reception was awful. We hardly spoke, and midway through the third quarter, Margolis dozed off, snoring like an old dog. When he woke up, he smiled dreamily. "How we doing?" he asked.

"Not too good," I said. "The Dolphins still lead, 31–7."

We watched to the very end. Then he cooked dinner. The kitchen was a disheveled nest of peeling linoleum and chipped Formica. The meal consisted of sautéed canned mushrooms, mushy rice, and boiled potatoes. To drink, he served warm sherry with lemon peels and nutmeg, a horrid concoction he claimed to have discovered reading Dickens. While gnawing on an oversalted and undercooked potato, I realized that I was glad to be there. Our silence was comradely, and when it was time to leave, he shook my hand and said, "Let me tell you something. These things have a way of righting themselves, though God knows I'm not the poster boy for this simple truth." My eyes were moist with tears.

*

Another night of insomnia. Lying in bed, I listened to a bird chirp. What birds chirp at night? Are some birds nocturnal? Owls, obviously, but they hoot.

When the chirping died down, I addressed my jury. I wasn't looking for an acquittal, just a reduction in sentence. So I pled my case humbly, fully acknowledging guilt, but asking my judges to consider the mitigating circumstances. "For what is the wrong of reading a diary compared to the crime of adultery?" began my stirring peroration. "Marriages are not controlled by the exclusionary rule! I am not proud of my actions. But wasn't I entitled to an explanation, a word of apology? What did I get instead? A vase hurled at my head!

"Obviously what followed was an accident. I'm not a violent soul. I've never struck a person in the face in my entire life. In Hebrew school, Scott Goldsmith split my lip and bloodied my nose because I was too astonished to punch back when he hit me in the face. For a week, I stayed home from school, nursing my pummeled features. I was a peace-loving child and am a pacific adult. She's the one with the temper. And she's the one who strayed. How's that for irony! She breaks the faith, and I get thrown out! Where is the justice in this? Where?"

Chalky dust covered my tongue. Speaking before a jury for hours on end dried the mouth. The unfairness of the situation chewed at my extremities, a bitter feeling. My heart slammed against my ribs unhealthily. Mute color skimmed the horizon. More than anything, I wanted R. I wanted to curl around her like a nautilus, and hold her tight. And stay like that.

*

This from Jonathan Stein:

> *Where to start? First I want you to know that I never expected my sister to do anything with your story. She knows we're friends, and I'm still furious with her. I never for a second thought she'd assign one of her reporters to research what I'd told her. It was all "off the record." Now why did I tell her in the first place? Sure, I've resented your success, but I'm not a bastard. I told her because we talk, and*

you happen to be one of the persons we talk about. So to repeat, I'm sorry. That said, I want to remind you that I'm not the one with the self-destructive streak a mile wide. Had you corrected the record, like you said you would at our lunch (not that I thought you really were going to do it), none of this would have happened, at least not like this. I warned you that it could only end in disaster, even if I never expected to be the one delivering the blow.

So what can we do about it? I've spent the last couple of nights re-reading Art and Atrocity. *It really is a damn good book. Obviously I don't know shit about the subject, but I can recognize good writing and thinking when I see it. It's damn seldom these days, and you've got it in spades. So your star will rise again, I'm sure of that. In fact, I allowed myself a talk with the dean about your situation. I'll admit, he wasn't tickled pink by your string of fuck-ups, but after an hour I had him agreeing that you remain one of the better things to have happened to Franklin in recent years. Of course, he's still going to bend you over the barrel. My advice: don't fight it. A year from now, you'll be largely rehabilitated. Of course, some folk are going to hold this against you forever. But those guys probably hated you already for making it onto the gravy train. In the long run, it will be a wash.*

What do you make of the new wheels? It's a bizarre story. Apple Grove Living told my mother that she had to dismantle the Mel Gibson shrine that she had erected in a corner of the senior recreation space. She moved most of it back into her bedroom, but decided to sell off some stuff on eBay. It turns out that one of her earliest acquisitions was Gibson's original handgun from the first Lethal Weapon, *a black Beretta 92. It fetched a small fortune at auction. She's the one who thought I needed a Bimmer. Either she hopes the car will help me find a wife and settle down, or she realizes it's hopeless, that I'll never have a family, and therefore deserve a consolation. In any case, I have to admit: I like it. The ease with which I've convinced myself that luxury is an entitlement is pretty breathtaking.*

So let's go for a drive one of these days. Maybe we can check out the new mini-golf course down on Route 7. My treat.

*

This time, R. answered my call. She had gone in for her final exam. The doctor said the measurements look good. Why don't her assurances assure? Did she go to an American medical school? I ask. Is she board certified? R. doesn't answer. She's called to discuss logistics. She agreed to phone at the onset of labor, but doesn't want me driving her to the hospital.

"Who's going to drive you? Vercin? M.D.?"

She hung up before I could add, "just kidding."

*

Last night's dream: I nudge open the door. Our bedroom is empty – the bed stripped, the walls bare, a single unmatched sock all that's left in the dresser. R. has returned to Chicago, to put down roots and live there forever. Her family anticipated the move. A cherrywood crib with a Babar motif bumper and matching crown stands at the ready in her old bedroom. She meets her boyfriend from sixth grade in a Whole Foods market. His wife died of basal cell melanoma the year before; they go out on a date and three months later are engaged. I take an all-night bus that gets me to our baby's first birthday party an hour late. I come laden with gifts – Legos, jigsaw puzzles, pogo sticks – but somehow they're all wrong. "He'll choke on these! Get them away!" The family treats me like a pariah. They don't want me near him. Fuck you, I whisper. Fuck all of you. I lift my boy. Look! It's Daddy! Daddy's here! The boy begins to cry. I try swinging him. Only now he's really howling. Aren't children supposed to like being swung? R.'s mother screams, "Someone *stop* him! He'll EAT HIM! Someone STOP THE CANNIBAL!" Everyone is screaming. I release the boy and escape before the cupcakes and song.

*

There's a bug problem here, no denying that. The rodents don't bother me: there's something comforting about the sound of mice scrabbling about the woodwork. The flies and moths are another matter. They flutter, buzz, and judder about, freely treating me as a landing strip or refueling station. It makes reading difficult. Sleeping, too. But does my bodily comfort justify the snuffing out of life, no matter how obnoxious and insubstantial? I think not. I try to shoo them away without causing death by smearing. In the case of moths, this is hard. I cup them gently in my hand and carry them outside, but still they leave deposits of life dust. Those that survive my transportation end up in spider webs. I remember R. telling me that only a tiny percentage of creatures in nature die of natural causes. Most conclude their lives in the alimentary canal of a stronger, faster, younger competitor.

*

"It was the doctor." This time, R. called me. She said it so quickly, without even a simple prefatory "Hi," that I didn't immediately follow.

"What was? What doctor?"

"The guy in the diary. It was the doctor who treated me for the miscarriage."

I had sworn to myself that when I finally found out, I would react with equanimity. "*That* asshole? You sucked off that stupid repulsive fuckhead?"

There was silence on the line.

"Well, did you or didn't you?"

"I just said I did!"

I tried to recall what he looked like. Tall. And handsome in the ruthlessly dull fashion of persons unburdened by introspection, imagination, and disorder.

"You sucked off that flaming shitbag . . ."

"Enough, Daniel."

"No, not enough. Let me ask you this, why'd you treat me like a psycho for being jealous, when all along I was right?"

"Because the business about Vercin *was* crazy."

"So I got the guy wrong, not the basic facts. And speaking of facts, did he come in your mouth?"

"Daniel, this isn't necessary."

"As long as you've decided to tell me, you might as well come clean. So to speak. Well?"

"Yes, if you really must know."

"Did you swallow?"

"I did."

Acrid, noxious fumes expanded in my chest.

"And when it came to your turn?"

"If it makes you feel any better, he was nowhere as good as you." Actually, it did.

"Now I assume from your diary that this was a single isolated event. Am I right? Wrong? By your silence I guess I *am* wrong. So how many other times were there?"

"Just two."

"*Just?* So what happened on these occasions?"

"We fucked."

"How frank. Both times?"

"Both times."

"Back in the hayloft?"

"There and his bedroom."

"And why did you go back?"

"I guess I wanted to."

"Of course. How silly of me. So why did you stop after only two fucks? Well?"

"I don't know. It just seemed enough."

"*Enough?* Enough for what?"

She sighed loudly. "It was a mistake, Daniel. It seems so long ago, so inconsequential. Not for you, I know, but for me. My tubes were tied, I wasn't over the miscarriage and your panic attacks. You had gotten tenure, I was feeling directionless, maybe resentful. I don't know . . . It meant very little. I wish you could let it go. If not for me, then for Zygote."

"Isn't that the purpose of having children? To punish them for the sins of their parents?"

"Whatever you say, Daniel."

"Well, it's not as if I've heard you offering any apologies."

"I'm sorry for what I did. And I'm sorry that you read my diary and cut me in the head."

"You have no idea how sick I feel about that. Just thinking about it makes me want to throw up."

"Me, too."

There was a pause, then came the click, the dial tone, and finally the recorded message. *If you'd like to make a call, please hang up and dial again.*

*

My program of remedial television watching is proceeding nicely apace. I watch at all times – morning, noon, night, the wee hours.

I'm particularly interested in gaining a working knowledge of all the shows I missed during the decade of submitting to R.'s television boycott – *Seinfeld, Friends, E.R., Law and Order, NYPD Blue*. Already I'm feeling more culturally relevant, attuned to the spirit of my land. On ESPN's U.S. Open of Competitive Eating, sponsored by Alka Seltzer, I watch a small Asian man thoroughly destroy a massive line-backer-type in the finals of the Pasta Scarf, bolting, virtually inhaling, 13.8 pounds of spaghetti in fifteen minutes. I also watch a lot of documentaries – the History Channel's weeklong biopic on Hitler, Discovery's series on UFOs, Court T.V.'s *Unsolved Massacres*. I happen upon TLC's special on the Somme, and there is Sir Charles Worthington, dapper as ever, discoursing on the battle: *The barrage was meant to cut the enemy's wire. Yet despite its historic proportions, the bombardment singularly failed in this respect. This proved most unfortunate for the soldiers who went over on the early hours of the first. Britain had sustained perhaps thirty thousand casualties by noon, fifty thousand by teatime.*

I watch in my underwear, snacking on Pop-Tarts. Still, I can't down more than two at a sitting.

*

Pulling into our driveway I nodded at Al, our neighbor. He was in his folding garden chair in the shade of his garage, a newspaper clenched in his bony hands, surveying the trickle of traffic. The old bastard didn't return my greeting. His squint was distrustful, measuring. Maybe R. had asked him to keep watch. Our lawn smelled freshly mown. Had he used *my* riding mower? The clapboards gleamed in the morning sun. R.'s car wasn't in the driveway, which was just as well, as I hadn't shaved or showered. I decided to go inside anyway, just to look around. My key slipped in, but the tumbler refused to turn. Then it dawned on me: R. had changed the locks.

I sat on the stoop. Sweetness pawed at me meaningfully through a window. I thought about the afternoon that R. and I had driven from New Haven to New York. A friend had given me the keys to his apartment in Greenwich Village, and we both believed that there we would make love for the first time. I remembered R.'s excited breathing as we stood by the door to the second-story walk-up. Only the keys didn't fit the locks. After a moment of confusion, I realized I had brought the wrong set. I leaned my head against the door and let my arms hang limply. "Hey, it's no big deal," R. said. "Come on, we'll spend the night on the town." So we went to Windows on the World, the hokiest and most romantic thing we could imagine. The maitre d' supplied me with an ill-fitting blue blazer, and from our table we could see the ant colonies of light stretching to the horizon. After dinner, we slow-danced to covers of Nina Simone and Rex Garland. Toward dawn, we drove back to New Haven and watched, tied in an embrace, the sunrise from West Rock. "I could imagine this working a lifetime," R. had whispered. "You and me."

I tapped on the window at Sweetness. She raised her paw, as if to touch me through the pane. The purr box was in gear. I sat for a while longer, then left.

*

Rosalind Roth wasn't expected back from San Francisco until the start of term, but in front of her building squatted the rust-devoured Dodge Rampage, hogging two spots.

"Wow," she said, answering her door. "You look awful."

"Thanks. I'm glad to see you, too. When did you get back?"

"Maybe a week ago."

"And you didn't call?"

"I didn't know I was supposed to. Was that how we left things? Well, don't just stand there . . ."

Rosalind looked strangely healthy – tanned, lips healed, freckles flowering across her nose and cheeks. I had pegged her as the type that burns.

Even the new apartment looked okay. It smelled of stale cigarettes, but at least it was tidy. The walls were bare save for a single picture, a framed poster of *The Battle of Algiers*.

"It was time for my semiannual clean-up," she said. "My parents are threatening a visit. The last time they came, they spent the entire weekend vacuuming and mopping. I can't afford a repeat of that."

Anubis was curled under the kitchen table, snoozing.

"Can I get you a bite?" She rummaged through the refrigerator. It was clean but basically empty. "Scratch that. We can order in, though. Or I can microwave some frozen mac and cheese."

"No, I'm okay."

"You sure? It's Kraft's."

"I'm positive. But you should go ahead and eat."

Once the macaroni and cheese was ready, I discovered my appetite. We shared it straight from the plastic dish, Rosalind scooping with a spoon while I used a fork.

"Kraft's is the best," she said, mouth full. "I really love this stuff. So what's wrong?"

"Me," I said. "I'm what's wrong."

I described my recent setbacks. She listened attentively. She was wearing a Swedish air force T-shirt and banana yellow vintage hot pants. Her legs were smooth and tanned, covered with a fine reddish-blonde down.

"So why'd you come here? Looking for a mercy fuck?"

"Hardly."

Still, I let her lead me to the bedroom. The blinds were closed. The air-conditioner, an ancient window unit, gurgled. There was little in the way of furniture. In the middle of the room was a simple futon covered with a Turkish throw. A hat rack displayed a single treasure: a Jackie O-style pink pillbox. Next to it, a peacock feather had fallen to the ground. In the corner sat an enormous TV-VCR surrounded by stacks of tapes: Godard, Pasolini, Buster Keaton, Fassbinder.

A scent of lavender potpourri competed with the smell of cigarettes. With unexpected force, Rosalind pulled me down onto the futon. The door opened a crack and Anubis wandered in. He settled himself in the corner with a yawn.

"So what's your desire?" Rosalind asked. She caressed very tenderly.

"You really want to know?"

"As long as it doesn't involve salami, yes."

"Well, if it's okay with you, how about if we just lie together? Would that be alright?"

Rosalind wrapped herself around me, while I curled up on my side. Why deny it? I was in a fetal ball. "It's going to be okay," she whispered, as I started to cry. "Everything's going to be okay." I never thought her edgy style would admit hoary cliché, but she administered a litany of encouraging words with smooth intelligence and only the slightest trace of irony. "Things have a way of working themselves out, even for human fuck-ups like you and me. You know, once my car was broken – it was running like shit – and I swear to God, it fixed itself."

I awoke at dawn. Rosalind was lying on her side, staring at me, as if she had never slept. "You have a cute nose," she said. "It twitches while you sleep." We kissed lighty. Then, in the crepuscular light, I noticed what I hadn't before: the long smooth "x"s that etched a scarified pattern on each of Rosalind's wrists. She saw me looking at them; her smile was shy, heartbreaking. "I told you I went through a bad patch. You see, we all do."

"Was this when you were with – "

"Sssh." She held a finger to my lips. I tried to touch the scars, but she pulled away. "Let's not. It's a long time ago and way too boring."

I must have fallen back asleep. Hot vaporous doggy breath woke me later in the morning. Rosalind was gone, but the futon was not empty. Anubis was lying in precisely the spot that Rosalind had occupied. We stared at each other and without stirring, his tail thumped against the futon. I wheezed and sneezed in the same instant – allergies. I raised a shade and opened a window. The sky was monotonously gray. Rain fell, windless vertical rain. Anubis stretched and groaned. "C'mon, pooch, let's find you some chow." I fed him and drank a glass of water. There was no sign of Rosalind. Maybe she had gone to retrieve food for humans. Then I found a brief note: *Went for a run. xxoo.* It came as a surprise, another minor complication in my image of this woman, though it did explain the superior legs: Rosalind, a runner. In a short message of my own, I tried to communicate how honestly and deeply and gratefully I was in her debt. As I closed the door Anubis whined plaintively.

In my apartment, I showered and ate a bowl of cereal. The rain continued to fall, but it was a nice, melancholy rain, the kind that returns color and shine. I was just tucking myself into a good documentary on tornado trackers when I noticed the answering machine's blink.

"Daniel? It's me. Will you please answer? It's about three, and I've been up since a little past midnight with contractions. It looks like the real thing. I called the midwife, and she wants me to keep tim-

ing them for now, but for once please make sure there's gas in your tank. Okay? And wake up!"

"Daniel? Daniel? Wake up, will you. It's 4:30 and the contractions are getting pretty intense. We'll have to leave pretty soon, so get up. And you might want to bring some food along. This can go on for hours and I'm sure the hospital cafeteria is awful. Daniel?"

"Where the fuck are you? It's six, and if you don't pick up in the next instant, I'll find alternative means of transportation."

"Hello? Hello . . . ? Okay, I forgot that I told you not to drive me. Where are you anyway? I'll see you at the hospital. Hello? You there?"

*

"You the husband?" A nurse with a vulpine nose and rebellious hair shot me a sly look. The maternity ward was bustling with activity. "Just catch your breath there, and dry your feet on that mat. Don't worry, you haven't missed the good part. Your wife's in Room 3, take a left and down the hall . . . No, hon, that's your right – other way."

En route I passed the neonatal ICU. A couple, holding hands, stared through thick glass at a tangle of tubes and monitors twisted about a small bundle. By the bundle stood a nurse in a surgical mask adjusting knobs, while another, also masked, wrote on a clipboard. Neither the man nor the woman glanced up as I hurried by.

R. was standing in the middle of her bright birthing room. She wore a hospital gown tied loosely in the back, her hair gathered in a bun. Standing akimbo, feet planted apart, she was swaying slowly back and forth, like an astronaut doing aerobics. I recognized the music – Liz Phair.

"Nice of you to show," she said.

I kissed her gently on her scar. "I came as soon as I could."

"Where were you – off evening the score?"

"I thought we were going to try to take the high road. I happened to be wearing earplugs. I've had insomnia so I took a sleeping pill."

"I don't like your taking pills. You're here now, that's the important thing. Do you want to take a shower? The showers are great."

"No, I'm okay. How are you doing?"

"I'm good. I'll be better when this is all over."

R. felt best when walking. I made a mental note to avoid the ICU, but inadvertently steered us straight to it. The father now held a lone vigil. Unshaven, collar loose, hands on chin, he was a picture of exhaustion and private grief. "Let's go back the other – " A contraction abruptly silenced R. Leaning against the wall, she focused on her breathing until it passed. "That was a pretty good one. Yeah, that one was for real."

Another lap around the ward, and we returned for the midwife's exam. A homely woman with thin oatmeal colored hair, the midwife touched, prodded and measured, then casually slipped on a surgical gown and wheeled a cart of instruments toward the bed. "The next time you feel one of those biggies coming," she said, "I want you to push." This was a stunning development. What of those last precious hours I had accorded myself to prepare for fatherhood? Everything happened awfully fast. On the first push, R.'s water broke: not the mild seepage described in *Planning the Birth*, but a titanic rupture, a biblical surge that smelled of English breakfast tea without the sugar. The midwife tugged and loosened, while a nurse panted encouragement in R.'s ear, freely jumbling the clichés of Deepak Chopra and Vince Lombardi. R. refused all pain killers – no surprise there. I mopped her brow with a damp sponge, my tears mixing with her sweat. She was heroic but all was not well. The fetal pulse raced wildly between contractions, only to grind to a near halt when she pushed. Another nurse materialized and a doctor, too. They wanted the baby out, and they wanted him out fast. With each push R.'s face turned purple. Blood vessels around her eyes exploded in a scarlet rash; the scar on her forehead stood out as a white cross. The midwives snipped, yanked, and sucked, and suddenly it flopped out, a slippery fish on a dry dock. They unwound the cord from his neck and rushed the blue mass to an adjacent table. There they slapped at claw-like feet until a mute cry rose from the stunned cringing body.

Murmurs of relief rippled through the room. "A peanut," the doctor said, commenting on the baby's size. He was wrinkly, as if left too long in bath water, and weighed a shade more than six pounds. Gradually he turned a reddish-pink, as a nurse extended the twitching legs.

"What's going on there?" Maybe I was speaking too loudly. "What are you doing?"

"His color's improving," the doctor said. "I wouldn't be too concerned about the cordulation. This one's brightening nicely, got good lungs."

Through the first night the baby remained indifferent to the bounty of R.'s breasts. "C'mon, little friend," she cajoled, "you can do better than that." When she tired, I called for the nurse with the fox-like nose, who returned the baby to the warming station.

"Is he okay?" I asked.

"Looks fine to me," she said, flicking sleep from the corner of her eye. "Now why don't you try to get some rest?"

"I've been resting. I'm not tired."

"Okay, Dad – but I am."

With the morning came our unceremonious discharge. "How does the baby look now?" I asked the nurse as she handed us the swaddled mummy.

"Still like a baby."

"But he hardly nursed. I mean, I was watching him. That can't be normal, can it? And what about his size?"

She shrugged. "Some take awhile to get with the program. Now by state law, I'm required to ask you whether you've brought an infant car seat."

*

R. consented to let me stay in the guest room for the first days to help out. I bring her mugs of Bengal Spice and Raspberry Zinger, and platefuls of tuna casserole and lasagna. (In a frightening display of efficiency, R. spent the early hours of labor baking and freezing.)

"Is he nursing?"

"A bit. Look at him – he's such a darling. And what a nose! It must come from my grandfather. He always insisted there was Roman blood in the family."

When he refuses food or sleep, I carry him around, cradling him in the crook of my arm like a football. He cries a forlorn tra-la-la, the weak singing of a kid goat.

*

I have to admit: the numbers don't look bad. Virgo – ruling planet Mercury. Likes health food, dislikes squalor. Intelligent and analytical, but prone to worry – little surprise there. September four – no major horrors associated with that day. The year: the second of the new millennium, with its nice Arthur C. Clarke resonance; 4698 in the Chinese calendar, the year of the proud golden snake, not to be confused with the untrustworthy white snake; 5761 on the Jewish calendar – adds to 19, not the most promising value in kabalistic numerology, but no major complaints.

Still, astrology goes only so far. I need certainty. I wait until R. is fast asleep to conduct my private exam. I place the baby on the changing table, remove his swaddling and diaper, and carefully inventory the relevant parts. Arms and legs, preposterously thin, like water-sogged chop sticks, but no apparent mistakes; umbilical cord, the shriveled piece of beef jerky, preparing to drop off as per schedule; fingers and nails, tiny but flawless, exquisite attention to detail; ears, nicely reticulated and obviously responsive to sound. Midway through the exam, Moses wakes up. Perhaps when I test his startle reflex. His eyes open wide and I brace myself for a terrified squall, but there is no distress, no importuning in his gaze. The expression is canny, trusting, and familiar. (They say all babies have blue eyes, but in the light his mirror his mother's brown.) It is as if he knows what I am searching for, and shares my curiosity. And then I find it, the imperfection, the defect that has escaped the notice of the doctors, the nurses, and the mother. On his left foot, between the second and third toes: a film of extra skin, a minute flap of webbing. I compare the left foot to the right, and so confirm the reality of the familiar flaw. I promise the baby that it will be our secret; he blinks his assent. And then, all at once, I surrender myself to yet another crying jag. "Thank you, God." I whisper burying my face in his warm body. "Thank you, thank you, thank you." The expressions of thanks have to total an even number.

*

Tonight, the Amtrak didn't wake up the little girl next door. Two nights ago, while reading in bed, I heard a strange sound: a dull soughing, like wind through dry weeds. Later I learned the girl had suffered an asthma attack. The father explained that it's worse in the fall. Three other children in her kindergarten also suffer, a veritable epidemic. He mentioned they might take her away for a few days, far from the golden rod, ragweed, and the tattered patch of ozone. Perhaps that accounts for the silence next door.

R. believes that nursing will protect against allergies. My mother didn't nurse, and I'm allergic to half the planet, but, logically, that proves nothing.

And R. considers all the crying normal, even healthy, a sign of sturdy lungs and strong personality. Though she cannot understand his tranquility in my presence. "It must be the rocking gait or the football grip," she says. "It probably reminds him of being back inside." But that's not it. While she slept, I again uncovered his toes, playing with them and kissing his imperfection. He's too young to smile, but not to know calm. The kissing turned frantic features placid. Moments later he was sound asleep.

Today I owe rent on this place, but the lease is month to month. I'll give Moses the first round of presents from friends and colleagues – the Whoozit Galaxy Rattle, the multiple copies of *Goodnight Moon* and *Pat the Bunny*, and from Rosalind, something for the future, a copy of Genet's *A Thief's Journal*. And I'll bring R. Tofu Home Style from her favorite Chinese restaurant. When she rests, I'll hold our baby, the beautiful webling, the little survivor with the canny brown eyes.

The sun has just risen on another night of fierce insomnia, but I'm not tired. Who could remain indifferent to such a brilliant dawn?

Acknowledgments

Lots of people helped. For comments on earlier drafts, I want to thank my friends Nick Bromell, Rand Cooper, Owen Fiss, Alex George, Robin Hessman, Nasser Hussain, Robert Karjel, John Kleiner, Laura Moser, Bill Pritchard, Jeff Rubin, Ira Silverberg, Molly Wynans, and James Young.

Daniel Greenberg, my agent, got the job done with humor and tenacity. Rosemary Ahern, my editor at Other Press, read wisely and made the book better. Bob Hack oversaw production with an expert hand. Judith Gurewich, publisher at Other Press, extended friendship and guidance. Finally, Nancy Pick, my wife, and Jacob and Milo, my boys – they dealt. It's not about them. Really.